Dead
Medium

Peter John Copyright © 2012 Peter John

ISBN: 1481879103
ISBN-13: 978-1481879101

This book is dedicated to my darling wife Jo, without whom this story would never have been written.

Prologue

Seventy Five Years Before

A chill rasped through the air, though there was no wind to carry it. The stars shone brightly in the clear sky above, clear but for a single dark cloud. It hovered above a wide empty meadow, empty but for the souls of the dead. It was a gathering of spirits.

On the crest of a hill overlooking the meadow, the dark figures of a man and a small dog stood motionless. They watched as wisps of sparkling smoke rained down upon the ground. Slithering columns of mist, like the tentacles of a great octopus, swept across the frost laden grass.

They continued to watch in silence as the smog of darkness enveloped each and every soul until nothing but a dead space remained. The man fell to his knees and sobbed, while the dog slowly wagged his tail.

Chapter One

There was little she hated more than the naive and gullible. People who were taken in by any scam or confidence trick, from chain letters to religious promises. If it cost money but promised more in return, the sheep like hoards would rush in and dish out their life saving on one improbable venture or another.

May Elizabeth Trump lived alone. She thrived on her own independence and sought the aid of others with a painful reluctance. She had always looked after her self and she relied on no one.

It was a Tuesday afternoon in late spring and May was taking a much needed break from her cleaning chores to watch one of her favourite TV shows. She didn't fully understand why she enjoyed The Adrian Farley Show as it left her feeling angry and frustrated as often as it made her feel a little superior, a tier above certain other people. May sat in one of her floral embroidered Queen Anne chairs facing her small television set that had once been state of the art about 15 years ago. She still wore her pinny over her pastel blue blouse and her charcoal grey slacks. It was her guard against spills and stains. Even at her age she still prided herself on giving a smart, clean appearance, even when there was no one around to appreciate her efforts. May Trump had worked hard for most of her 75 years and the toll paid was evident in her wrinkled skin and sagging jaw line. Her eyes had the flickering light of a dying fire which could still issue a flame if stoked, fuelled by a source buried deep beneath the ashes. She knew her age and the pain she felt from her tired joints made sure she didn't forget. She suffered no ills apart from the passage of time but she could feel the downward spiral as her body slowly withered with age.

The television was small but the picture was clear and sharp.

"What do you think people are going to say after that kind of behaviour?"

May's clenched fist flew back and forth through the air. Her lips were gnarled as she growled at the images on the screen.

"What would your mother say if she saw you right now?" Her fist dropped back down and rested on the arm of her chair.

"Oh that is your mother," May's voice took on a surprised tone but only for a moment.

"How do you expect your kids to turn out with you as their only role model?" Her voice regained its previous harshness.

The Adrian Farley Show was an arena for petty squabbles. Adrian Farley was a smartly dressed young man who paced back and forth across the stage firing demanding questions at his guests, who were usually people who couldn't solve their own personal problems without a TV camera pointed at them. May watched as a young woman wearing an ill-fitting pink tracksuit explained to the studio audience about how she loved the father of her child, if only she could remember who he was.

May looked up at her brass carriage clock that sat on the mantelpiece above her wood effect gas fire. More time had passed than she had realised and she still had a few things to do before Margaret arrived.

It was another Tuesday afternoon and that meant another day of listening to mindless gossip. Her one and only friend Margaret was coming over for her weekly visit. She was only a few years younger than May and had worked with her for the decade before they had both retired. May didn't particularly like her company but continued to allow her into the house, more through familiarity than friendship. Margaret was a loud and boisterous woman whose huge waistline was only dwarfed by her ever compassionate heart. When ever she entered

5

May's house her booming voice would make the windows rattle ever so slightly. The noise of vibrating glass was almost inaudible but May had attuned herself to it over the years. May found Tuesday mornings particularly unpleasant. It felt like the slow turn of thumb screws, waiting for that soft tap on the door that was always followed by Margaret's signature greeting.

"Coo-wee' it's only me". The sound generally brought a chill down her spine. She never once wondered why Margaret chose to visit her every single week. She only ever considered her own view of the habitual friendship.

It was a quarter to two, which gave May only fifteen minutes before Margaret arrived. She switched off her television set and slowly rose from her chair. Her knee joints complained sending sharp pains up her thighs but she did her best to ignore the discomfort. She stood still and straight for a moment to allow her aches to settle and soothe, before she made her way slowly into the kitchen. She leaned against the sink and filled her old iron kettle with water. The kettle was heavy and she struggled to transfer it to the stove. She promised herself a new electric kettle for the hundredth time, before switching on the gas. While the kettle began to warm up she brought out a tea tray and started arranging items on it. She knew that if everything was ready as Margaret arrived she would finish her tea sooner and have less of an excuse to stay. May placed her old stained teapot on the tray and heaped three spoons of loose tea inside. After placing the matching sugar bowl and milk jug on the tray, she removed a brand new packet of Bake well slices from the cupboard. Another of May's few pleasures was Bake wells' and she sorely begrudged having to share them. Sadly they were part of the weekly charade and to withhold them would cause more trouble than they were worth. Margaret would get the crazy idea that May wasn't well, or was becoming forgetful in her old age and then smother her in unwanted concern and compassion. She would start nagging at her about visiting a doctor or, even worse, staying with her for a few weeks convalescence. May had made that mistake only once before and she had vowed that it would never happen again. After less than a day she had made her polite excuses and left. It had taken her more than a week to get over the stress.

   May placed four Bakewell slices' on a small plate, that had two others stacked below it, making sure that she didn't leave any finger marks on the soft fondant icing. She fetched two small dessert forks and then she heard the kettle begin to whistle.

   May almost spilt the boiling water as she poured it into the teapot. The tap on the door and the loud shrill greeting always made her jump. She carried the tea tray into the living room and placed it on a small table between her two Queen Anne chairs. She took one last look around the room. Everything is tidy and in its place, she noted with a sigh and then brushed herself down with the palms of her hands. There was another tap on the front door. A booming voice, which was only slightly muffled by the thick wooden panels, caused a slight rattle in the closest windows.
   "Hello, May are you in there? Coo-wee it's only me!" May hesitantly stepped towards the front door, dug deep within her reluctance and found the strength of will to open it.

   Margaret was a big woman or as she was fond of saying "No skinny mare me". She had given birth to four children and she would often tell of how each pregnancy had left her more of a woman than she previously had been. She was a grandmother to 'My two little treasures', which was a subject May rarely discussed. If ever the topic of her little Timmy or Mary, 'My little heart melter', was broached, there was no stopping her. It was like firing a gun at the top of a snowy mountain and then watching the resulting avalanche form.

   "May dear, you are in. How are you?" Margaret pulled May towards her and dwarfed her in an encompassing cuddle.

"I'm fine, how are you?" May muffled a reply, as her face was squashed up against Margaret's chest and her nose was thrust between her ample cleavage. Margaret's grin stretched across her face and her eyes emitted a faint glow, as she released May from her squeeze. May took an unsteady step backwards while trying to disguise her gasps for air. It will take hours to get the smell of lavender out of my nose, she thought.

"Glad to hear it," Margaret boomed. She stepped past May and, like a heat seeking missile, zeroed in on the tea tray perched on the table. "I see the tea is all set and ready. Oh my and Bakewell's, I really shouldn't". Margaret flashed May a quick wink. "But I shall". She sat down on the chair furthest from the television set, while May closed the door before sitting in her favourite of the two chairs. Her knees flared up again as she bent them but she managed to hide the pain from Margaret.

"I'll be Mum," Margaret announced, as she grabbed the teapot from the tray. May shuffled forward in her chair. She was about to protest but before she had raised her hand an inch, Margaret had already begun to pour. May bit her tongue but watched nervously, as Margaret handled her prized china in, what May considered to be, a reckless manner. Hold it by the base; careful don't clink the cups together. That's expensive porcelain not your cheap stoneware, I'll have you know. May kept her concerns silent and forced out an uncomfortable smile.

"Did you hear about poor Penny Saunders last week?" Margaret asked, as she heaped two spoonfuls of sugar into one of the cups and stirred it vigorously. The spoon rattled against the porcelain causing May's smile to loose much of its cohesion.

"No Marge" May replied dispassionately, knowing that she would soon hear the entire story in unnecessary detail. May relaxed a little when she saw Margaret place the spoon into her saucer.

8

"Oh it's a terrible shame it is," Margaret said, as she slipped an empty plate from the bottom of the pile. May reached out and turned her cup, pulling it closer.

"Yes Marge," she said, as she picked up the Milk jug and poured. Her eyes were on her task not her friend. Margaret cupped her mouth with both hands in a gesture of sombre surprise.

"Oh May! It's all over the town, even the Vicar is said to have been in tears over it". Margaret swiftly dropped her hands again and, in one fluid movement, selected a Bake well slice from the tray. She placed it on her plate delicately, before kissing the crumbs off her thumb and forefinger.

"Is she alright?" May asked, she was still only half listening and her mind was beginning to wander onto more important issues than small town gossip.

"No May! She's not all right, not alright at all!" Margaret's face adopted a serious expression, one which May had rarely seen before. Maybe there was something more going on here than illicit romance, sponge cake recipes and fashion taboos. I've been here before, May thought. She could remember at least two other occasions where she had expected something serious and important to come out of Margaret's mouth, only to be met with the same pointless trivia. It's going to be about the tom-bola stall at the summer fair again, May picked up her cup and raised it to her lips.

"I'll tell you what happened, it's terrible it is," Margaret said. "They say that she was trying to fix her power shower in the bathroom. Eric, you know Eric the Plumber from down the high street near the fountain with the benches. Well he said that she had no business messing with that kind of equipment. He said that she should have called him down to do it. I couldn't help but agree May, he's very reasonable you know. He fitted my Chris's bathroom suite last month and he didn't charge no arm and a leg either I tell can you". Margaret paused for half a second to breathe and then continued. "Anyway; it seems that she had forgotten to switch off the mains electricity. Now my Alf,

9

you remember Alf? He's always saying that you should never mess with electric unless the mains thingy is switched off and he knows a thing or two about that electric". Another pause, another breath. "She only got herself electrified, poor woman. I tell you it's that young Chloe of hers I feel for, the poor girl must be in such a tizzy". May put her cup back down on the table.

"So how is she?" She asked. Actual concern was a rare emotion for May, she found herself experiencing an unexpected motion in her stomach. She cared but didn't know why and she found it confusing.

"Not good May, not good at all," Margaret replied in a slower, softer voice. "She's dead!"

"No! Surely not, that's terrible". The unfamiliar feeling of sadness flooded over May but she couldn't help thinking about how avoidable and pointless it was. Maybe she asked for it, messing about where she didn't belong. Maybe everyone was better off now, without her around taking stupid risks. Maybe they were lucky no one else was hurt. May just couldn't muster her usual frustration at the stupidity of others. She had to admit to herself, she felt sad.

"I know, I said didn't I. I told you it was bad. They buried her yesterday out by the old church. It was a bit of a rush job if you ask me". Margaret picked up her plate again.

"How's her Chloe holding up?" May asked, as she returned her cup to her lips. Margaret had just taken a large bite of cake; she waved her hand to indicate that she would answer as soon as she'd managed to swallow it.

"Not good at all May" Margaret said, wiping the crumbs from her mouth. "It seems that she's been lumbered with an awful lot of debt. What with there being no insurance and her mum's wage not coming in, she may have to give up college or lose the house I reckon. I know dear Penny wouldn't have been happy about it; she always used to talk about how proud she was of how her girl was studying. She used to boast about how smart she was and how she wouldn't have to struggle through life, like she had done, once she got her degrees. It's a real sad affair I can tell you". May finished her tea and placed the cup back down as Margaret polished off the Bake well slice.

"You know what else?" Margaret said as she picked up her own tea to wash the cake down. "You know Barbara, that friend of mine who works down at the supermarket in the high street. You know the one; she's got that big red hair do". May shrugged, she assumed she would recognise her in the street if she saw her but she didn't care to remember her name.

"The one that got into trouble when the customers at the deli-counter kept finding red strands in their coleslaw?" Margaret continued, while May held her blank expression. "Well anyway, she does those Tarot card things. You know predicting the future and what not. A group of us meet up on a Thursday night at her place and play a little gin rummy, sometimes more gin than rummy. Don't go mentioning it to my Alf mind you but we sometimes dabble with...other things. Barbara has a bit of a gift for the spiritual. Well she says that she gave a reading to her sister last month and turned over a death card, which ain't no good sign. Now her sister has got a friend whose son attends the same college as Penny Saunders's daughter Chloe. He's not in the same classes mind you but the exact same school. Strange that isn't it, puts a chill right up your spine things like that".

The conversation continued in a similar trend for another twenty minutes. Margaret had devoured three of the bake wells and two cups of tea by the time she finally rose from her chair.

"Well I'd better get off home now," She announced and May was relieved to hear it. Margaret had spent the last twenty minutes talking about the summer fair, the bargains to be had at the local market and how Alf keeps leaving his golf clubs laying around the house. May hardly registered any of it. She made the right noises whenever Margaret paused for more than a second, which wasn't often. May just couldn't get the Saunders family tragedy out of her mind.

"Oh! I'm sorry to hear that," she lied. "Can't you stay just a little longer?"

"Well I Guess I could stay," Margaret wavered, causing May to panic a little.

"No I really can't May. Times getting on and I've got to get the dinner ready before Alf gets back from playing golf. He'll probably be in a bad mood again; he's useless at the sport".

May stood carefully from her chair and saw her friend to the door.

"Same time next week?" Margaret said, as she stepped through the front door.

"Of course, you are always welcome". May lied but surprised herself by adding: "If you see Chloe Saunders do give her my best". Margaret stopped in her tracks, as if she had just walked into an invisible brick wall. She shot May a confused stare.

"May Elizabeth Trump!" She gasped. "In all the years I've known you I have never once heard you give your best to anyone".

"Maybe I'm getting a bit soft in my old age?" May admitted to herself, as much as to her friend. Margaret let out a heavy sigh that seemed to reverberate through her entire body.

"You've left it a bit late old girl, are you feeling quite right?"

"Now you can get right off that train of thought, I'm perfectly alright. I feel just fine thank you very much".The problem was that she didn't.

May leaned against the closed door and gave a sigh of relief. She had managed to convince Margaret that she wasn't in need of a recuperation break and she had seemed happy to leave it at that. May had found it a particular struggle today and she was glad it was over.

May walked back to her chair and sat down, careful not to irritate her knees. She couldn't help thinking about Penny Saunders and her daughter Chloe. May cupped her chin, feeling the few whiskers she had missed while plucking early that morning. What a waste of life, such a stupid way to die. Anger welled inside her. Mixed with her still turning stomach, she was beginning to feel decidedly unwell. She switched the television back on with the remote control. There was another repeat of Adrian Farley Show on; she had just caught the beginning of the second half. There was a young man sitting on a velvet green sofa spouting on about how he was 'The innocent party in this whole sordid affair'. It soon became clear to May that he had married twelve women, all from the same family but not one of them knew about any of the others. May shook her fist at the screen.

"Are you stupid or some such? How didn't you know?" She picked up her teacup, it was empty. Her stomach still felt queasy, I need to eat something then it will settle. She lifted the lid of the tea pot and it was also empty. She looked down at the last solitary Bake well slice. As one of her few vices, it stared back at her like a wonder pill with the promise to cure both her body and soul. She took a large bite that saw over half the sticky, sweet slice disappear into her mouth. The cake had been left uncovered for over an hour and it had become dry and flaky to the touch. May chewed for a moment and then tried to swallow. The mouthful of stale pastry stole what little moisture that had remained in her throat. She couldn't swallow; she couldn't breathe. She started to panic and tried to spit it out but all she could muster was crumbs. It had become wedged in her throat and the fragments of fondant gripped at her gullet like putty, preventing her from coughing her airway clear. She fell forward, bending over double, trying to dislodge the cake but with every attempt her strength faded. She eventually lost consciousness and life gradually slipped from her grasp.

Chapter Two

May opened her eyes but the blackness remained. She had a blurred memory of choking and her throat felt raw and blistered. Frightened to move, she tried to make sense of her fractured mind. While searching through the confusion a voice filtered out, it was clear above the humming chaos.

"Never give nothing to no one," May recognised the coarse throaty voice.

"A penny earned is your frickin' penny and nobody else's". The image of Mrs Collins appeared in May's mind and she remembered the lessons she had learnt from her favourite nurse at the orphanage. May's earliest memories were of Mrs Collins which was probably why she was at the top of her mind. May's parents were as strangers to her. She had never sought to find them, even though she had considered it when she was young. They had left her at the orphanage while she was just a small baby, so the strong willed nurse had become the closest thing to mother that she had ever known. Mrs Collins had been her champion and mentor; she held dear all her teachings.

"The world's full of evil doers and lazy cretins, are you listening girl. Look at me when I'm talking. If anyone asks anything of you, you tell them girl, you tell them to get off their arse and earn it for themselves".

"Mrs Collins where am I, what do I do?" May pleaded, still trapped in a dark swirl of patchy memories.

"Charity starts at home and that's where it should frickin' stay". The voice seemed louder, closer. May's jumbled mind started to take form, the confusion was beginning to fade.

"God helps those who help themselves; who are we to argue with God" The image of Mrs Collins was suddenly replace by another image, this one was of Margaret. She was holding a 2ft long Bakewell slice up to her mouth, as if she was going to play it like a trumpet. Like a scene from an old cartoon, Margaret stuffed the entire cake into her

14

mouth before fading into the blackness and May could remember everything.

She moved her right hand, which seemed to work, she moved her left hand. Maybe it was a dream, May pondered, as she used both her hands to prop herself into a sitting position. As soon as her head was a few inches from the floor she could see again, as if a blindfold had been removed. May looked down and found herself sitting in her freshly vacated corpse. It lay flat on its back across the lounge carpet. Her legs were still in perfect sync with her body's but the rest of her was at right angles with herself. So it was no dream, you dammed old fool. You killed yourself with a frikin' cake. Death by confectionery; what an epilogue that's going to make. She scolded her self some more and then raised herself gingerly to her feet. Looking down at her own body, May felt her stomach tighten and twist. Her face had turned blue, her eyes were wide open and her mouth was gaping; it wasn't a dignified look.

May examined the way that she had fallen and, in one respect, she felt relieved. Her arms where outstretched and her right leg was twisted under her left. I might be dead, May considered and I may look as if I'm a hungry chick waiting to be fed a worm but at least I'm not spread-eagled across the carpet in some undignified manner.

May's eyes became moist and a single tear teetered on the edge of existence. The uncomfortable feeling in her stomach rose up through her chest and settled at the base of her throat, where it felt like patient bile. May bowed her head a little and clasped her hands in an unsettled grip. She realised that she would be missed by few and her passing would go unnoticed by most. She expected that there would be no tears at her funeral and no empty hearts would be left wanting. The most she could expect was that Margaret would have to find something else to do on Tuesday afternoons.

May had never really concerned herself about the way

other people felt about her but now something was different, something fundamental had changed. Something other than life had left her, something she had held most dear.

"You've been so tied up in yourself, selfish and alone". May spoke the words aloud but they lacked any real enthusiasm. "I'm alone because that's how I like it". The only reason May hadn't moved up into the mountains, to live like a real hermit, years ago was because she preferred to look down on people symbolically rather than physically take the higher ground. She began to pace up and down the length of her corpse.

"I have no regrets," she told herself, shaking her head as if to add strength the statement. "I can't expect the world to stop turning just because of me. I wouldn't stop for anyone else; I wouldn't even change my ways to save the world". May had led an independent life and she now faced Death the same way, independently. She had no need for mourners or tears of sorrow but, somewhere deep inside, she felt it would nice to at least have been missed. She had an inward perspective that refused to allow herself to believe that her passing would be treated in any other way. That was the way her mind worked and it made sense to her to assume that everyone else thought in the same way.

"So that's it then, I'm dead". Her life was now over and there were no second chances. She had led her life faithful to her principles and was confident in a life well spent, yet she still felt that it had all ended too soon. Life has deserted her too early. There were so many things left undone, there was washing up in the sink for a start.

May suddenly felt as if she was being watched. She stopped pacing and, unsure whether to be scared or surprised, turned slowly towards the kitchen door. Familiar eyes starred back at her. The cat looked plump but it was mostly fluff encompassing a hardened stout frame. Years of hunting the small creatures that used to populate May's rear garden had cultivated a gnarled muscular body beneath the bushy ginger fur. He was the size of a small dog and had eyes like polished dinner plates, that starred adoringly up at May.

"See! I can't even feed Mr Kibbles," She thought aloud. "Now that I'm dead". May's recently rebooted memory took a few moments to jog her conscious mind. Mr Kibbles had died over ten years ago.

It had been a difficult time, May hadn't realised until he had gone just how much emotion she had invested in her scruffy ball of fur. Mr Kibbles looked up at her and mewed. It was a simple sound but it wrenched May's heart from her chest. He strode towards her with his tail held high. May's legs felt weakened and numb as he weaved around them, purring contently. The knots in her stomach began to loosen and she felt an unfamiliar warm glow. She picked him up and held him in her arms for the first time in a decade. The softness of his fur and the slightly fishy smell of his breath, brought old dormant emotions bubbling to the surface. Another tear formed in her eye but this time it broke free and trickled down her face. It fell but didn't touch the ground. She watched as it passed ineffectively through the carpet and disappear beyond.

With Mr Kibbles still purring in her arms, May started pacing again. What now? She thought. What happens next? Do I get swept up by a column of light and ferried upon high into the heavens? Or do I stay and haunt this place? As I have already for so many years. Mr Kibbles began to struggle for freedom. His body wriggled in her arms, so she was forced put him back on the floor. As she bent down she noticed the lack of pain in her knees. She smiled as she remembered how Mr Kibbles had always set a limited duration when it came to cuddles. He stayed by her feet washing his paws, as if no time had passed and nothing much had changed.

"OK Mr Kibbles," May asked. "What do I do now?" Mr Kibbles seemed to ignore her; in the usual way cats do.

She began to wander around the house, looking at her belongings. Trying but not actually touching anything. She was quite glad she had made her bed earlier and that the majority of the house was tidy. She hated to leave things in such a mess. The kitchen was in need of a little attention but she could live with that. The living room, however, was in a wholly unacceptable state. There were crumbs on her armchair and broken crockery scattered across the floor, not to mention the dead body lying on the carpet. She stopped and considered this fact for a moment, biologically. Her sense was still a little clouded and she had to admit to herself that she wasn't running on all cylinders but she still had enough awareness to realise that the atmosphere in that room was not going to improve any. In fact, as she didn't expect anyone to call on her for at least another week, things were going to begin to smell pretty bad in there. May turned away from the sight of her own body and tried to detach herself from the more emotional aspects of her predicament.

"OK girl, a clear head and a sensible approach is what's needed here". She forced herself into practical thought. She knew that she couldn't touch anything, except for Mr Kibbles that is and this had made little impact upon her until now. A real sense of helplessness began to wash over her, it was a feeling that May had not felt since she had first left the orphanage to make her way in the world. Stepping through those great iron gates and leaving behind what little family or sense of community she had ever known. May could remember Mrs Collins face as she offered her mentor a stiff wave goodbye. Her eyes looked on in a critical stare, watching for any sign of weakness in her prodigy. May rewarded her with a tough fearless appearance, while inside her heart pounded like that of a startled deer. Mrs Collins stood with her arms folded across her chest. A slight nod was all the acknowledgement May received as she left, never to set foot within those great iron gates again.

May took a slow deep breath. Physically it was a pointless action but it still helped her gain focus. She gradually swept the feeling aside and regained her composure. It became clear to May but she wasn't the least bit happy about it, that she couldn't solve this problem alone. She sighed, there was no other option left open to her and it grated against her principles like course sandpaper. She took another glance at her stiffened body and steeled herself for the inevitable. She would have to go outside and seek help.

She stepped towards the front door, reached out and tried to turn the handle. She watched as her hand passed through it, without reaction or sensation. May had half expected as much but this didn't stop her from trying a second time. Faced with the same result she turned to Mr Kibbles, he was watching her with doe-eyed interest.

"OK cat," she knelt down to his level. "How do I open this door? You've been dead ten years now, so surely you've picked up a few pointers". He rubbed himself across her knees and then flopped, belly side up, on the floor beside her. She tiggled him for a moment and the raised herself back to her feet. Mr Kibbles rolled over and stood beside her. She turned to face the door again. The thought had occurred to her a while ago but she had buried at the back of her mind. Yes I agree; if my hands can pass through solid objects then the rest of me should follow suit. May just couldn't help thinking of it as an unnatural act of some kind. People do not walk through walls but I guess I'm not people any more. Normal people walk through doors! It was the only justification she could find for what needed to be done.

May closed her eyes and took a slow step forward. She felt no unusual sensation other than trepidation. She allowed one of her eyes to crack open to discover that she had not yet reached the door. Her nose was still half a centimetre away from the wooden panel. She closed here eyes again and took another step, still no change. No resistance, no sense of pressure or the sensation of the air around her thickening, as she had imagined it would feel like. Another step followed another, until the ground seemed to disappear beneath her feet. She tumbled forward, falling head over heels. She opened her eyes and it dawned on her, she had forgotten about the three steps that led away from her front door. She suffered a strange sensation as she fell. It seemed to happen in slow motion, because gravity had a lot less to grab onto now. She didn't feel the concrete steps as she rolled down them; it was like they were padded in some way. It was akin to falling over in a bouncy castle but without the rebound or the risk of getting landed on by overexcited twelve year olds. She finally drifted to a halt, like a leaf falling from a tree, coming to a rest half on and half off the pavement. She rose back to her feet gingerly and, with a face as red as a clown's nose, brushed imaginary dust from her clothes.

May's house was situated on a wide, busy street. It was mainly residential, but still a popular cut through for traffic trying to avoid Main Street at rush hour. May looked up and down the road. There was very little traffic; it was still too early for the evening rush. Trees lined the road; their branches overhung both sides and had grown to a shape that accommodated the passing buses. May could see a large red shape in the distance. As it slowly approached it gained clarity and May saw that it was a number 46. Regular as clockwork that bus, May thought to herself, outdated, unreliable and prone to seizing up at the first sign of wet weather. It was the slowest moving object May could see and she figured that buses were generally used to being flagged down. May took the opportunity and stepped into the road. She waved her arms wildly and cried out for help, which made her think of Penelope Pitstop and the Wacky Races. The bus kept approaching and showed no sign of slowing. May kept waving her arms above her head and the bus kept coming.

"He's going to stop," May announced to herself. "He's going to stop". The bus kept approaching and its speed remained unchanged. May could see the drivers face, it was filled with fierce concentration and purpose. The bus was so close now that May realised, all too late, that it wasn't going to stop at all. With no time to move, May braced herself as the 12 tonne vehicle bared down on her. May screamed in another Pitstop moment and thought she saw the driver twist his head sharply towards her. There was no impact and again no sensation, as she merged into the bus. May flowed through the windscreen and then slipped rapidly down the centre aisle of the bus. She finally passed through the engine compartment and found herself back out on the road. She was shaken and confused but she could have sworn that she saw Mrs Wiggins sitting in an aisle seat by the middle doors. She was wearing that stupid blue cloth hat with the little pink feather in it again. May had always thought that it gave her an odd appearance and an aura of instability. May felt embarrassed about her scream.

"You soppy old mare". Screaming was an automatic and understandable reaction, had it been performed by anyone else. A 12 tonne, double-decker, bus hurtling towards you with no means to avoid it, was a suitable situation for the employment of such an outcry. May would have made no comment, derogatory or otherwise, had she been just a spectator to the event. She was different however. She was May Elizabeth Trump and May Elizabeth Trump didn't make a public spectacle of herself, no matter what the circumstances.

She turned and saw Mr Kibbles sitting on the steps by her front door. May skipped out of the road just as a green van, with the word 'Gracie's' stencilled on the side, hurtled passed, just missing her by an inch. She walked up to the old ginger tom cat and made a fuss of his head.

"Did you see all that?" Mr Kibbles just looked up at her and mewed. "I think that bus driver might have heard me, I'm just not sure though. It happened so fast, he could have just been looking at you. No he can't see you either, can he?" May turned away and took another look up the road. A few cars were in sight, passing through from either direction but they were travelling too fast for her to try the same approach again. She knew if anyone was going to see or hear her, they would have to be close up and slow moving.

She started to walk up the street, following the same direction as the bus but travelling at a much slower pace. She kept catching glimpses of Mr Kibbles as he followed her by way of the gardens to her left. She would occasionally see him leap a hedge or scurry past an open gate. It gave her comfort to know that he was there. She had loved very few things in her life but Mr Kibbles was at the top of the list among them.

It wasn't long before she saw someone approaching from the opposite direction. She started waving her hands above her head as they both walked towards each other. She recognised him, it was Mr Chimer from next door book one. He was only a few metres away; Mr Chimer seemed oblivious to May's presence.

"Hello...hello!" May yelled, as the gap between them closed to just a few feet. "Can you hear me? Hello!" Mr Chimer continued walking towards and eventually straight through her. May was becoming a little annoyed.

"Mr Chimer!" She yelled at the top of her voice.

"George!" She could feel her tonsils rattle against her throat. Almost immediately, Mr Chimer stopped still and begun to look around. He looked left and then right. He turned around in a pivot and looked straight through May; there was no reaction or recognition in his eyes. May waved half-heartedly and then watched, as George turned his back on her. He shook his head and continued to walk away.

"George...George, it's me! May from two doors down. The old Witch! I've heard you call me it. I don't mind George, really I don't mind. Just hear me, just hear me please!" He didn't stop again.

She tried to contact another three people in a similar fashion but received no reaction from any of them. She didn't even get a puzzled pause, as she had from George. They had been strangers to her and their lack of response did not concern her as much. George had been the first familiar face she had seen since her death, not counting Mr Kibbles and for some reason that fact mattered. May and Georges relationship had hardly been close. They were neighbours and not even fence to fence neighbours for that matter; Mrs Brown's house stood between them. May had always thought of him and his family, as the noisy ones from down the road and she knew they all thought of her as the skinflint witch. May understood just how her lifestyle alienated her from other people and, as far as she was concerned, that had always been a benefit. She enjoyed being on her own and at that precise moment she couldn't have felt any more alone. So why doesn't if feel right? She thought. Why does it hurt?

She reached the end of her road and turned right onto the main carriageway that led directly towards the town centre. The main road was wider and much busier, cars and vans were hurtling by from both directions. The pavement ended on May's side of the road, giving way to a steep grassy verge than ran the entire distance to the large roundabout that marked the beginning of the town centre. She waited until there was a larger enough gap in the traffic for her to cross. Mr Kibbles didn't suffer the same delay, as he bounded through the fast moving traffic, merging in and out of the speeding vehicles. May half knew that she could have walked straight out into the road and not encountered any real difficulty. It was partially habit and partially uncertainty that made her wait. Mr Kibbles was preening himself for the umpteenth time when May finally reached the other side of the road. He looked up at her and mewed.

"Yes, yes smarty pants," she said to him. "Where's the fire anyway?"

They began to walk down Main Street towards the town centre. May used the pavement while Mr Kibbles kept pace on the wall that ran parallel to the road, leaping over gaps and alleyways. There were more pedestrians on the main road. Most of them seemed to be heading towards the shopping precinct, the main hub of the town. May waved her hands in their faces as they passed by, oblivious of her efforts. May was still trying to grab anyone's attention, just not as optimistically as before. They were half-hearted gestures now; she was getting tired of being ignored.

The town centre was not far ahead and the journey didn't seem as long as it had previously. May's knees would normally be aching something fierce by now and she hadn't stopped for her usual sit down breaks. Mr Kibbles had disappeared into some gardens to her left but she was sure he would turn up again soon. The road began to widen to accommodate a large roundabout, which stood as a local landmark to indicate to people that they had reached the town centre. To her left was a large detached house, three stories high and surrounded by a large garden. The house faced the roundabout as the road bent around it. Its position created a triangular plot of land in front of the building, large enough to park several vehicles. As May passed by, she saw someone crouched down on the large driveway. It was a woman in her forties, wearing yellow summer dress with light blue flowers scattered randomly over it. She was stroking a large ginger cat, which weaved contently around her. May took a further two steps before she realised exactly what it was that she was seeing. That woman was petting Mr Kibbles.

May turned around and stepped up to the waist high, wrought iron gate that marked the entrance to the driveway. The woman was still there and so was Mr Kibbles.

"Excuse me; I do believe that's my cat". The woman looked up, she seemed surprised.

"Can you see me?" She asked standing up; Mr Kibbles continued to weave about her legs.

"Yes of course I can! Can you see me?" May replied, just as surprised. The woman skipped more than walked over to May.

"Yes...yes I can thank God". The woman smiled inanely, as if she was cooing over a small child.

"Who are you?" May asked, leaning over the gate, she could see that the woman had recently been crying.

"Who am I? I'm Penny Saunders, this is my house". The name struck a chord with May; she remembered her conversation with Margaret

"Penny Saunders? Didn't you die? Aren't you dead?" May asked bluntly. Penny stumbled backwards, as if the strength in her legs had momentary left her.

"Yes...yes I guess I am aren't I". Penny put her hands up to her face but May could still see the tears as they glistened through her fingers. May realised that her approach had obviously been a little too harsh for Penny, the woman was clearly fragile. May had never been very good with social interactions when she was alive and death wasn't about to warm her spirit any. She wasn't comfortable with compassion and she had little experience dealing with emotional people. She remembered Mrs Collins teachings and how she had handled May when she had been young and, May hated to admit it, a little delicate.

"Pull yourself together woman. I mean no harm by it". The brash outburst seemed to have had the desired effect. Penny wiped her eyes with the back of her hand.

"Yes...yes you're right!" She said, bleary eyed and red faced. "So who are you then? Some kind of psychic or medium?" It was May's turn to take a stumble backwards, she felt horrified. To be compared to such charlatans. Such people who preyed on the weak and gullible, profiting from another's grief. She gave neither time nor compassion for the naïve and gullible but the con artists and tricksters of this world were in a league of their own. They had no morals or principles. She had spent many hours moaning and complaining about their victims and how they shouldn't have been so trusting and so easily swayed, while sitting in front of her television set. The perpetrators, however, she had no words for. They filled her with disgust and no words, that were acceptable in decent society, could describe how she felt about them with sufficient wrath.

"How dare you! I certainly am not!" May erupted, her face turned red and her lips became as thin as a razors edge.

"Oh...I...I'm sorry," Penny replied. The tears were threatening to return. "I... I just thought, what with you being able to see and hear me. I assumed you had The Gift, or what ever it is they call it?" She bowed her head and rubbed her eyes again. "This is just typical of me. The first person I talk to in over a week and I'm already insulting them". May stepped through the closed gate and took Penny's hands in her own.

"It's alright," May said, her voice was smooth and quiet. It wasn't a tone she was used to and took a lot of effort to maintain. "As I said, I mean no harm. I'm always a little brash and easily provoked, it's just my way". Penny looked up and gave May half a smile, before looking back down at their hands.

"You can touch me? How come you can touch me? Who are you?"

May struggled to keep her voice smooth and free from sarcasm. "My name is May Elizabeth Trump and I am just as dead as you are".

Chapter Three

May stared at the woman standing in front of her. Her eyes were still red and blotchy but a faint smile was showing at the edge of her mouth.

"I'm not being a very good host," Penny admitted as they parted hands. "Please do come in". Penny gestured towards the house and then began to walk up the driveway. May looked back towards the town centre, the street was becoming busier.

"What's the point," May shrugged. "Nobody's listening anyway". May looked around for Mr Kibbles but he had wandered off again, as was his way. She set off up the driveway after Penny. They entered by the front door, though they clearly didn't need to. May was slowly coming to terms with being beyond tactile contact with the living world; the journey through the big oak door was less of unnerving experience. They entered into the passage way and Penny begun pointing out the off shooting rooms. It was a very large house; twice the size of May's and probably double the value. She remembered what Margaret had said about the possibility of an issue with money here but the house must have been worth a fortune. May peered into each of the rooms. They were old fashioned in décor, nothing seemed modern or new. The papered walls and painted woodwork seemed to be in need of some attention in places. She recognised the smell of rising damp and the tell tale signs where mildew had recently been wiped away. There was great value in the building and the land but the interior told a different story. She could tell that there was hardship here. This place was being poorly maintained with little more than sweat and tears.

"This house has been in my family for generations," Penny said, as she showed May around. "It was built in 1754. It's full of history and very personal to me". 1754, May thought, that must have been the last time it had been decorated.

"It's all left up to my daughter Chloe now. I'm not sure how she's going to cope with it. She's still at college for the moment but my meagre savings won't last her very long. When that runs out, she will have nothing to live on. I really don't want her to give up her education but I also don't want this house to fall into the hands of strangers. It's not my decision now anyway, even if I had answers I can't get her to hear me. That's why I haven't answered the calling; I'm just not ready to go yet".

"Calling?" May asked, "What calling?"

"When the angels summon you to heaven," Penny explained. "Or at least that's what I hoped it was. It's a warm welcoming feeling that gently tugs away at you, trying to draw you closer. You don't actually move with it. The pressure seems to want you to fold into yourself. It was only about five minutes after my death, the first time I felt it. It comes and goes and is easily rejected. It's as if it won't take you unless you give yourself up to it and I'm not ready for that quite yet". I've not experienced anything remotely like that, May thought and I've been dead for a good few hours now.

"Are you sure it's not just indigestion?"

"You must be kidding. Unless I'm just not explaining it right? It's definitely no belly ache, that's for sure. It's the pull of the angels, I'm certain of it and it seems to be gradually getting stronger".

"And you get this quite often?"

"Yes, once or twice a day. I'll let them take me as soon as I'm sure that my daughter will be alright". May was beginning to wonder if she had something wrong with her. The thought also occurred to her that maybe whatever was calling for Penny just doesn't want her. Maybe she had been too independent, too selfish. If that much was true then maybe it was just a matter of time before she feels the hot, downward pull of talons.

"What would you say if I told you that I haven't felt the calling yet?" May asked. Penny fell silent for a moment.

"Well! Obviously I don't know anything for sure but I

28

would hazard a guess that it's a sign that you still had some kind of work to; before you move on so to speak. You might think your ready but someone or something might have a special plan for you. Like a holy crusade or some such thing". May hadn't considered that possibility; the thought gave her some hope. What she had heard about the underworld might turn out to be untrue. Either way, she had never been a great fan of hot weather.

"I take it you don't mean that I have to conquer Jerusalem," May said sarcastically.

"Oh no of course not," Penny replied, shaking her head. The sarcasm was obviously lost on her. "It's probably something smaller and a lot more local".

"That's possible I guess," May acknowledged, mostly because it was easier to swallow than the alternative. "We'll see".

"Anyway, why were you wandering about out there?" Penny asked.

"I was trying to tell someone what had happened. I live...lived alone and no one even knows I'm dead yet".

"I'm sorry to hear that. At least I know now, so you're not alone any more," Penny said, smiling sympathetically.

"I like being alone! I don't need anyone's pity," May barked. Penny showed no reaction to May's harsh tone. It was as if she had gained a little more strength of confidence. Whether it was because she was now in her own home or because May had let a little vulnerability show, it wasn't clear.

"That may well be true but you're here now in my house. You didn't have to come in. You didn't have to talk to me but you did. Things aren't the same as they were. It might not be wise to burn any bridges so soon". May wanted to disagree but she could see the sense in her words.

"Alright Penny," May relented. "I'm sorry if I come across as rude but I'm used to being alone and fighting my own corner. My social skills are a little rusty; please forgive me if I come across as brash".

"We are both confused and unsure of ourselves," Penny Smiled. "It's all going to take some getting used to. Anyway, did you have any luck? Did you get the message across to anyone?"

"No not really. It's like I'm not even there. I was unseen and unheard".

"Yep, that sounds about right". Penny nodded her head. "I've been at it for a week now and all I can manage is a few faint orbs and that was only when I concentrate really hard. I've not had any luck with sound yet".

"What do you mean by orbs?"

"They're little white lights. They are supposedly the beginning of a manifestation. My orbs are so faint, however, they could be easily mistaken as just flecks of dust floating in the air". May considered this and realised that, if it was going to take a week just to make a room appear dusty her plan of explaining her predicament to a living person within a day was unlikely at best.

"So you have had no progress in getting yourself heard either?" May asked.

"No I seem to be having a lot of difficulty with that. I screamed myself hoarse trying to communicate with my daughter, all she did was walk straight through me as if I wasn't there. It was rather disheartening".

"So you've not managed even the smallest of sounds?"

"No, not a squeak. Why have you?" Penny replied and May thought about George.

"Maybe, There was this one man on the street where I lived," May explained. "It could have been just coincidence but it's possible I triggered a reaction from him".

"Why? What happened?"

"I knew him and I called out his name. He stopped and then started to look around. He seemed puzzled. He looked straight at me but I'm sure he couldn't see me. Eventually he just turned around and carried on walking. I kept calling after him but he didn't react again". May kept running the event over and over in her mind. If it was a coincidence, it had been perfectly timed.

"That is strange," Penny agreed. "How long is it since you...passed?" Penny was showing a little more tact when talking about death than May had been able to muster.

"Only a few hours, maybe four or five. I can't be sure; I don't even know what the time is now".

"Well if it's not a coincidence you are showing a lot more potential than I am," Penny pointed out. May felt Penny was selling herself a little short and, against her usual nature, informed her of the fact.

"You've managed to do those orb things that you told me about. I can't do anything like that".

"Yes but I'm a week ahead in the game! I should be doing public appearances by now". Get over yourself and stop being such a drama queen! May kept the thought silent so as not to upset Penny further. May began to notice how her conscience was behaving rather strange of late.

"It probably takes time and a lot of effort to master these skills; you may need to show patience".

"Time is something I haven't got," Penny complained. "I've got to solve these problems for my daughter and then convey the solutions to her somehow". May then did something that she has no memory of ever doing before. She freely offered Penny her help.

Chapter Four

Chloe Saunders was only nineteen years old and already alone. There were plenty people ready and waiting to offer her their compassion but she was tired of well wishers. Chloe couldn't help visualising them as a rugby scrum, all trying to push their own shoulder forward for her to cry on. She understood their concerns but she didn't need them reminding her, every minute of the day, just how empty her life had become.

She had lost the only close family she had. Her father had left while her mother was still pregnant with her and he had never returned. There had been no contact, not even a letter or a post card, she didn't even know if he was still alive. She hadn't tried to find him in years. She had gone through a phase, when she was about fourteen years old but it had been short lived. She was aware of an aunt who lived abroad but she had very little recollection of her. She had been no more than five years old the last time she had seen her. Her mother was all she had and now she was gone.

Chloe was throwing herself into her studying; distracting herself from her grief whenever possible. Her tutor and fellow student's relentless compassion made it difficult. They had suggested that maybe a short break, time away from hustle and bustle, would help her mourn. She disagreed; she had no where else to go but back home. She felt that the big empty house drained her of strength; too many things reminded her of what she had lost. She preferred to fool herself for now. She knew it was only a temporary solution but she couldn't afford to let herself become overwhelmed with grief.

She had no income and very little savings. The house would be her only equity, once the solicitors had done their work. The legal fees were going to eat into the meagre savings that her mother had left behind. She knew that it would be in her best interest to sell up and buy somewhere smaller, somewhere cheaper to maintain. She couldn't do it though. It was the family home and had meant a lot to her mother. Chloe knew that she had been loved and cherished by her mother and that she was the only thing more important to her than the house. She had watched her mother struggle to keep it within the family and she didn't want to let it go without a fight. The house was Chloe's responsibility now that it had been left entirely to her in her mother's will. Her solicitor had explained about how her estranged aunt was contesting the will. Which in it's self would have been no bad thing, she was family after all, if she had intended to keep it and help with its running costs. Her Aunt had ambitions that didn't mirror her own or her mothers. She wanted to sell it to a property developer who would probably convert it into flats. It would be gutted and stripped of all its character. It was just another pressure that Chloe had to endure at a particularly difficult time.

Chloe pulled her jacket collar up close around her neck. There was a chill breeze in the air as night lingered on the horizon. She walked slowly; she wasn't in any hurry to get back home to an empty house. Her journey took her close to the shopping precinct and she felt herself drawn to the lights in the shop windows. She stared into the window of a closed shoe shop; nothing caught her interest because she wasn't really looking. She was just staring time away. It was similar delay tactic which lead her to one of the few local fast food restaurants.

Buster's was the only burger bar in town but that wasn't the only reason why it was such a popular place to eat. The sign outside boasted: "Buster's Burgers, the best in town," which was considered as local humour. Buster's had made the local paper last year when it saw the competition, a large national company, close it's local branch and move to a town five miles away. Even the lack of completion and the best beef patties within walking distance were not the reason why the restaurant was never empty; the main attraction was Buster himself.

He was a born and bred local who was considered, by many of the town's older residents, as "Our little entrepreneur". He had opened the restaurant with other people's money and now, after only ten years, he was debt free. He owned the freehold to the building and even let the flat above to one of his employees, at a thin sliver of a discount.

Chloe joined the queue for the counter. It was busy as usual. Most of the avocado and brown tables were occupied and she could hear Buster singing from the kitchen at the back. He had a passable voice and could perform a reasonable vocal impersonation of Elvis Presley. There was a karaoke machine in the kitchen and one of the strict conditions for any prospective employee was the ability to sing. Buster didn't expect his employees to be opera singers or have any actual vocal talent as such. You just had to be able to hold a tune while turning the patties at the same time.

Buster was currently performing his very own interpretation of the classic Heartbreak Hotel. Some of the patrons were singing along while waving their milkshakes from side to side. Chloe wasn't in the mood for singing and it seemed neither was the guy standing in front of her in the queue. She recognised him as a local boy who she had known for many years. His parents used to be friends of her mother, not particularly good friends; they were more like social acquaintances.

Stephen Chimer was only sixteen, a few years younger than Chloe and she had a suspicion that he had a little crush on her. He turned around to face her, as if he had felt her eyes upon him.

"Hello Chloe" Stephen greeted uncomfortably, "How are

you keeping, what with....um".

"I'm doing OK," Chloe lied, "How's the family?"

"Well it's been a bit of a strange day" Stephen admitted. "Dad was on his way home from work and he said that he could have sworn that he heard the lady who lived two doors down from us call out his name. He swears that there was no one in the street at the time but it did get him thinking about her. He decided to check up on her, she was pretty old and lived on her own and he figured it wouldn't be any bother as he had to walk passed her house to get home. He knocked on her door but there was no answer. He said that he could hear the noise coming from her T.V so he guessed that was why she couldn't hear him knocking. He was going to walk away at that point but something stopped him. He couldn't say what it was exactly. It was just a feeling he said that made him go around to the side of the house and looked through the window".

Stephen abruptly stopped talking, as if a button had been pushed in his head and then continued in a quieter voice. "Oh sorry maybe I shouldn't be telling you this what with...what happened?" Chloe was getting used to it; everyone seemed to be stuttering and pausing around her lately. She understood their hesitancy but only to a point. Her mother had been a popular local figure and was missed by many but Chloe was getting tired of people walking eggshells around her.

"No you carry on" Chloe insisted, "I'll be fine". The story had caught her interest and the queue was slow moving. Stephen didn't seem to need much encouragement.

"Well, when he looked inside he saw old Mrs Trump laying cold stone dead on her living room carpet".

"Oh God, that's terrible!" Chloe said. "It's lucky your dad found her when he did". Chloe was shocked. Even in this day and age somebody could end up dieing alone and be noticed by no one, she thought. "What happened next?"

"Well it scared the life out of my dad for one thing, seeing her lying there. He was as white as a sheet when he stumbled into our house. Mum poured him a generous malt to perk him up." Stephen indicated just how much alcohol was in his dad's glass by the two inch space between his thumb and forefinger. "I know it was generous because he offered me one last Christmas and all I got was this much". 2inches became less than a centimetre. "We had to call the police and everything; that's why I'm here. After all that commotion mum just didn't feel like cooking tonight".

"I guess that's understandable," Chloe replied. "Do you know how Mrs Trump died?" She felt a little mercenary for asking such a question but she didn't know what else to say.

"We don't know; after the ambulance had gone the police taped off the house," Stephen explained. "They're treating her death as suspicious I think".

Chloe knew the procedure all too well. They had done much the same thing at her house when her mother had died. They only closed it off for two days and Chloe had to stay in a hotel until they finally discovered the faulty electrics in the bathroom. They said it was cased closed; death by misadventure, which Chloe thought was a barbaric thing to say to someone who was still grieving. Eric Spanner showed her far more respect when he called by the following day and he replaced the whole shower unit free of charge. He said that the bill had been taken care of but he wouldn't say by whom. Chloe hadn't pushed the matter. She guessed that her mother had taken out some kind of insurance that she wasn't aware of and Mr Spanner had seemed a nice enough man; he even disposed of the old shower unit to save her the bother.

Stephen was at the head of the queue and ordering his food. Buster was singing Hound Dog; slightly out of key but full of passion and gusto. Chloe was waved forward to the counter and Stephen stepped aside.

"I've got to wait for Dad's Belly Buster" he shrugged.

"Hello Chloe, how are you keeping up?" Jean asked from the other side of the counter; it was a very small town.

"I'm OK thanks," Chloe replied with fake zeal. "Can I have a Buster Burger and a small fries to takeaway please Jean". Jean tapped at the console in front of her.

"Would you like a drink with that?" Jean asked robotically, as if reading off an autocue. "Can I have a medium Buster's Berry Juice, diet please and no ice". Chloe paid for her food and Jean began to gather it together. She was glad that the Buster Burgers were all ready and waiting on the hot shelf. Buster was just starting to sing Wooden Heart and she was well aware of his usual set list. She didn't think she could cope with hearing his famous rendition of Old Shep. Jean bagged the food and handed it to her.

"Enjoy your meal" Jean said and then in a slightly quieter voice, "Call me if you need to talk". Chloe thanked her for the food and the concern but assured her that she was doing just fine. She said goodbye to Stephen, who was still waiting for Buster's famously huge burger. When she left the restaurant, buster was just tailing off Wooden Heart and he didn't usually pause very long before starting the next song. Chloe considered it as a close shave.

The short walk home had been uneventful and the slight chill in the breeze was refreshing after the heat in the restaurant. She had drunk half her berry juice before she had even reached her garden gates. She opened the gates and they squeaked slightly. She fancied that she saw a flash of orange disappear around the side of the house but she assumed it was a just fox or another wild animal. The gardens at the back of the house were at best overgrown and at worst a jungle. She was used to wild creatures roaming the grounds at night.

She opened the front door with her keys in one hand and her food and college bag in the other. She struggle down the hallway and into the kitchen with her berry juice perched precariously. She was worried that she might drop it; berry juice could create a stubborn stain. She knew this because her mother had given her a bit of a tongue lashing while she was trying to remove the last one Chloe had spilt. She managed to ferry her burdens to the kitchen table without incident. She pulled up a chair and sat down to eat.

The house was quiet and the rustling of her burger wrapper sounded very loud. She opened her college bag and pulled out a text book; which she flicked through as she ate. It helped distract her from the silence that was only broken by the occasion creak and groan, which was usual of such an old house. Chloe finished her food and tidied away the packaging into the recycle bin. She closed her book; her mind was wandering and her eyes were tired. It wasn't particularly late in the evening but she already had thoughts of turning in for the night. She glanced at her watch, I've not gone to bed this early in years. I'll take a bath first, she decided, a nice warm bath. She switched off the kitchen light and made her way up to the first floor. Her footfalls made the staircase creak and the noise echoed through the house.

Suddenly she heard a voice, a whisper. It sounded like someone was speaking loud and brashly but from very far away. She stopped and listened but didn't hear it again. I'm tired and stressed, she told herself. She hadn't been sleeping well this past week and obviously exhaustion was beginning to set in. She decided to forgo the bath and head straight to bed; maybe she would feel better in the morning. Even as she lay in bed drifting into overdue sleep, she felt confused. Why on earth would I image hearing the words: "Frickin' calm down woman?"

<u>Chapter Five</u>

The two ghosts were on the first floor of the house, in the room that Penny used to sleep in. May paced the room; she was beginning to regret her moment of weakness. Penny was reasonable company, when she wasn't having panic attacks or fits of hopelessness, but May stilled preferred to be on her own. She had been considered many things during her life but unreliable wasn't one of them. She had made a principle of never going back on her word. Her general rule was: don't make any promises and you'll have no promises to break. However occasionally she had found herself with no choice but to put her reputation on the line and give out personal guarantees. This was one of those times. No matter how much she regretted it, she had given her word. You can tame the beast by trapping it and May felt more than a little caged. May wanted to solve this problem as soon as possible but Penny's emotional out bursts were not helping.

"For fricks sake! Calm down woman" May's temper was wearing thin and she wasn't the most tolerant of people at the best of times.

"I'm sorry," Penny sobbed, "I just hate to see her so alone like this. The poor girl's really going through the mill and there's nothing I can do about it".

"Sobbing and screaming not going to help her none," May pointed out, "but it's sure giving me a headache". May began to realise that her unsympathetic approach wasn't working particularly well but she didn't feel that she had the strength for compassion at the moment.

"Now calm down and be quiet so I can think," May ordered. She didn't have the faintest clue of how the resolve Penny's dilemma. She had no real experience with death or its after effects other than when Mr Kibbles had passed away. All she knew about ghosts and ghouls were what she had seen in old Abbot and Costello movies. It seemed that the supernatural never had much trouble snatching the limelight on the silver screen. In the real world it was a different matter entirely. The last thing she thought she would be doing eight hours after her death was trying to mediate between Randal and Hopkirk.

"I guess we should start with finding an answer to the financial problem first and then worry about how to convey it later," May suggested. Penny didn't look any more hopeful.

"And how do we do that?" Penny asked sarcastically, "it's not like we have a great, big pile of cash lying around is it?" May held her tongue. She had plenty of spare money just sitting there in her building society account but there was no way of getting to it. Besides, she thought, it's my legacy even if there is no one to inherit it.

"Obviously not!" May lied. "We have to come up with some kind of plan, some way that Chloe can earn an awful lot of money in a short period of time. Some kind of well paid job maybe; something she can do during the evenings and at weekends. Something that won't interfere with her education". Penny took a sudden step backwards. Her hands shot to her hips like hydraulic clamps; her eyes widened and her nostrils flared ever so slightly.

"How dare you suggest such a thing! I can't believe you even mentioned it".

"Calm down! It was just a suggestion". May didn't understand why Penny was getting so flustered. A bit of hard work never hurt anyone in her opinion; it was how she had earned every penny she had ever owned. She remembered what Mrs Collins used to say about such things: "Sweat and toil feeds the soul as well as the body," and it seemed to make even more sense to May now.

"It's disgusting is what it is!" Penny hadn't calmed down as May had instructed. "I've managed to keep this house running for years without ever lowering myself to such depths; I never even came close. Yet you waltz into my house offering to help at our time of crisis and all you can suggest is that my dear, sweet Chloe prostitutes her self on dirty street corners like some kind of low life whore!"

"Oh God no!" May felt mortified. "I didn't mean that! I didn't mean anything like it. I don't even know how you could think I could suggest such a thing. I meant working behind a bar or...Oh I don't know just something productive but not that! Not that at all".

"Oh! Bar work you say," Penny replied with a puzzled expression. Her hands dropped away from her waist. "Not prostitution then?"

"No! No way," May quickly replied.

"Oh, oh right". Penny said but then one of her hands returned to her waist while the other started wagging a finger at May. "No I'm still not happy. Serving drunk men while they ogle her all night long? No not my Chloe; not my baby".

"Well it's not like we can go out and get a job now is it?" May was getting a little bit impatient with Penny's reluctance to put her daughter to work. "They tend to serve spirits, not employ them!"

Even May herself had once worked in a pub to earn extra money. She had to admit though, it had been a long time ago and much had changed since then.

"So what! It doesn't change anything; I'm not sending her out to work in a pub and that's final". Penny stamped her foot; quite literally putting her foot down on the conversation. "There must be some other way?"

"Well ok, do you have anything worth selling? Any antiques or jewellery maybe?"

"Not really," Penny admitted, "Not anymore. I've already been down that road and have sold everything of value that I could bare to lose. I've got nothing but items of little more than sentimental value". May had expected as much, going by what she had seen of the house so far. She found it frustrating; they were just two ghosts and they were fast running out of options.

"I can't see any alternative," May confessed. "She will have to sell the house; I just don't see any other way".

"There must be another way," Penny cried, "This house has been our family home for generations".

"There's very little choice," May regretfully informed her.

"No I don't accept that," Penny pleaded. "There has to be

another way, there just has to".

May couldn't see any other way. They had nothing to sell and no earning potential. They needed money and that wasn't something that grew on trees, it didn't just appear out of thin air. It had to come from somewhere and, to May's experience, it generally came out of other people's pockets. Nobody parted with their hard earned cash without expecting something in return. They were just two ghosts and a young girl in mourning. What did they have that would be worth anything to anyone? What could they do that somebody would be willing to pay for?

May looked at Penny and sighed; maybe they just needed more time.

"We'll keep working on it, don't worry. You just have to except that this house is the only asset she has right now. You have to decide just how much you are willing to sacrifice to save it; you have to consider Chloe's education for a start".

"I won't let her sacrifice her education," Penny said. She seemed to surrender to the idea, if only partially. "If push comes to shove then she should sell the house". She paused, "however I just want to make one point quite clear: that's only if it comes down to it; it's early days yet".

They both heard the sound of a door being opened downstairs. The sound was quiet and drawn out, as if the door was being opened very carefully. May couldn't place the sound but Penny seemed to recognise the particular creak.

"That's the front door, who could that be?" Penny said and then sank straight through the floor feet first. May took an involuntary step backwards and stared at the floor where Penny had just stood. Now that's impressive, she thought, I didn't know we could do that. She walked up to and stood exactly where she had seen Penny disappear. Nothing seemed to happen so she tried bending her knees in an attempt to force her weight downwards. She found herself almost crouching before she began to feel a little absurd and stood up straight again. How did she do that? It puzzled May that some things where completely intangible while other things, such as the floor, were an impenetrable barrier. She looked around sheepishly to check if anyone was watching and then performed a quick, two footed jump. She jumped again but the floor still didn't surrender to her efforts. She sighed; there was obviously a knack to it that she had yet to acquire.

May could hear the sound of heavy footsteps climbing up the stairs. A few creaks from the floorboards of the landing and then a loud banging on the bedroom door.

"This is the police! I know you're in there so I want no funny business do you hear?" A familiar voice shouted gruffly through the door. The door handle began to slowly turn.

"I'm coming in so don't be starting any trouble!" The door opened and May recognised Constable Davis immediately. They had met on a couple occasions in the town centre and he had also paid her a few home visits after she had called the local police station to complain about one thing or another.

Constable Davis stepped into the room with his truncheon held high. He had the nervous expression of a man who was aware of his duty but not accustomed to performing some of the more dangerous aspects of it.

"I can't see anyone Miss Saunders," Davis announced as he scanned the room.

"Have you looked under the bed?" Chloe asked nervously from the doorway. The Constable crouched down and peered under the bed.

"No one there," He said, "Are you sure you heard voices?"

"Yes clear as day; one voice at least," Chloe explained. "They seemed to be talking to someone but I couldn't hear any of the replies. I guess they must have been on the phone or something. Have you checked the wardrobe?

They could be hiding in wardrobe!" Constable Davis sighed and cautiously pulled opened the wardrobe door. May stood by the window watching silently; taking in the scene. A realisation was slowing forming in her mind. Something unexpected was becoming possible. This will require further testing, she thought.

"I'm sorry Miss Saunders but there's no one in here," Davis confirmed his belief in the statement by putting his truncheon back into his pocket. "I understand that sometimes, during moments of great stress or aguish, the mind kind play tricks on a person. I know it seems real to you now but you have been through a lot lately; maybe you just need some rest".

"Maybe you're right," Chloe admitted reluctantly, "but could you check over the rest of the house just to be sure. I won't be able to sleep a wink otherwise".

"Of course I can, that's not a problem". Constable Davis stepped out of the room and closed the door behind him. Moments later Penny reappeared through the floor.

"Well isn't that interesting," She said. "Now that answers a few questions that does". May couldn't agree more; there was definitely something worth investigating going on here.

"I just saw Jean, you know Jean? Works at Buster's burger place. She's out there now in Constable Davis's car," Penny said, smiling proudly. "I always knew those two had something going on together". May groaned inwardly; it was a typical small town.

May walked over to the door and gestured for Penny to follow her.

"Come with me; we're going outside," May whispered as quietly as she could.

"Where are we going?" Penny asked but May didn't answer. She put her finger to her lips and walked through the door. May crept down the stairs and only looked back once to check that Penny was following her. They slipped through the front door and into the front garden. May wasn't sure where in the house Chloe's bedroom was located so she refrained from speaking until they were all they way up to the front gates.

"I think this is far enough away," she whispered.

"Far enough from what?" Penny whispered back through a puzzled expression. "Why are we whispering?"

"Because I think your Chloe can hear us, or at least one of us, by what I overheard her saying to Constable Davis," May explained.

"Oh!" Penny said aloud and then dropped back into a whisper. "Oops sorry! Do you really think she can hear us? I've been trying to talk to her for ages but she's never shown any reaction to me"

"No Penny I don't think she can hear us both; I think she can just hear me". May had been puzzling it over ever since Constable Davis had left the room; it was the only thing that made any sense.

"As you said," May explained, "You've tried to talk to her before but have always failed. She admitted to Constable Davis that she had only heard half a conversation. Somehow, I don't know how, my voice is getting through".

"Do you think she can hear everything you say?" Penny asked with a glint of hope in her eyes. This could be the answer to Penny's prayers but May wasn't willing to bet the farm on it quite yet.

"I don't know but I plan to find out!" May announced with purpose in her mind. She took a step back towards the house. Penny grabbed her shoulder.

"No not yet," She pleaded. "Let her sleep for now. She needs her rest; we can try in the morning".

"OK Penny," May reluctantly agreed. She was biting at the bit to find out just how much Chloe would be able to hear; It could solve her own problems as well as Penny's. "What do we do now then? Just wander around your house, haunting it all night?"

"No I've tried that before," Penny replied shaking her head. "Believe me it gets really boring after a while. However I've found that, when it's late like this, I tend to call it a night and go to sleep".

"You go to sleep? We don't need to sleep... do we?"

45

"No we don't need to sleep as such but we can sleep if we want to," Penny explained. "I think it's more like a kind of meditation. Centring your spirit and all that new age hippie stuff. I find it quite relaxing". May had never taken to such flower power mumbo jumbo.

"Why would you want to sleep if you don't need to?"

"Because of the dreams mainly but it also seems to revitalise me sometimes. We all need to stop and get our breath back and I guess this is how we do that now". It was beginning to make sense to May. When she was alive she used sleep as a way of detaching herself from whatever pressures life was throwing at her at any given time. Now that she was dead, she was permanently detached but it seemed that the same pressures still haunted her.

"What do you dream about?" May asked, "Are they the same as when you were alive?"

"No they're not quite the same," Penny explained but May sensed that she was just realising the truth as she spoke. "They are much more vivid; it's often hard to tell the difference. It's as if your not dreaming as such but it's almost as if you've entered another world. To tell you the truth I call it dreaming but who knows what's really possible?"

"And you do this every night?"

"Yes, it's easy. You just close your eyes and relax. As you let yourself drift away you seem to fade into another world". That didn't sound very relaxing to May; she wasn't happy relinquishing control at any time.

"And that's it?" May asked a little suspiciously. "You just close your eyes and dream, or what ever it is?"

"Pretty much yes," Penny replied. "And then you find yourself in a different world meeting people who have passed before you. You can even end up watching your own personal history, like a fly on the wall documentary, that's always interesting. This is just what I have experienced; it could be completely different for you". May hoped it would be; it all sounded too fluffy and pleasant to her. She never trusted anything nice that she hadn't had to work hard for. An easy victory was a suspicious one as far as she was concerned.

"Come on May," Penny said as she took her by the arm. "You need a break; it's your first day dead. You should take a little time to come to terms with it properly". Penny led May back into the house. May barely resisted, Penny was making more sense than she could find the strength to contest. May smiled, it had been a life changing day.

She allowed herself be led up the stairs and back into Penny's bedroom. She found a little comfort when she saw Mr Kibbles; he was snoozing on the end of the bed. Maybe not on the bed exactly but just a shade above it. Penny laid herself down on one side of her bed. It was a large king-size bed and there was more than enough room for two people and a cat without becoming too cosy. May sat down on the opposite side. There were plenty of empty bedrooms in Penny's house and May could have chosen to sleep in any one of them but she knew that Penny would find comfort in her presence. If she was truthful she would have to admit that she felt more comfortable with the company of both spirits close by.

"Now just close your eyes and relax," Penny explained softly. May laid down on her back. She hovered, at an almost unnoticeable height, above the bed. She folded her arms across her stomach and then gradually closed her eyes. She had a warm feeling inside as if she was slowly melting. She felt as if she was a single snow flake falling from the sky, unaware that she would become part of something much greater once she reached her journeys end. Her mind began to fade and she lost all awareness of her spectral form.

Chapter Six

May awoke gently. She felt like a leaf drifting down to the ground, waking as she slowly became aware of her surroundings. It was as if she had melted away and then returned, gracefully solidifying. She was alone; Mr Kibbles was god knows where but she knew Penny wouldn't be very far away from Chloe.

May could hear the sound of the sound of pots and pans being knocked together. Either Chloe was in the kitchen or a travelling circus had popped in for a spot of breakfast. May rose from the bed and made her way down the stairs. She still hadn't mastered the art of falling through the floorboards. Penny was exactly where May had expected her to be, in the kitchen hovering over Chloe.

"I kept telling her to use the plastic spatula on the non-stick frying pan but she obviously never listened," Penny moaned. "She's going to ruin that pan". May stepped into the kitchen; Chloe was at the cooker frying eggs. May waved to Penny but didn't speak. She wanted to reveal her presence to Chloe when the situation would be easier to control. To start speaking to her now could cause hot oil to be splashed across the room. Which May knew to be not only dangerous but also a real bugger to clean up.

"She's using way too much oil," Penny pointed out. "I've been watching her and she's not been eating healthfully at all lately". May just smiled and tried to signal to Penny that she couldn't speak openly. Penny seemed to get the message.

"Oh yes sorry," Penny acknowledged, "Just in case eh?"

Chloe dished her eggs up onto a plate and added toast from the toaster. She pulled out a chair and sat at the kitchen table. Her college text book still lay on the table where she had left it on the night before, she began to flick through it while eating at the same time. May was impressed by this. Chloe was showing no small amount of dedication towards wanting to better herself through education. May was also surprised to discover that Chloe's small and almost unconscious action had, in no small amount, helped her begin to see beyond the prejudice she usually held against young people; though her cooking skills left some what to be desired.

May watched as Chloe slowly sipped from her coffee cup and it made her realise just how much she missed her usual morning cup of tea. It was something she hadn't really thought about before, how she was now denied the little pleasures she used to enjoy. She would miss her bakewell slices particularly so; she held no grudge against them.

May was thinking about the dream she had last night while she watched Chloe eat. It had seemed rather bizarre but so much else had seemed as equally as strange since her death that she held no concern for it.

She had found herself standing at the beginning of an old western style town. All the buildings were wooden and painted white, with a wide dusty road that cut straight through the middle of them. People came out of the buildings in they're droves to welcome her. She was mobbed by the crowd of strangers, none of which recognised her but made her feel welcome all the same. She was led and almost carried towards an old saloon bar; she remembered the waist high doors. There were women dancing on a small stage while groups of men played cards around the tables. They all stopped what they were doing when May entered the room. There was a cheer of welcome and she was placed at a table; a shot of whisky was slammed down in front of her. She felt composed to drink it and enjoyed it's warmth as it flowed down her throat. The women started dancing again and May had a feeling that this new dance was for her. There was lively music and she felt more alive than she had ever felt. She felt welcome; she felt that she belonged. She had lived her life alone and without family. For the very first time she felt amongst kin. Nobody knew who she was but everybody loved her all the same. Cowboys danced with empty holsters and the women swayed to the smooth rhythm of the music. May felt happy and she recognised that it was probably the first time she had ever felt real joy. It was a place of acceptance; it was where she wanted to stay. The people were nice and they showed no ulterior motives behind their friendliness. It was only the pull of promises un-kept that drew her back into the waking world. Penny had told her that sleeping helped her relax. May felt more than relaxed, she felt released. There was another world out there and May wanted to be a part of it but first she had work to do.

Chloe had finished her breakfast. She closed her text book and slipped it into her bag. She was preparing to leave for college and May knew that if she didn't act soon she would have to wait until this evening to test her theory. It wasn't the perfect time but May still took a deep breath and spoke.

"Now don't be alarmed," May said in what she considered a soft and calm voice. It was more like quiet and firm as if she was scolding a small child. Chloe screamed and threw herself away from the table, knocking over her chair in the process.

"I mean you no harm," May attempted to consol Chloe with a smile but then realised the she couldn't actually see her face. Mr Kibbles slinked into the kitchen; he was obviously curious about all the noise.

"Who are you? Where are you?" Chloe screamed hysterically. She had gone as far as she could; her back was now against the wall.

"I'm here in this very room with you," May replied and immediately regretted it as Chloe pushed herself into the wall as if trying to break through it. The words had sounded better in her head.

"Tell her I'm here," Penny suggested. She was obviously concerned for her daughter and watching her slide down the wall was bringing tears to her eyes. "Tell her she's safe; tell her I'm here with her". May hesitated; she thought it could make matters worse. The poor girl was still grieving and I'm about to reintroduce her to her dead mother. She was beginning to think that this wasn't a very good idea after all.

"Your mother's here as well," May announced and Chloe promptly threw up on the floor. "She wants me to tell you that you're safe and she's here with you". May looked down at Chloe who was slumped in a dishevelled heap next to a small pool of vomit; things weren't turning out quite as planned. Penny crouched down by her daughter; she was so close but still beyond touch.

"What have we done? I can't even comfort my own daughter!" May watched as Chloe surprised her for a second time.

"Mum, are you there?" Chloe asked in a voice that was little more than a squeak. She lifted he head and looked directly at Penny; it was as if she could sense her mother's closeness.

"She is here but she can't speak to you. Well no she can speak to you but you can't hear her. She can speak to me and I can tell you what she says". May finally worked it out and allowed herself a small prideful smile.

"I don't understand," Chloe confessed. She rested her head in her hands and began to sob.

Mr Kibbles jumped up on the table and stared up at May. As she looked back into his big round eyes he began to purr and something inside her changed. It was a memory, a stark vivid retelling of a time of great loss. Part of her was still standing in the kitchen with Penny and Chloe but another part of her was reliving the days, weeks and months that followed the death of Mr Kibbles. She couldn't remember the exact moment he had died but her time of mourning, the time in which she had missed him the most was now locked in her memory as if etched in stone. She felt fire in her heart and ice in her gut and out of the pain a seed of compassion grew. May turned back towards Chloe and an unfamiliar voice escaped her lips.

"You lost your mother at a time in your life when you

needed her the most. When we lose somebody a part of ourselves dies with them as if a part of our very soul is torn away. In time the soul begins to heal but it never heals completely. It leaves a scar that can open up again when we least expect it and we start the grieving process all over again. Most people in this world will never see or hear from those they have lost until their own dieing days and for some not even then". May stared back down at Mr Kibbles. "But for other's the loss just becomes a change in circumstances. They are the lucky ones; they are the ones the lost come back for. Your mother died but, as tragic as that is, she's not lost to you. Your mother is here, maybe in another form and maybe not exactly as you remember her but she's here regardless and she's here just for you".

Mr Kibbles swished his tail and jumped off the table. May watched him saunter out of the kitchen and her mind began to clear. The memory was still sharp but the uncomfortable feelings in her stomach and chest had gone. Chloe raised herself to her feet and dragged the chair from the floor. She sat down and grabbed a tea towel off the table to wipe her eyes and mouth.

"Who are you?" She asked.

"I'm...," May had to think for a moment. "I'm a friend of your mother's". Penny threw May a smile.

"And you're dead as well?" Chloe asked, "If it's not rude to ask".

"Yes I'm afraid so," May replied.

"So how comes I can hear you but I can't hear my Mum?"

"Well ghosts can't usually speak to living people, at least that's what I've come to believe. It would seem however that I have a particular talent for making myself heard if you like. Quite frankly, we've only just discovered it. I'm not even sure it will work with anyone else but you". Chloe seemed to take a moment to digest it all.

"So why are you here? You said that most people don't get a chance such as this, so why are you and Mum here?"

"Your Mother's worried about you," May replied. "She's worried about how you are going to cope now that she's not here, in a physical sense that is. She's worried about your finances, your education, your emotion well being. You know Mum stuff".

"So am I, especially about the financial stuff," Chloe admitted. "I'm sorry Mum but I think I may have to sell the house. If Aunty Anna doesn't steal it out from under me that is?" Now this is a new angle that I hadn't seen coming, May thought. I had always assumed that the very least, Chloe had sole ownership of the house. Now it seemed even that was under protest

"I though I had that covered in the will," Penny seemed shocked at the news as well.

"You mother just said that she left the house to you in her will, it should be legally yours," May conveyed for Chloe's benefit..

"But my solicitor said that Aunty Anne has every right to contest the will," Chloe explained.

"That's possible I guess," May agreed. "But the odds would be stacked against her, if your mother's will is legally sound".

"Which it is," Penny added.

"Which it is, you're Mother's just assured me," May relayed.

"But that doesn't change the fact that I don't have the money to keep this place running," Chloe pointed out.

"No that's true," May said, "but we're working on that".

"Where are you exactly?" Chloe asked scanning the room.

"I'm just by the door and your Mother is over by the sink," May told her. Chloe looked towards the kitchen sink and then turned her attention to the door. She seemed to be a lot calmer now but May could tell that she was still a little uneasy.

"Who are you exactly? Other than Mum's friend," Chloe asked while looking in May's direction but not actually seeing her.

"Oh yes of course, my name is May Elizabeth Trump. I passed away yesterday and just happened to bump into your mother outside".

"May Trump?" Chloe asked.

"Yes that's right," May confirmed, "Why? Do you know me?"

"No but your name was mentioned last night at Buster's," Chloe explained. "An old friend of mine told me about how his dad had discovered your body yesterday evening".

"That's great news! I've been really worried about that," May felt relieved. It was like a great weight had been lifted but then her suspicious nature cut in. "Hold on though, I've got to ask. How did your friend's father know to look?" May was beginning to envision her physical remains being involved in some kind of failed burglary.

"My friend said that his dad thought he heard you calling his name so looked in on you as he passed by your house. That was when he discovered you," Chloe explained to May's relief.

"Your friend, what's his name?" May asked.

"Stephen Chimer," Chloe replied.

"That's George's boy!" Penny piped up but May had already worked that out for herself. So George had heard her but there was still one thing she needed to know.

"Did anyone mention the state of the living room?"

Chapter Seven

May wasn't sure how much of a good idea this was. Chloe had taken a few days off college just so she could watch. It was assumed that she had finally taken the advice of her peers. Penny was excited to be spending the day with her daughter so she didn't care where she was going but May was still unsure.

They had talked about it in the kitchen while Chloe had made herself another strong coffee. Chloe seemed to have gotten over her initial shock and was taking to the new situation with apparent ease. May guessed that her words had helped Chloe see things in a different light. Maybe she just wanted to make the most of the renewed time she had to spend with her mother but May was cautious. She refrained from mentioning it as she feared that Chloe's emotional stability was still as fragile as thin ice.

May conveyed Penny's input to Chloe, as much as seemed fitting. Penny was a typical worried mother. May found that she was passing on messages about eating fresh vegetables and other tips on healthy living more than anything else. May had spent her life eating pretty much anything she fancied and it never did her any harm. She was glad that she had kept that thought to herself as she remembered the incident involving the bakewell slice. She still felt embarrassed by her cause of death and was glad to hear that the police were not making it public as yet. She felt a little guilty as she considered it to be wasting police time but she figured that the longer they kept the details secret the better.

Chloe was the one who had originally suggested it. She had referred to it as fun, while still being productive and educational. May disagreed, there must be another way, she thought. There must be a more discreet way, something that wasn't so public. May had voiced her misgivings but her words seemed to fall on deaf ears. Penny had sided with her daughter, no surprises there and May had begun to realise that she was being ganged up on. This is hardly fair, May thought, I'm being railroaded here. It ran against her very grain but she held her temper at bay. She would have never let herself be coerced in such a way before but she felt that she had been left with little choice. She could just agree to go along with Chloe's plan, or pull out the big guns and let her temper run free. May just didn't think that Chloe could cope with a full on Trumping and her sapling of compassion wouldn't allow her to even test the theory.

It hadn't taken long before all four of them were outside the house and walking down the driveway towards the town centre. As far as May could imagine anyone with a paranormal gift would be able to see a young woman being accompanied by two ghosts and a dead cat. Most other people would only be able to see Chloe, which included Chloe herself.

"This is nice isn't it?" Penny observed with a slight skip in her step. "It's like a little family day out".

"Not in the slightest," May objected, using a quiet voice as she feared that she might be overheard. Penny shot May a big grin; her mood would not be easy to lower.

"Cheer up May, it'll be good fun". Like mother like daughter, May thought. She doesn't realise the gravity of the situation. They're both acting as though it was a game. May wasn't in the mood for playing games, which was nothing unusual in it's self. She was feeling rather nervous about the whole thing and having fun was the last thing she had on her mind. Here she was heading into a busy town centre to discover the full extent of her gift, as Penny had described it. May had to attempt to make her self heard by as many people as she could but without causing too much of a scene; the last condition had been her own suggestion. She also had to figure out a way of turning it off when she didn't need it; she was getting tired of whispering all the time.

Penny' house was only a short walk from the town centre and the street was already getting busy. People were walking up and down the pavement and May found that she had to keep swerving out of their path as they strode past, completely unaware of her presence. Penny had opted to walk in the road after almost falling through a hedge and into somebody's garden when a large man in a tracksuit had jogged directly towards her, giving her little room to manoeuvre.

"What about her?" Penny suggested while pointing to a woman in a purple hat who was walking briskly towards them. "Say something to her May... or him even". Penny gestured towards a man on a bicycle. She was clearly eager for May to start but May didn't feel ready. She didn't want to start randomly shouting at people on the street. What would I say? How would I gauge a reaction? What if other people heard me at the same time? What if my words became misheard of misunderstood? And what if they began accusing each other of those words? I could end up starting some kind of riot! May knew in herself that it was a highly unlikely outcome but it gave her the excuse to bide her time until they found a more controllable environment.

The town centre had been declared a pedestrian only area about three years before, so people were free to just wander in and out of the road as they pleased. May could remember countless occasions where she had been forced to complain about the cyclists who tended to use it as a cut through. It had been on one of those occasions that she had met Constable Davis for the first time.

Chloe stopped outside Buster's and pulled her mobile phone out of her pocket. May could hear singing; it was a woman's voice.

"I think that's Jean singing in there," Penny remarked. "She's not very good is she?" May had to agree, her squeaky voice was beginning to grate on her nerves and her timing was out by a mile. However May had to admit that she could still hold a tune, it was just a pity that it was the tune from a different song entirely.

"I prefer Buster's singing," Penny said, "but he never performs the matinee".

"Hello May," Chloe said while holding her mobile phone up to her mouth. "I think we should meet up in the coffee shop and discus things in a more controlled environment". May was impressed for a third time in one day, which was a bit of a record considering her general lack of respect for the younger generation. Chloe had not only managed to suggest a perfect place in which to test out May's gift but she also did it in such a way that any passer-by's wouldn't begin to doubt her mental stability.

The spectral group followed Chloe into *We Sell Coffee*, the town's most popular café. It used to be called Finnegan's but the owner had fallen in with the new trend of: *saying it how it is.* Chloe chose a small table in one of the corners which had a good view of the entire café. It was dimly lit and shrouded in a thin layer of smoke that came from the many candles, which had were wedged into the tops of the empty wine bottles and adorned on each and every table. It seemed a little unnecessary to May considering that it was still broad daylight outside.

May sidled up next to Chloe and Penny followed suit. Mr Kibbles was nowhere to be seen but that could mean he was just obscured by the tables and chairs that were scattered about the room. May had the suspicion that he was investigating the kitchen. He may be dead and unable to eat but old habits died hard, especially if there was fish on the menu.

The waiter slowly ambled towards Chloe's table.
"I'll try with him first and see how it goes," May whispered into Chloe's ear. The waiter pulled a small pad and a pencil from his pocket.

"Would Madam like to order?" He asked in a faded Italian accent.

"Just a small Cappuccino please," Chloe replied politely. The waiter scribbled something on his notepad.

"Would there be anything else you would like today? We have a special on lemon sole with new potatoes and seasonal vegetables?" The waiter suggested, which confirmed May's suspicion regarding the whereabouts of Mr Kibbles.

"No thank you. Just the coffee will be fine," Chloe replied.

"Very well Madam," the waiter acknowledged as he slipped his notepad back into his pocket and turned away from the table. May saw this as an opportunity and stepped up behind him.

"Service!" May cried directly into his right ear. The waiter suddenly took a hopping step to the left and turned his head sharply to the right. He stared directly at May for a moment with a puzzled look on his face and then twitched his head from side to side. Bewildered, the waiter slowly turned away again and continued to walk towards the kitchen.

May returned to Chloe's table where she received a short round of applause from Penny and a subtle nod from Chloe.

"That was really good May," Penny said excitedly. "You made him turnaround and everything". She clapped her hands another three times.

"Yes Penny it did seem to work as planned," May said with far less enthusiasm. She agreed that it had been a successful test but it was hardly worth applauding.

"I guess this means you can talk to just about anyone, doesn't it?" Penny deducted. May figured that she was right. The chance that they had just stumbled on the only other person in the world that could hear her, other than Chloe, was slimmer than a twig on a diet. However, May had just recognised someone on the other side of the room and she couldn't fight the temptation to pay them a quick visit.

May strode across the room and Penny followed her; she obviously didn't want to miss out on any of the action. May tried to avoid the scattered tables but still ended up skimming a few as she passed. Moments later she found herself standing directly behind her oldest, closest and probably her only living friend.

Margaret was busy trying to decide what to choose from the cake trolley. May knew that if Margaret was given free reign she would have chosen it all. Margret looked rather jolly as she finally selected a large slice of chocolate gateaux. This worried May but only until she realised that her friend probably didn't even know she was dead yet. For just a moment, May had entertained the thought that Margaret was eating cake in celebration of her death. She felt relieved when the moment of anxiety had passed.

Margaret sat with the gateaux in front of her. She picked up a fork and plunged it into the sweet light crumb. She scooped up a fork full and brought it to her lips.
"You really shouldn't eat that you know," May whispered into her ear. The fork stopped just an inch from her lips. Margaret seemed hesitate for a moment with the fork full of chocolate gateaux hovering just in front of her open mouth. May was beginning to think that Margaret would actually put the fork back down but then she watched it continue its journey into her mouth. Margaret scooped up another fork full and May thought about speaking again but she held her tongue. She felt a little guilty for trying to trick her oldest friend but she had made a promise to herself many years ago. When I die, May had sworn, I'm going to come back and haunt her into loosing weight. She should have known it wouldn't be that easy.

Mr Kibbles was sitting on Chloe's table when May and Penny returned. He stood up, stretched his back and purred at May. She gave him a quick fuss while Chloe was drinking her coffee.
"We're back," May whispered, which made Chloe jump

and spill coffee over the table. Conversing with the dead was obviously some thing that took a little time to get used to, May thought.

"What do you want to try next?" Chloe asked as she mopped up the spill with a napkin.

"Well we know that I can be heard when I want to be," May said, "I guess I've got to try not to be heard now".

"Is Mum with you?"

"Yes she's right here".

"OK then, I've just got to pay for the coffee and then I'll meet you outside". Chloe suggested, "I've got an idea".

"Very well," May replied, "I'll see you outside".

"I won't see you though," Chloe said with a cheeky smile, as she stood up from the table. May and Penny headed back towards the entrance of the café. Once outside May allowed herself a quiet chuckle.

"I won't see you," May mimicked Chloe, "I do like that".

"Did you see that man standing by the kitchen door?" Penny asked in a nervous voice. May turned and looked at her, she seemed a little distraught.

"What man?" May asked, a little concerned by Penny's change in mood.

"I was watching him and he seemed to be following your every move," Penny explained.

"Is he still there or did he follow us out?" May asked quietly, as she had become aware that there were still a lot of people walking around.

"I don't know, he disappeared just before we left," Penny said, "I think he might be another ghost". May didn't like the sound of that. There was a possibility that they were being watched by other ghosts. She found the idea strange and unnerving. What would the dead want with us?

"Keep your eyes open Penny," May advised in a whisper. "Let me know if you see him again".

Chloe stepped out of the café and walked straight across the road towards an automated toilet cabin. May and Penny crossed over behind her, puzzled at why she hadn't waited outside the café for May to confirm their presence. By the time they had caught up with her Chloe was waiting outside the metal, oval shaped cabin. May noticed that the display window by the door handle showed: Engaged.

"Shall we wait out here?" May whispered discreetly.

"I don't need to go if that's what you're thinking," Chloe replied. She kept her voice low and her face partially hidden by her hand. "I thought we might get some privacy inside, so we can talk more openly".

"Good thinking!" May replied, impressed yet again. The cabin door suddenly slid open and a man stepped out shaking his wet hands.

"The hand dryers aren't working again!" He moaned for Chloe's benefit as he walked passed. Chloe inserted a coin into a slot on the side of the cabin and stepped inside; the two ghosts hurried in behind her before the door slid closed.

"She takes us to all the best places," Penny remarked.

"Sorry about this but I was beginning to get funny looks in the café," Chloe explained. "I guess I wasn't being quite as discreet as I had planned. I spoke aloud on a couple of occasions and what with me sitting alone at the table, well people noticed".

"Oh dear I didn't realise," May admitted.

"Neither did I," Penny said.

"Neither did your mother," May repeated.

"That doesn't matter now," Chloe said. "I've brought you in here because, not only is it private, but it's small and cramped. If you can talk in this big, tin can and stop me from hearing you; you'll have no problem doing it elsewhere". May couldn't find any fault with her logic.

"Alright then," she said.

"I heard that," Chloe announced.

"You were meant to".

"And that!" May tried to concentrate on not being heard. It felt alien, like trying to breathe through your ears.

"Can you hear me now?" She said. Chloe showed no reaction.

"How about now?" May asked but Chloe still stayed

silent. Her head was tiled and her teeth were clenched, as if she was straining to listen.

"I can hear you," Penny said and May tried her best to ignore her.

"If you're still here and talking I can't here a word of it. Try something louder. A shout or a scream, or something". Chloe suggested. May bolstered herself; she hadn't screamed since she was a teenager and even then it had been more of a yell. May smiled, The Jenkins twins never crept up on her again, not after the beating she had given them.

May filled her lungs and screamed. Both Chloe's and Penny's hands shot to their ears.

"Stop! I can hear that just fine," Chloe cried. May stopped screaming; it had felt quite invigorating.

"My ears are going to be ringing all day long now," Penny complained.

"Obviously loud is still loud whether you're dead or alive," Chloe pointed out.

"Well it worked when I concentrated really hard so that proves that I have some control," May announced. "At a sensible volume that is". Chloe nodded in agreement and pressed the button that operated the cabin door.

"Let's see if you get the same results outside," She suggested. The doors slowly slid open and Chloe stepped out. A small crowd had gathered outside the cabin, they all stared at Chloe with obvious concern on their faces. A man stepped out of the crowd.

"Are you ok Miss?" He asked. "It's just that we heard screaming".

Chapter Eight

The next morning May reluctantly pulled herself from a dream. It had been almost the same as before, just a continuation of the first. This time she had been welcomed back by people who were no longer strangers.

Yesterday, Chloe had spent the entire walk back to the house with a cherry red face. She admitted that she had never been so embarrassed before in her life. She had made up a wild story about screaming when she saw a large hairy spider in the toilet cabin in an attempt to disperse the crowd. Instead of accepting her excuse, a few of the men decided to search the cabin for her eight legged tormentor. The spider obviously didn't exist but Chloe hadn't expected a full scale man hunt to begin.

They had enjoyed a pleasant evening, just the three of them. May couldn't remember the last time she had really felt comfortable in the presence of others. Even during Margaret's weekly visits, May had spent most of the time anxious for her to leave.

May and Chloe had a long chat and got to know each other a little better. Penny had joined the conversation but only at irregular intervals. She had decided to make a real effort at improving her manifestation and telekinetic skills. She had said that if she couldn't improve her talents she would feel as useless as a spare wheel in a rowing boat. While May and Chloe were talking, Penny was practising making orbs. She admitted that she had seen a little improvement, especially after Chloe had opened a window in an attempt to clear the air. She was still finding it impossible to move even the smallest of objects. Chloe had voiced her support but May figured that orbs might be all that Penny was capable of.

It was late in the morning and May was the last one to

rise. Chloe was drinking coffee in the kitchen downstairs, along with Penny who was trying to move a teaspoon along the draining board.

"I swear I made it rattle, I swear I did!" Penny said as May walked in. May could smell Chloe's coffee and found that she was still pining for a fresh brew.

"I'm sure you did Penny," May humoured her. "Good morning Chloe".

Chloe looked up from her coffee cup, even though she had no idea where May was.

"Good morning," She said. "Is my Mum in here?"

"Yes she's standing over in the corner by the fridge," May replied.

"Oh I thought so; I had to open a window earlier." Chloe explained and then called over to the fridge. "I'm not complaining Mum. It's nice to be able to sense your presence one way or another".

"Thank you dear," Penny replied, smiling.

"Your Mother says thank you," May conveyed. Chloe smiled and looked back down at her coffee mug.

"I know it's still early and you've only just woken up, if that's the right thing to call it". Chloe said without looking up. "It's just that now we have all slept on it," Chloe lifted her head. "Do we have any ideas how to stop my aunt getting a hold of this house?" May sighed, she hadn't really thought about it. She had drifted straight into the dream world with plans to only stay for a couple of hours. She had thought that she had stuck to that plan. It felt like she had only stayed for two, maybe three hours at the most but when she awoke it was already morning. Who ever it was that said: 'time flies when you're having fun' wasn't exaggerating.

"Sorry Chloe," May admitted. "I've got nothing yet".

"That's too bad," Chloe looked dejected. "I really can't afford to keep this house going for much longer. I mean no disrespect May but how are you and Mum supposed to help me with this. You're both just ghosts. You can talk to people but I'm still not sure how that's going to help. Mum I'm sorry but the only use I can come up with for your special talent is to start a business refilling snow globes. I just don't know what to do about any of it!" May was about to protest but she realised that Chloe was right, in her own hysterical way. May didn't know of what use she could be. She was only a dead woman talking; I guess I could always become a radio presenter.

"Chloe please, I'm trying everything I can!" Penny had tears in her eyes.

"Maybe I can help?" May and Penny both heard a man's voice and turned their heads towards the kitchen door.

"Oh my god that's him!" Penny cried. "That's the guy from the café". The man stood in the door way smiling at the two women. He wore a plain grey suit over his average to slim frame. He held the appearance of a man in his forties but May knew that was just the age at which he had died.

"Who the frick are you?" May yelled at the trespasser, she felt both angry and scared. "What do you think you're playing at? Get out of this house at once or I'll call the police!" May knew her words didn't make any sense as soon as she said them; I can't even pick up the telephone.

"Who are you talking to? What's going on?" Chloe asked nervously. She could only hear May's voice but that seemed enough to put her on edge.

"I'll get Chloe to call the police!" May amended her previous threat when she remembered that at least one person present could still pick up a phone. Chloe pulled her mobile phone out of her pocket and held it up.

"Shall I make the call?" She asked. "What do I tell them?"

"You should tell her to make the call if you think it's really necessary May," The man in the doorway suggested calmly. "But I don't think the local police station even has a paranormal department".

"Call the police Chloe," Penny yelled. "May, tell her to call the police. I don't like the look of him".

"Put your phone away Chloe; the police are of no use to

us here". May couldn't find fault with the man's logic. She even felt a little embarrassed for voicing such an empty threat. The closest the local police could ever get to putting a spirit into custody would be if they raided a gang of bootleggers.

The initial shock subsided and May's anger and fear became curious annoyance.

"How do you know my name?"

"You told me it yesterday," Chloe replied as she slipped her mobile phone back into her pocket.

"It's alright Chloe I wasn't talking to you," May lifted her hand up and pointed a finger at the man in the doorway, as if it were a loaded gun. "I'm talking to him!"

"It's nothing sinister; I just overheard it yesterday when you were in the café". The man shrugged his shoulders.

"I'm sure you over heard a great many things yesterday," Penny said accusingly. "While you were stalking us!"

"That's a fair cop I guess," The man admitted. He held up his hands in a gesture of surrender. As May still hadn't retracted her pointing finger it made for an amusing picture. "But I only followed you after I overheard your conversation about May and her unusual talent. I guess that this could have gone a little better and I solely blame myself for that but I'm only here to ask for your help".

"Is there still some body here? Some dead guy I'm guessing but I don't know what's going on! What's happening May?" Chloe pleaded.

"It's all alright Chloe. He's still here but I don't see any harm in him now. I'll explain everything to you very soon". May turned back to the man, who seemed more like Oliver Twist asking for more than the dangerous house invader that she had first thought he was.

"Now then, how are we supposed to help you?"

"Exactly like that! I need you to contact a living person for me; I need you to speak with my son".

Tempers and nerves began to settle as the man explained

his predicament. His name was Gary Johnson and he had died just over 10 years ago. It had been sudden and unexpected. He was driving home from a meeting with a client when an oncoming lorry had skidded into his lane; he had died instantly.

"I left behind an ex-wife and an eleven year old son," Gary explained. "I've spent the last ten years trying to find ways to contact my son but I've found nothing but disappointment. I even approached living mediums and psychics but no matter what I tried none of them seemed to hear me or even sense that I was there. Even within the second realm I could find nobody who could help me and it was the ghosts there who put me onto the living mediums in the first place. I give them their dues though; they did say that it would be pretty hit and miss. It's all got something to do with channelling. I'm not sure if I'm getting this completely right but it would seem that for a ghost to be able to speak to a living medium they both had to be on the same channel. Even then, I spoke to this one guy and he told me that when it does eventually work it can be like trying to have a conversation in a busy night club; not every word might be heard and poor assumptions could be made. Then yesterday I saw you May, playing your tricks on people in the café".

"I wasn't playing any tricks! It was a serious experiment," May said defensively.

"That's such a sad story Gary," Penny said. She seemed to have gotten over her first impression of him. She walked up to him and took his hand in hers; she looked directly into his eyes and smiled. "You've done all this just to be able to speak to your son one last time; you really are a sweet man". May sighed; Penny was trying to get the man arrested five minutes ago and now look at her. May watched as Gary stared back at Penny with the same doe eyed look on his face. It's like I'm an extra in an Australian soap opera and I should know, I used to watch them all. She decided to break up the moment.

"Why do you want to talk to your son now? It's been more than ten years you said, he's hardly likely to even remember you after all that time". Gary and Penny both turned to look at May; their fingertips stroked as their hands slowly slipped apart.

"If there had been any other choice, I wouldn't have left it this long," Gary explained. "You're the first person I've ever met who has the skills I need. I do hope you're wrong about my son May but I'm not so naïve as to disregard the possibility. I do want to meet my son and have the chance to say my goodbyes but that's not the only reason that I need to speak with him. Not long before I died, I created a bank account in his name and deposited ten thousand pounds into it. I have no idea how much is in the account now but, what with ten years of compound interest, it must have amounted to a fair sum. I had planned to give it to him on his twenty first birthday anyway, so that much could still go as planned I guess. I just expected to be there and give it to him in person; I hardly expected to be dead. In hindsight, I guess I should have told someone about it or even made up a will? I didn't so what does it matter now? I need you to pass on the all the account details so he can access the money. I want him to have the little head start in life that I had worked so hard for".

May was impressed by Gary's dedication towards his son but not by his lack of foresight. May could hardly condemn the man; even at the ripe old age of 75 she hadn't expected death to take her so suddenly. However, she though, if only Chloe had a dad like Gary then I could slip back into the dream world with a clear conscience.

"That's so nice Gary; you must really love your son to do all of that for him," Penny said with an unwavering smile.

"Yes I do. Of course I do; he's all I've got," Gary replied with a similar smile.

May had to admit that Gary wasn't without his charm but Penny seemed completely smitten by him. She's going to be of little use once the negotiations start. May put her game face on, which was hardly flattering but usually effective.

"So Gary, what do you offer in return?"

"I hadn't really thought about that," Gary said, obviously surprised by May's demand.

"Well I'm not a charity you know," May growled, "If you want something you had better be willing to pay for it!"

"You're helping me for free aren't you?" Penny piped up, she looked a little concerned.

"That's different Penny," May replied. "You're also helping me in your own way".

"Oh ok that's nice," Penny sighed with relief.

"I don't know what I can give you; I have nothing to offer. What is it that you need?" Gary looked panicked and Penny was giving May a disapproving stare.

"I don't need anything," May pointed out. "It's Penny and Chloe who need help. They need money! Can you help with that?" Gary stepped forward and tapped at the air with his finger angrily.

"That money is for my son and my son alone. I won't let you take it; not any of it!"

Chloe had sat quietly cradling a mug of coffee ever since May had promised to explain to her what was currently going on. She could only hear May's contribution to the conversation and her patience had obviously grown thin.

"What's happening now?" She yelled. "Can somebody tell me what's going on? I know it concerns me because I just heard my name mentioned. I've been patient but now I think you're all being down right rude!"

"Sorry Chloe," May apologised. "I don't mean to be rude but could you just hold for just a little while longer. We are just about to start haggling". May turned back to Gary who, in the meantime, had re-holstered his finger.

"So you expect me to fill your son's pockets yet ask for nothing in return. This young girl faces the prospect of either losing her home or her education. If you can't help us with that then what use are you?"

"All I ask is that you perform one séance. Just one séance

and I'll do anything you want in return," Gary pleaded. "I really need your help; surely you can perform this one, solitary séance for free?" May was about to bring Gary's world crashing down upon him with a resounding 'No' but then his expression suddenly changed.

"Of course!" he cried and clapped his hands together. The noise was so loud and sudden that Penny jumped into the air and, for no apparent reason, Chloe's coffee mug fell over on the table.

"Who did that?" Chloe asked as she picked up the mug, fortunately it had been empty.

"Before I died I worked as an entertainment agent," Gary explained his outburst. "It was my job to represent an assortment of different acts and artists. I was the one who booked the venues; I was the one how arranged the gigs. If I know anything, I know how to get the punters in! If you do this one séance for free, I'll make sure you've got plenty of paying customers for the ones that follow".

The thought at never occurred to May. All her life she had condemned those who preformed such services. People who preyed on those who were weakened and vulnerable through grief; selling false hope as if it were candy. Charlatans and swindlers the lot of them. This was different because she was real. She had a genuine ability and, if they had the ghosts already lined up, those who still mourn would not be disappointed. The offer was beginning to make sense. Gary probably knew more about being dead than both Penny and her combined. Ten years was a long time to be a wandering soul without learning a great deal about the facts of death. Also his experience in the entertainment industry would probably come in useful; they would need to sell the idea. She still had her doubts; she didn't like the feeling of having to rely on yet another person. However, Penny seemed excited at the prospect of working closely with Gary.

"That's a smashing idea!" She said, almost hopping on

the spot like a school girl. "It's a great idea, isn't it May?"
May wasn't as enthusiastic about it as Penny. She wasn't
the one who would have to perform in front of strangers
but the idea had potential.

"I really think the decision should be Chloe's," May
suggested. "It's her house now and there for her problem".
She hadn't meant it to sound as harsh as it did, which was
yet another first for May.

May ran back through the entire conversation for Chloe's
benefit. She had to start right back to where Gary had first
announced himself because Chloe hadn't been able to hear
two thirds of the people involved. May didn't begrudge the
task; you couldn't blame the girl for living. Chloe took a
moment to process the information that she was receiving
from a seemingly empty room. May could tell she was
worried and so would she have been in her situation. It was
all very well for the ghosts to suggest that she should turn
her house into some kind of spiritual meeting place but
they were beyond harms way. She would be inviting
complete strangers into her home on the pretext of
communing with the dead. It was a lot to ask of a young
woman living alone, to open her doors to strangers on the
advice of a disembodied voice.

"I don't know," Chloe finally admitted, "It sounds like it
could work but I don't think it would be safe to do it on my
own".

"She's right you know!" Penny agreed as if she had just
realised the implications. "There's no way she's doing this
alone! I won't let you put her in any danger". May
understood her concern. Penny crouched defensively
beside Chloe and Gary had the worried face of a man for
whom every open door had a brick wall hidden behind it.

"If there were other people around, people I could trust, I
think it might work," Chloe said. "But all my friends would
either just laugh at me or totally freak out. I don't know
anyone who could deal with the situation as it is". May
didn't think she would be any help in that department. At

least Chloe had friends; Margaret was all the friends May had ever known. The thought hit May like a wet kipper. Someone who had an interest in the spiritual and the supernatural and someone who had the kindness and the compassion that Chloe would need to see her through. Margaret and her Thursday Night Club; it seemed too perfect to be true.

"I think I know just the people we need!"

Chapter Nine

It was clear to May that the best course of action would be to approach Barbara first. She was the leader of the club, so to speak and the most experienced when it came down to spiritual matters. The first problem they discovered was that no one knew where she lived, so they decided to make contact with her at her place of work.

The local supermarket was owned by Mr Poise and his two sons, which is why it had been named Gracie's. Just like most of the other businesses in the town, it had seen off all its competitors with local support. Mr Poise was able to compete with the big nationals because of a rare sale or return agreement he had with the farmers and other local food producers. He only paid for what he sold and anything left over was sent back to be made into pigswill. If he was forced to reduce something he listed it down and paid a reduced price himself. The farmers were happy enough with the deal. It was only a small part of their production and, because young Terry Poise collected, there were no transportation costs. Besides, the pigs would still need feeding and Mr Poise always paid them on time.

They had decided to let Chloe do the talking for now. May was more than willing but it was suspected that Barbara wasn't acclimatised to speaking with the dead at such a direct level. Penny was the one who suggested inviting them to the house on a pretext of contacting her. Penny's death had been a bit of a gossip gold mine and the Thursday Night Club would never turn down a chance to hear the inside scoop.

May and Penny accompanied Chloe to the supermarket. Gary had left the house earlier in the morning saying he was going to try and get a feel for the prospective market. They had left Mr Kibbles chasing a mouse around the garden, even though the mouse was oblivious to his presence.

Chloe walked into the supermarket and picked up a basket, she needed milk and coffee anyway. The two ghosts followed a few yards behind. They weren't sure if Barbara would feel their presence or not. There was no way of knowing how much of what they had heard was true or just hype on Barbara's part. Chloe had never met Barbara before socially but at the first mention of her big red hair she had figured out exactly who she was. As Chloe approached the deli counter Barbara's hair acted like a homing beacon drawing her in. Chloe pulled a ticket from the dispenser on the counter and waited for her turn. There were two customers in front of her and Barbara seemed in no hurry to serve them.

"I tell you I felt something last night," Barbara said. The two customers were ladies of between sixty and seventy years old. One of them listened quietly and nervously to Barbara's story, the other one didn't.

"I haven't felt anything in years," The customer cackled loudly. "Chance would be a fine thing". The quiet customer turned a light shade of red.

"You know I don't mean anything like that Vicky love," Barbara scolded. "I'm talking spiritual here". Vicky, the louder customer seemed to be the youngest of the three.

"I didn't expect you to be talking any other way, not at your age" Vicky sneered.

"I'm only four years older than you, young lady and I'm still fit enough to be working," Barbara replied.

"Part time and for your own nephew," Vicky pointed out. The other customer, the oldest and shortest of the three, tried to calm the situation.

"Can I have four slices of the cured ham please Babs," She said in a soft voice. Barbara turned to face her and smiled.

"Who's first out of you two?" Barbara asked.

"I am," Victoria said. Barbara appeared to ignore her.

"Who's first Debs?"

"Vicky is," Deborah said quietly.

"Sorry you'll have to wait until I've finished with her then".

May was getting a little impatient watching from behind a pile of washing powder. She decided to try and hurry up proceedings.

"Barbara!" She called out in a loud but low pitched voice. "There's a queue forming at the deli counter". This caused Barbara to look up and acknowledge Chloe and the red faced man who had joined the queue behind her.

"OK Vicky," Barbara barked. "What do you want? I'm trying to do a job of work here". Victoria smiled as though she had won some kind of contest.

"Two scotch eggs and a small tub of coleslaw please," She said with false grace. Margaret had once told May that Barbara and Victoria were close friends though she could barely believe it. Barbara hurriedly served Victoria and then bagged the ham for Deborah

"Is there anything else Debs?"

"No that's all thanks Babs, see you tonight". Deborah and Victoria walked down the aisle; May overheard them chatting.

"I need milk and teabags. Oh yes and some kind of cake for Margaret".

"Next Please," Barbara called over to Chloe who gestured for the man behind to go ahead of her.

"Serve him first; I'm in no hurry" Chloe said with a smile. The man stepped forward and nodded in lieu of thanks.

"Half a pound of cheddar please," The red faced man asked. He was obviously in a hurry but had been too polite to complain. Barbara handed him a bag of cheese and he hurried away to the checkouts.

"Now then, what would you like dear?" Barbara asked. Chloe stepped closer to the counter.

"I would like to speak to someone about ghosts," she said. "Oh and a portion of those stuffed olives please".

"They're her favourites," Penny informed May.

"Is quarter of a pound alright?" Barbara asked as she

readied a serving spoon and a plastic container.

"Of the olives?" Chloe asked in an unsure voice.

"Obviously dear," Barbara said with a big grin. "We don't sell ectoplasm by the pound".

"Yes of course. Thank you, a quarter will be fine," Chloe replied with a red faced smile. Barbara bagged and tagged the olives.

As she handed them to Chloe she seemed check for a queue, there wasn't one.

"So what do you need to know?" Barbara asked.

"It's true then, you do know about ghosts and things?" Chloe replied.

"Of course I do! They don't call me Madam Smith of the inner circle of sacred seers for nothing". May scuffled a giggle but Penny didn't have to. Her laugh was loud and dirty like a witch's cackle.

"Can you help me Madam Smith?" Chloe said with gritted teeth hidden behind a strained smile. "I don't know if you've heard but I have recently lost my Mum, Mrs Penny Saunders and there's been strange goings on around the house ever since". Barbara's eyes seemed to light up for a moment but then she forced a frown into existence.

"So you're Chloe Saunders," She said softly. "I'm so very sorry for your loss".

"Thank you very much for your concern but can you help me?"

"I have a meeting with a circle of friends tonight who also have an interest in such matters. Maybe we could arrange to meet at your house instead".

"Yes, that sounds good," Chloe agreed, "I'll make some sandwiches if you like?"

"That'll be very nice thank you. We'll be over to yours at about seven".

"I had better give you the address".

"No need, we know where you live". Barbara said and then quickly added. "It's a small town".

"Seven o'clock it is then, thank you." Chloe gave her a quick wave and walked off down the aisle. May walked up behind Chloe, as she was placing sandwich ingredients into her basket and whispered into her ear.

"Don't buy any cake; I think Deborah's got that covered".

Chapter Ten

Chloe was busy buttering bread while May and Penny looked on helpless. Chloe was moaning about how much it had cost her to gather the ingredients to feed seven people. It didn't help when May pointed out that she and Penny couldn't physically eat so she only had to cater for five. May agreed that Chloe had made a point though; they were doing all this to make money not spend it. Penny, as hopeful as ever, had called it a wise investment. May wished that she could have shared in her confidence.

Chloe started moaning again, this time she was griping about whether there were any vegetarians in the group or not.

"You brought cheese," May pointed out. "Let them eat cheese. They're lucky to get fed as it is". Penny agreed but suggested adding some kind of pickle. Mr Kibbles didn't care for condiments; he had his eyes on the ham. May shooed him off the table, purely out of habit, he couldn't touch the meat anyway.

"I guess it'll be alright," Chloe said as she assembled the sandwiches. There were three plates spread over the kitchen table, all with little quarter slice triangles piled upon them.

"Afternoon all," Gary greeted as he suddenly appeared through the wall. His abrupt entrance caused Penny to jump but she quickly regained her posture.

"Afternoon indeed! It's gone six o'clock in the evening. Where have you been waltzing off to for all this time?" May growled at Gary and then added before he could reply. "And use the door in future. You'll liable to cause someone an injury, jumping out of the wall like that!"

"I'm glad to see your mood has improved since this morning May," Gary replied sarcastically.

"Hello Gary, how are you?" Penny asked softly.

"I take it we have another visitor?" Chloe asked as she

made the finishing touches to her finger food feast.

"I'm fine thank you Penny and how are you this evening?" Gary smiled and slightly bowed.

"It's just Gary," May informed Chloe.

"I love the way you always make me feel so welcome May," Gary said.

"I'm alright actually and thank you for your concern," Penny replied, returning Gary's smile.

"You're welcome as always," May retorted. She was beginning to suspect that three different conversations were on the go at the same time.

"Did he have any luck with finding possible clients?" Chloe asked as she washed her hands. She had finally finished and the food, to Mr Kibble's disgust, was now covered over with cling film.

"I did as it happens," Gary said and May relayed for Chloe's benefit. "There is quite a bit of interest in the service on offer, from the dead side of things. Sadly though, the money's got to come from the living and I have no way to predict how that will go". May didn't have any clue either. That was a question she hoped would have a positive answer and soon.

"Well we have arranged a meeting tonight with a group of people, who I affectionately refer to as The Thursday Night Club," May said. "If we can gather the dead together, maybe they will be willing to seek out their living counterparts. Also, Barbara seems to know a bit about all this psychic business. Maybe she knows what the going rate is?" May assumed, even though she still wasn't entirely convinced about Barbara's spiritual qualifications.

The time was getting on to a quarter past six.

"I'd better get showered and ready," Chloe said and then walked out of the kitchen. Gary had to quickly dodge backwards, to avoid her walking through him.

"I forget that she can't see me sometimes," He admitted with a grin. May eyed him suspiciously.

"Don't you dare go up to that bathroom while she's in there!" May barked.

"What do you take me for? I wouldn't dream of doing something like that! It hurts me that you would even think it May!" Gary shot May a disgruntled stare.

"Well you are a man, aren't you?" May snapped back.

"Is that much not obvious? Regardless that I happen to be dead, along with my hormones and any kind of sexual urges you might care to mention. I have no interest in such things anymore, not that I had harboured any voyeuristic desires while I still lived and breathed".

"A likely story if ever I heard one!"

"It's the truth May! We're no longer driven by the urge to reproduce but I take it you haven't noticed the change as yet," Gary pointed out. May had no choice but to agree, in part at least. She couldn't remember the last time she had suffered feelings of such a nature. Even in her youth, she hadn't been very active in that department. She had weathered a few fleeting relationships but they always withered and died in a relatively short period of time. She had never found the right man. She had never met that one special person who could live up to her many expectations. May had decided many years ago that no such man existed and even if he had, she couldn't see herself ever opening up her soul and placing it at another's mercy.

"Does that mean we can no longer love?" Penny asked, she sounded disappointed. May knew that Penny had taken a shine toward Gary, that much was clear but was it pseudo attraction or a connection from beyond the physical form

"Of course we can still love," Gary winked at Penny. "Everything I have ever done since my dieing day has been for love. I wouldn't be here right now if it wasn't for the love I feel for my son. Are your feelings for your daughter any less strong?"

"I understand that," Penny replied. "But what about love in the other sense; what about romance".

"I only know what I feel," Gary looked directly at Penny and May began to feel as if she should be somewhere else. "The physical attraction may be gone but I still feel the need closeness. Unlike most other things still available to us now, romance is far from dead. That which brings us together has lost none of its hold on us; the concept of kindred spirits is more appropriate now than ever". Penny seemed to find comfort in his words but May could sense that not all of her issues had been resolved to her satisfaction.

"So all we have left is emotion. There's nothing else, no physical displays of affection available to us?" Penny seemed to be clinging on to a sliver of hope.

"As far as I know, yes. However I have heard talk of a special bond that can sometimes occur between two kindred spirits. The bond allows them to make a spiritual connection so strong it's almost tangible," Gary explained. Penny gave him a broad smile; she seemed happy but not just about his answer.

May and Penny had moved into the living room by the time they heard Chloe walking down the stairs. She had called out to them from the kitchen, obviously expecting them to still be in there and May had called her over into the living room. Gary had already left the house again, on what he referred to as an advertising crusade.

It was ten to seven and May was hoping that Margaret wouldn't be allowed to announce The Thursday Night Club's arrival. May didn't think she could face another high pitched Coo-wee. There was a sudden knock on the front door and May braced herself as Chloe went to answer it. May could hear the door opening but there was no shrill greeting.

Chloe showed The Thursday Night Club into the living room. Barbara led with Margaret behind her. Deborah handed Chloe a small box wrapped in a plastic carrier bag and Victoria, the last to enter, was shaking a bottle of red wine in the air.

"Have you got any glasses dear?" Victoria asked, before putting the bottle on the coffee table.

"Yes of course. Make yourselves comfortable, I won't be a minute," Chloe announced and then scooted out of the room.

May watched as the four old ladies shuffled out of their coats and sat around the coffee table on. Chloe returned a few moments later with five glasses. She had left the box in the kitchen; it was obviously cake. She placed a glass in front of each of her guests and then collected their coats, which were being held up expectantly. She took them to the wall hooks in the hallway. The coats were thick and heavy, she seemed to struggle a little with the burden. When she returned she took the only vacant seat, which was opposite Barbara.

"Oh do you need a corkscrew?" Chloe said as she started to rise back out of her seat.

"No dear, it's not a posh plonk". Victoria said as she unscrewed the wine bottle.

"So we should start with introductions I guess," Barbara said as Victoria filled the waiting glasses.

"Of course," Chloe agreed. "My name is Chloe Saunders and I'm so very glad you all were able to come tonight".

"Yes I remember you from Gracie's don't I?" Deborah said. "I'm Deborah but you can call me Debs if you like". Margaret reached out for her glass.

"My name's Margaret," she greeted as she sipped her wine.

"And Victoria you met earlier today as well," Barbara pointed out. "Now what seems to be the problem?" Chloe took a deep breath; they had gone over this initial statement many times.

"My mum has recently passed away," Chloe announced.

"God bless her soul," Deborah interrupted her with the best of intentions.

"Yes bless her soul," Victoria agreed, raising her glass. They gave a toast to Penny and then Chloe continued.

"It has been a hard time for me, which has been made even more disturbing by some strange events that have recently been occurring in this very house". Each of the group leaned forward in their seats.

"Ever since my mother died, I've been hearing strange sounds and even voices in the night. Things that I have never previously experienced. To tell you the truth, I'm beginning to feel quite uneasy living here". May and the other Penny listened intently, the speech had been a joint effort.

"I need to know if the spirit of my dear departed mother still resides here. I'm at the end of my tether, I'm worried I might be losing my mind". Margaret reached over and patted Chloe lightly on the hand.

"You're not going mad dear," she soothed. "During time of stress, your judgment can become clouded. If we can't find any evidence of your mother's spirit here, don't worry yourself. You're probably just reacting normally; this is a particularly traumatic time in your life". The rest of the group nodded in agreement.

"That's only *if* we don't discover anything supernatural here tonight" Barbara confidently added.

"Drink some wine, settle your nerves," Victoria suggested. "It's alright; I've got another bottle in my bag". Chloe picked up her glass and took a token sip.

"I think we should start by lighting some candles," Barbara suggested.

"Always with the candles, I don't see how they help?" Victoria groaned. Barbara pulled four small, red tea-light candles from her bag.

"They work I tell you!" Barbara said as she placed the candles on the table. She put coasters underneath them to protect the wooden surface.

"How do you know?" Victoria asked, "Have you ever tried without them?"

"We have never had a reaction from the spirit world without them," Margaret pointed out. Victoria looked over at her.

"We have never been without them to know!" Victoria said. Deborah put her hand in the air.

"I quite like them; I think they're rather pretty," She announced.

"They calm the spirits and make them more amiable and approachable". Barbara explained as she begun to light the candles. May watched the candles burn and felt no calming effects; she was more worried about them becoming a fire hazard. Penny seemed to like them, how ever, so maybe Barbara did have something there.

"We should all hold hands around the table now," Barbara said, reaching out to Deborah and Victoria who were sitting either side of her on the sofa. Victoria swapped her wine glass to her free hand. Margaret, who was in one of the arm chairs, could just reach Deborah's other hand. Victoria quickly downed the last of her wine before putting the empty glass down and taking Chloe's hand across the table; she had to move one of the candles for fear of burning herself. Chloe reached out with her other hand and held Margaret's free hand at an uncomfortable stretch. They looked a little awkward and unevenly stretched.

"It's usually more comfortable with a round table," Barbara pointed out, even though she had the position of greatest comfort. May walked around the group and tried to work out who was going to fall out of their seat first. Her money was on Chloe; she seemed to be making the most effort to be within reach.

"Right then, if you would all now try to relax," Barbara instructed.

"Not likely!" Victoria pointed out.

"Well try your best, it helps".

"What as much as the candles?"

"Please Vicky we are trying to help young Chloe put her demons to rest. Can you please concentrate," Barbara closed her eyes. She started to hum softly and sway a little, or as much as the conditions would allow.

"Come hither to us restless spirits. Tell us your woes and let us help guide you on the path to peace and contentment". Margaret leaned towards Chloe slightly, which in turn threatened to lift Deborah from her seat.

"She wrote those chants herself," Margaret whispered. "They're rather good don't you think?" Chloe smiled back at her, either way the words were pointless. The ghosts were already present and waiting.

May still wasn't sure about the initial greeting that they had finally agreed upon. She was worried that it was a corny, stereotypical way to instigate communication. She Stood by the doorway and cupped her hands over her mouth, in an attempt to create a muffled echoic voice.

"Woo!" she called out self consciously. The group reacted with surprise and Chloe tried to mimic them.

"What was that?" Margaret yelled in shock.

"Keep concentrating everyone; I think we've got something here," Barbara said.

"Woo...woo! Who disturbs the cosmic forces and summons me to this place?" May said as she began to get into the swing of it. Margaret's shock seemed to give way to nervous confusion.

"It is I, Madam Smith of the Inner Circle of Sacred Seers, who summons you here today," Barbara replied. Her voice sounded confident but her facial expression suggested that this was probably her first real spectral encounter.

"For what reason do you summon me into your presence?" May was beginning to adlib a little. Margaret kept trying to grab Barbara's attention. Deborah was a white as a sheet and Victoria was trying to reach for the wine bottle, while still not releasing Chloe's hand.

"Barbara!" Margaret called but appeared to be ignored. She tugged at Deborah's arm to get her attention but Deborah was as stiff as a pole.

"We summon you here today to help Young Chloe Saunders ease her suffering after the passing of her mother. Are we speaking to Penny Saunders?" Barbara called out.

"No I am not she," May replied through her cupped hands. "She's standing over by the window". Margaret clearly wasn't having any more of this charade as she released her grip from Deborah's and Chloe's hands and stood up from her chair. Victoria took the opportunity to release Chloe's other hand and make a grab for the wine bottle.

"May Elizabeth Trump!" Margaret yelled. "Is that you?" May was stumped; she hadn't expected that.

"I know your voice any where so there's no point in pretending. Come out and show yourself; this is really not funny". Then May suddenly realised that Margaret didn't even know that she was dead. Her closest friend was unaware of her plight and in such a small town this was disturbing news. Chloe sat open mouthed; her surprise was no longer false. May looked towards Penny for ideas, who merely responded with gestures of bafflement. May decided to own up to at least some of which she was being accused of.

"For God's sake Margaret!" May yelled. "You've completely ruined the atmosphere". Margaret fell back into her chair, which creaked noisily with the impact.

"I can't believe I was actually right," she admitted. "Where are you May? What are you doing here?"

Now May was faced with another problem. If Margaret really didn't know about her death, how was she supposed to inform her of it without causing her too much grief? May looked around the room. Deborah was still white and motionless, except for the faint evidence of breathing. Victoria was drinking wine straight from the bottle; her trembling hands were causing the glass to rattle against her teeth. Barbara sat with a shocked expression on her face, which was threatening to soon break. Chloe however, just looked on in amused interest; she was beginning to crack a cheeky smile. You're beginning to really enjoy this, May thought. She couldn't think of any other option but to just come out with the stark facts. She just hoped that Margaret's reaction wouldn't be too severe.

"I'm over here Margaret," May admitted. "I'm standing right in front of the doorway". Margaret, along with everyone else in the room including Deborah, who hadn't moved a muscle in the past five minutes, looked towards the door.

"Where?" Margaret said nervously. "I can't see you".

"I know," May agreed. "This is going to come to you as a bit of a shock Margaret but I'm dead. I died Margaret and now I stand before you as a ghost".

Margaret stumbled backwards a step and her eyes began to well.

"No... That's not true! I only saw you two days ago," Margaret protested. "This is not like you May, playing such a nasty trick. Where are you really?" Chloe stood up and offered Margaret a supporting embrace.

"I'm sorry but it's all true. Everything she says is true," Chloe assured as Margaret began to sob into her shoulder. Moments later, she suddenly lifted her head and pushed Chloe away.

"How do you know?" She yelled at Chloe through her tears. All the eyes in the room, dead and alive, turned towards Chloe.

"Well technically I first heard it from Stephen Chimer in Buster's burger bar," Chloe explained. "Though it didn't really sink in properly, not until she told me about it herself". The whole of the Thursday Night Club looked on in confusion.

"Why did you ask us here if you already knew that this place was haunted?" Barbara asked. "Let me rephrase that; why ask us here if you are already on talking terms with the ghosts who's haunting you?" May didn't like the sound of that remark.

"Hold on that's a bit strong don't you think? I'm wouldn't say I'm haunting the girl!" May protested.

"Then what are you doing here?" Victoria asked; it seemed that wine was helping to bolster her courage.

"She's here to help me," Chloe explained. "If I don't get some cash flow going here soon I'm going to either lose this house or I'll have to give up on my education". Margaret knelt down by the sofa and turned her attention to Deborah, who was now showing obvious signs of shock.

"That's convenient for you," Victoria sneered. Penny seemed very unhappy at the way they were speaking to her daughter.

"Why didn't you just tell us the truth in the first place?" Barbara asked.

"It's money Babs!" Victoria answered in Chloe's stead. "She's just after the money. She trying to do number on us; con us out of our money somehow". Penny was clearly having no more of this. She rushed forward across the room towards Victoria.

"How dare you speak to my daughter like that!" Penny screamed and attempted to slap Victoria across the face. May watched as Penny's hand passed ineffectively through Victoria's head. She lost her balance and fell backwards through the coffee table. She clambered back to her feet, red faced and dizzy.

"I'm not trying to con you," Chloe protested. "I need your help! We have a plan to make money by holding séances for people who want to contact the dead or visa versa".

"Visa versa?" Barbara asked, surprised. "Do you say to tell us that there are ghosts out there who need of our help to contact the living?"

"Yes, that's exactly what I mean," Chloe replied.

"Don't listen to her Babs she's just trying to scam us!" Victoria yelled. Penny stared long and hard at Victoria's wine glass. It suddenly shattered and red wine was thrown all over Victoria and the coffee table.

"Yow... They're attacking me now!" Victoria screeched. "We have to leave this place. They mean us harm I tell you". Victoria jumped up from her seat and dropped what little remained of her wineglass. She was covered in red liquid and thankfully it was all wine.

Margaret stood up from Deborah's side and slapped Victoria hard across the cheek. The impact forced Victoria back into her seat and the shock kept her silent. "Now calm down Victoria!" She yelled and then announced in a much calmer voice. "I have no idea what's going on here but if May Trump is involved then you can be sure that the motives are honourable. I know that some of you consider her to be hard, brash and a little rude even but she's no

trickster and definitely no liar. Now obviously we have
started off on the wrong foot here. I don't know about
you? But Deborah could do with a hot, sweet tea and I'm
way over due a sugar rush". Margaret helped Deborah up
on to her feet. "So when you've all calmed down and
settled your differences; you'll find me in the kitchen
serving tea".

Chapter Eleven

May stood by the fridge, watching Margaret as she gathered what she needed to make the tea. She seemed to have no trouble finding everything; she clearly knew her way around a kitchen. Chloe was sitting at the table next to Deborah, keeping her sat upright. Deborah was mumbling something incoherent, while Chloe tried to keep her from sliding off the chair. Barbara and Victoria were still in the living room discussing their options. May suspected that it was more likely that Barbara was just trying to convince Victoria not to run out of the house and start shouting hysterically into the night. Penny had chosen to stay and keep an eye on them.

"So you really didn't know what happened to me?" May asked. Margaret had her back to her, so her expression was hidden.

"No I didn't May," Margaret replied. "I saw you on Tuesday and I expected to see you again next Tuesday as normal. It never crossed my mind that you had passed on, though I did think about you at the café yesterday. I could almost hear your voice. It very nearly put me off my gateaux, in a nice way obviously". May smiled, Margaret was coping quite well considering. She had always assumed that she would be useless in a trauma, not unlike Deborah. Her oldest friend had surprised her with such strength of character that she would never had given her credit for.

"I must admit though," Margaret pointed out. "My emotions are in a real muddle at the moment. Part of me wants to grieve for you, yet another part of me can't get over the fact that you're still here. I've not been this confused since Dirk Bogarde came out of the closet".

Margaret put a cup of hot sweet tea in front of Deborah and Chloe encouraged her to drink it.

"That's understandable Marge," May sympathised. "To tell you the truth I've been a little emotionally unstable the past couple of days".

"That's saying a lot coming from you," Margaret said.

"I guess you're right," May agreed. "I did spend most my life withdrawn from people. I was happy that way but now I feel more vulnerable. I'm finding it hard to turn down the company. Maybe I'm just trying to keep a hold on to whatever semblance of life I can. Maybe I quite literally left my backbone behind in my body".

Margaret pulled a chair up to the table and sat down opposite Deborah. She put her cup of tea on the table in front of her and started to examine the food laid out by Chloe.

"Strength like yours doesn't come from the body it comes from the soul. That's why they call it spirit, when someone stands behind their principles no matter what. Even if that means they stand alone. You haven't become weak May, far from it. I don't see you relying on anyone here; I see people relying on you," Margaret said without looking up from the table. "Do you mind if I help myself?" She pointed at the sandwiches.

"Of course not," Chloe replied as she stood up from her seat, "I'll fetch some plates. I'm sorry; I've been a terrible hostess. I'm just not used to entertaining".

"The one thing you can't say about this evening is that it's not been entertaining," Margaret grinned. Deborah had regained a little colour and was sipping gently at her tea.

"I think maybe I should eat something as well," She suggested quietly.

"Are you back with us again Deborah?" Margaret asked softy.

"I guess so," Deborah shrugged. "It would be a shame to waste such a nice spread anyway; Young Chloe has obviously made an effort". Chloe returned to the table with a small pile of plates.

"It's no trouble," Chloe explained.

"It is trouble," Margaret disagreed, "Trouble and money. Believe me, we appreciate the gesture. That includes Victoria, when she eventually calms down. She will need something to soak up all that red wine she's been drinking".

"Thank you for your words Marge," May said, "They mean a lot. You're probably the closest thing I have to family". Margaret unwrapped the sandwiches and selected two cheese and tomato triangles.

"Does that mean you've left me all your money?" Margaret said in jest. May suddenly felt guilty, she hadn't even considered Margaret. She had left no will because she thought that she had no one to name it in. If only I'd got my frickin' head out of my backside before I died.

"I'm sorry Marge," May regretfully admitted. "I should have made some kind of will; I should have considered you and your family more".

"I was just joking May, don't worry yourself about it," Margaret said reassuringly.

"I know you were Marge but I'm being completely serious. All I owned will become the property of the state and we are here trying scrape together what little money we can". May really understood the meaning of closing the gate after the horse has bolted. The money she had saved would have been more than enough to see Chloe through comfortably and that wasn't including the value of her house.

"I see your point May, I really do, but it'll do you no good dwelling on it," Margaret said between mouthfuls. "If you want to see this bizarre endeavour through to the end; you really shouldn't focus on the past".

"Margaret's got that right," Barbara said. She led Victoria into the kitchen. Penny and Gary followed closely behind. May hadn't realised that Gary had returned. "If I understand this undertaking correctly we will all need to conserve our strength". Barbara said, as she guided Victoria into the last vacant chair at the table. Chloe stood up and relinquished her chair so that Barbara could sit.

"Thank you very much; it's nice to see courtesy is still alive and well". Barbara said as she accepted Chloe's offered chair. "Eat something Victoria; it'll make you feel better". Chloe passed Victoria an empty plate.

"I think they've calmed down a bit now," Penny said. May noticed that Gary was holding Penny's hand but decided not to mention it.

"Is that tea on the go?" Barbara asked "I won't say no but I think Victoria would benefit more from a strong coffee". Chloe switched the kettle back on.

"Won't be long, I was thinking of making myself one anyway. I'm not really a tea drinker".

"Right then!" Barbara announced. "What do we do now?" Deborah looked up at her.

"Are you seriously considering going along with this séance idea?" She asked.

"Of course we are," Barbara replied. "After all the time we've spent searching for some kind of contact with the paranormal do you truly expect me to not get involved? I've been waiting for this opportunity all my life. It may not be exactly as I had imagined it but it's still the real deal. I haven't spent all my spare time trying to contact the dead just to say, 'no sorry not interested', as soon as I get an answer. I'm sorry if you disagree but I don't care. With or without you, I'm going to be knee deep in this and no mistake" .Deborah just sat there for a moment in open mouthed silence.

"I...I didn't mean nothing by it Babs," Deborah finally stuttered." You know me, whether it be the church roof or a jumble sale, I'll do anything for the benefit of the local community. I suppose Chloe's a local and part of the community? There's no real difference if I don't think about it too much".

"I don't know Debs," Victoria joined the discussion, "It all seems a bit freaky to me". Victoria had forced herself to eat a couple of sandwiches and she seemed to have regained a little control.

"Surely no freakier than what we've been doing every Thursday night for god knows how long?" Barbara asked. Victoria shrugged.

"Well I guess it's kind of different; now that it works properly". Barbara shot Victoria a look that could have fried onions at fifty yards.

"Are you saying that after all these years you've never believed in my psychic abilities?" Barbara almost roared at Victoria, she was obviously none too pleased.

"No... Not at all!" Victoria replied. "I just thought it was a little unreliable. A bit hit and miss if you prefer?"

"A bit hit and miss!" Barbara Yelled. May was beginning to realise that this seemingly gentle group of old ladies could be quite volatile at times.

"Oh come on Babs," Margaret confessed. "It's not like we've been bouncing from one supernatural disaster to another. On the really quite nights, I thought you knew it was me who made the Ouija board spell cake".

"She's right Babs, it's not like we were over run with ghostly encounters," Debra added nervously. Barbara looked at each of her friends in turn and sighed.

"OK you lot," Barbara relented. "I can see your point to some degree but that's all changed now. We sit here now, in the presence of two ghosts who are asking *us* for help".

"Three ghosts," May corrected her. "Actually no, four if you count the cat".

"There's you May and Penny Saunders; who else is here?" Barbara asked.

"Gary," May replied. "He's kind of our agent. He's the one who will be bringing in the dead, so to speak".

"And a cat?" Margaret added.

"Mr Kibbles Marge. You remember Mr Kibbles don't you?"

"Oh...oh yes. He was just a big ball of fluff, if I remember correctly," Margaret replied. There was a quiver in her voice as she spoke.

"Right so we are sat here in the presence of three ghosts and a dead cat, who are asking for our help," Barbara repeated. "Are we really going to say no?" Victoria looked at Margaret and Margaret looked at Deborah. They were clearly trying to gauge each others reactions.

Chloe stepped forward and put a large mug of coffee in front of Victoria and asked if she wanted any sugar. Deborah watched Victoria as she gave Chloe a negative gesture.

"All I know," Deborah suddenly announced. "Is that I don't have a very full schedule nowadays and some things in life are more important than crochet; you can count me in". Victoria finally agreed, after stipulating the conditions that she wouldn't have to miss bingo and she wouldn't have to listen to any of that head banging music that the young people listened to these days. Margaret was easily recruited; May knew she could rely on her. She suffered another pang of guilt; she had never appreciated just how good a friend Margaret really was.

The Thursday Night Club left the house with promises to return and Chloe had announced her desire for an early night. May lay upstairs on the bed of the spare room she had chosen for herself. Mr Kibbles was curled up at her feet. Gary and Penny were still down stairs chatting, or at least that's what she had assumed they were doing. There was another meeting planned for late tomorrow morning, to discus the game plan, as Victoria had described it. May was relaxed and ready to drift away. Chloe had her company at last and May couldn't help thinking of it in the military sense. She had been dead for just over two days and she had more friends now than she had managed to make in her seventy five years of life. She started to regret her lifestyle choices, so she cast the thoughts from her mind. As Margaret had told her, there was no use dwelling on the past. May drifted off to sleep and she met with the friends of her future in an old saloon from the past. She agreed with Deborah; there was definitely more to life than crochet.

Chapter Twelve

May awoke from the dream world. She began to notice that each time she visited it, the harder it was to leave. There had been no party atmosphere this time, just a sense of a relaxed acceptance. She had toured the town and spoken to many that resided there. She was surprised to discover that she had met some of them before. May didn't know them well but at one time or another, their paths had crossed. She had searched the town but found no one closer than brief acquaintances. She guessed that there were so few people in that particular category that the odds of them meeting again were slim. It had been a comfortable and safe reminiscence.

May realised that she had woken up late again when she heard the rattle of cups coming from the kitchen below. Muffled voices and the scraping of chairs; the Thursday Night Club were already here.

May walked into the kitchen and glanced up at the clock on the wall, it was just after eleven in the morning. Chloe's army were sat around the table, each of them cradling a cup of tea. Victoria looked a little worse for wear but she was grinning and bearing it. She's probably used to heavy mornings, May thought. Chloe was leaning against the draining board holding coffee mug with both hands.

"I'll tell you this for nothing," Margaret said. "Alf didn't even care where I was going this morning, let alone start making enquiries about it. He's not even on the same planet as everybody else at the moment. He was out late last night at the golf club. He told me that he had a double bogey at the nineteenth hole and now he feels squarely in the rough". May listened to the groups chatter for a moment but then decided it was probably impolite not to announce her presence.

"Good Morning" She said in a calm voice, as an attempt

to affect the least surprise. Deborah jumped up in her seat and Victoria almost dropped her teacup. Barbara casually scanned the room and Margaret just smiled.

"Good Morning May," Chloe replied with little facial reaction; she was clearly getting used to the situation.

"Oh yes," Barbara said, "Good morning May". She paused for a few seconds. "If it's not rude to ask, where are you? It's just so I know which way to look when I'm talking to you". May smiled, she crossed the room and stood in front of fridge. If it puts them at ease, she thought.

"I'm standing by the fridge Barbara," she said. "It's not rude to ask either. Well at least not as far as I'm concerned". All living eyes looked towards the fridge. May received an uneasy hello from both Deborah and Victoria. Margaret just flashed a big, bright smile in May's general direction..

"Thank You May," Barbara acknowledged. "It just makes it seem less weird".

"How are you today May?" Margaret asked, still smiling.

"Stone dead but otherwise fine," May said in an attempt at humour. The joke didn't seem to translate too well to the living.

"Oh...that's good I guess," Margaret replied in an unsure voice.

"How are you today Marge? I'm sorry to hear that Alfred is feeling under the weather," May remarked. Barbara spoke out before Margaret could respond.

"This is all very good and dandy," She said. "But can we dispense with the pleasantries and get on with the work at hand". May respected Barbara's outburst in both content and style, she couldn't have said it better herself. There was much that needed doing. The morning had almost passed with nothing yet achieved. If the trend was allowed to continue, there was a risk of the whole day being wasted with pointless distractions.

"That was rather rude Barbara, don't you think?" Victoria said. Deborah and Margaret nodded in agreement. May was about to step in with her own opinion but Chloe beat her to the post.

"I really don't think that's true ladies," Chloe explained. "We need a day of hard talk and solid decision making. Barbara's right, we don't have time for idle chat. You've all been here for forty minutes already and we haven't got a single thing organised. If we don't make some plans soon we'll lose the day. We need form plans and make decisions, while we still have some of the day left to implement them". Chloe quickly added. "Although your help is much appreciated, of course".

"A firm head on her shoulders and she makes a good cup of tea; this girl has a got a lot going for her," Margaret joked. May had to agree, even though she had never tasted her tea.

"We'll need to make notes," Deborah announced as she dug a small black notebook and a pen out of her bag. "There's no point doing anything without writing it down". Margaret had once mentioned to May that Deborah used to work as a secretary and it was clearly beginning to show.

"This will do for now," Deborah said, holding up her note book. "Anything official I can type up later".

"Anything official?" Victoria remarked. "What do you think we are doing here?" Deborah smiled as if she held the winning hand in a poker game.

"Not reading shorthand for a start!" Deborah pointed out as she opened her notebook.

"OK fair enough, good point". Victoria relented while wearing a slightly sulky expression.

May could read shorthand, though she had never found a use for it professionally. She had been put off the idea of an office career just in the nick of time. She had been set up with a temporary position where she had discovered that, working in an office frequently meant having to be in close proximity to other people for long periods of time. There was also a hierarchy system that she just couldn't abide. You would never catch May running around after some jumped up manager who's life, so far, had only been a construct of lectures, seminars and exams. Some spotty young man with no achievements other than grades, it would have never worked.

"Right then, where do we start?" Barbara threw out an open question.

"I guess we have to set up a room somehow," Chloe suggested. "You know dimmed lights, tasselled tablecloths and a crystal ball. That sort of thing".

"Barbara normally gets by just fine with candles," Victoria said sarcastically.

"No she's got a good point," May said. "It doesn't matter if this stuff works or not it's all about creating the right atmosphere. The dead don't care about candles and tassels but the living will need something real to hold on to".

"So job number one is to decorate a room to look spooky," Deborah said as she wrote.

"Which room?" Victoria asked. "It'll need to be upstairs or somewhere not too close to the front door. You'll have nervous people sitting in a strange dark room talking to May who, let's be honest, is hardly cute and cuddly. They'll be having heart attacks every time there's a knock at the door. What more, What if you have other people waiting? Where do you suppose to stick them?" That was the first sensible thing I've ever heard Victoria say, May realised. She didn't say much of any use but when she did, it made up a little for her normal useless chatter.

"That's…that's a very good point Vicky," Barbara said, she seemed a little surprised as well. "Write that down Debs, we need a waiting room as well".

"I don't want to worry anyone," Chloe looked concerned. "But won't this all cost money. I really don't think that I can afford to decorate two whole rooms".

"Don't worry yourself Chloe," Margaret said. "Barbara's probably got everything we need stuffed in her garage".

"Oh yes," Barbara agreed "Don't concern yourself Chloe; I've got plenty of that kind of stuff. I can even put a few copies of my Psychic Monthly on a table in the waiting room, just for effect mind you".

"We know how to work with a budget if nothing else," Victoria added.

"You're not kidding," Deborah agreed. "My pension doesn't stretch half as far as it used to".

"Why do you think I'm still working my nephew's deli counter? Not for the love of cheese that's for sure," Barbara admitted.

Deborah checked her notes.

"OK we've sorted out the venue, what's next?" she asked.

"I guess it's bringing in the punters?" Victoria suggested. May realised that this was where the living had little control. This was Gary's department, wherever he and Penny were this morning. There's was no point asking anyone else in the room because they wouldn't be aware one way or another.

"At this stage we need to wait for more information from the prospective dead clients, before we know who amongst the living we need to contact," May explained. Chloe put up her hand as if she was a small child in a classroom.

"What about Gary's son?" She pointed out. "I wrote the contact details down somewhere last night, where did I put it?" Deborah lifted up her teacup and peeled the small piece of paper that had stuck to its base.

"Is this it?" She said as she held up the tea stained scrap of paper. "Sorry, I didn't want to ruin the surface and I couldn't find a coaster". She pointed at the table and shrugged.

"Yes, that's it," Chloe replied. "Anyway, we could invite him over as a sort of test run". Deborah examined the scrap of paper and deciphered the address through the damp brown circle her cup had created.

"This address is a good bus journey into the next town," Deborah noticed. "And there's no phone number here". Margaret leaned over the table.

"Let me see that," She said and plucked the scrap out of Deborah's hand.

"I know that road" Margaret announced. "I'll go and talk to this one, see if I can't convince him to come over tomorrow evening sometime. That's if he's in, if not I'll leave a note or something".

"Well I guess I should pop home and sort out a few bits from my garage," Barbara suggested.

"I'll help with that!" Victoria offered too swiftly to be without motive. Deborah could go with Marge; you know I'm none too fond of buses". Deborah seemed to be about protest but then didn't. May suspected that her sudden change in body language was in consideration of Margaret's feelings but she was wrong.

"There's a really good wool shop in the next town," Deborah said in a hopeful voice, "We'll have time for a quick visit won't we?"

"Only if we get going straight away," Margaret stipulated, as she slowly rose from her Chair. Deborah quickly tided her notebook and pen back into her bag and followed Margaret to the coat hooks in the hallway.

"Right then Vicky, let's get going," Barbara said.

"I can come with you and help carry...stuff?" Chloe volunteered.

"No, you should stay here," Barbara said. "You've got enough to do. You need to organise two rooms, one upstairs and one down".

"Oh yes of course," Chloe realised.

May bade farewell and watched the group leave the house. Finally action was being taken; things were beginning to get done. She did feel a little useless, being unable to help at this stage, but she was aware of her own unique contribution. That was something that still worried her though: How was she going to talk to the living without scaring the life out of every visitor?

She followed Chloe, who had begun her search for suitable rooms and considered her options. She finally decided that the best course of action was to approach the whole process from the prospective of a ventriloquist; all she needed now was a dummy.

<u>Chapter Thirteen</u>

A few hours had passed since The Thursday Night Club had left on their separate errands. Chloe had chosen the living room as a waiting area and had cleared it out of anything personal to her. Family photographs and particular ornaments which had the most sentimental value. She had explained to May that she felt more at ease with them safely tucked away. Safe from any bored or clumsy people who may fiddle around with them while they wait for May's mystic wisdom.

To May's relief, Chloe had chosen a different spare bedroom to the one that May had claimed as her own. Excepting the good with the bad, May watched Chloe move the unwanted clutter from the new séance room and stack it into hers. May didn't mind that much, she just asked Chloe to keep the bed clear. Both finally seemed to be ready for Barbara to decorate with her collection of supernatural accessories.

Chloe had only just returned to the kitchen, to make a well earned coffee, when Penny and Gary appeared through the outside wall. May made a mental note to have a word with Gary about his unconventional entrances. He was beginning to influence Penny with his unhindered movements. May didn't know if there was a spiritual code of conduct already in force but if there wasn't, she would soon implement one. So you can walk through walls can you? Well that didn't mean that you should.

"Now where have you two been?" May asked.

"Hello May," Penny greeted, smiling girlishly. "Gary was just showing me around his regular haunts. He introduced me to a few of his friends".

"I hope you don't mind," Gary said, also smiling inanely. "You were away when we left and it's not like we could leave a message with anyone. We have made a few

arrangements for tomorrow night, it that's alright; just a
few eager spirits who would like to discuss the opportunity
we have on offer". Chloe turned away from the kettle with
a coffee mug in her hand.

"Is that my Mum come back?" She asked in the direction
of the fridge.

"Yes Chloe," May replied. "It would seem that she's been
out on a date with Gary". Penny flushed red. It was just an
emotional or psychological reaction; her actual blushing
days were over.

"No not a date as such," Penny protested with little real
effort. "We were working, kind of. Putting the word out,
gathering prospective clients, that sort of thing. I'd hardly
call it a date!" Then, under her breath, she added. "Mores
the pity".

"Hello Mum," Chloe greeted. "How did it go?"

"She says it wasn't a date," May conveyed.

"Oh OK then," Chloe looked a bit disappointed. "Is Gary
here as well? Have you told him about his son?"

"What about my son?" Gary jumped in, leaving not a
moments silence between Chloe's words and his own.

"Margaret and Deborah have gone to his house with the
intention of inviting him here tomorrow night," May
explained. "Obviously that's if he's in and if Margaret can
coax Deborah out of the kitting shop".

"Oh...oh right," Gary replied apprehensively. "It's going to
be a busy day tomorrow then". Gary didn't seem as happy
about the news as May had expected. He seemed worried.

"Is there a problem?" May asked. Gary shook his head
slowly.

"No, there's no problem," He replied. "I'm just a bit
nervous is all. I've waited for this moment for ten years and
now that it's here... I just don't know. I'm not sure what I'm
going to say to him, if anything at all. It's been such a long
time now that he might not even remember me. Who am I
to take him through that grief again?" Penny put her arm
around his shoulder.

"You're his father and, if he doesn't remember that, it's
your responsibility to remind him". Penny said. "I know you

didn't have the perfect relationship but you were a good father. You've dedicated your life and your death to him. Even from beyond the grave you've done your best by him and he should know of it. He should know just how much his father loves him!" She paused and then continued in a softer voice. "But I'm sure it will all go just fine. I'll be right here by your side the whole time, if you'll allow me?"

"Thank you Penny," Gary replied. "That means a lot to me".

"What's going on now?" Chloe asked; there had been a long pause in the conversation from her prospective.

"Sorry Chloe". May replied, as she realised that Chloe had been left out of the loop again. "Gary's worried that his son won't remember who he is. It's just a bit of stage fright if you ask me. I just hope he grows a backbone by tomorrow or I'll be the one left high and dry!"

"That's a bit harsh May, don't you think?" Chloe said. "Don't worry Gary. I never knew my father at all; he left before I was born. You were an active father to your son for eleven years; I really don't see how he could forget you". May didn't think that Gary's son would have forgotten him either but if he had, ten thousand pounds would jog anyone's memory. One look at that bank account and it'll all come flooding back to him.

There was a knock on the front door and Chloe went to answer it. Barbara and Victoria had returned with three large bags of tassels and candles, among other things. As soon as they had taken off their coats, they set to work decorating the living room. Chloe offered to help but was instantly relegated to tea making duties. Victoria produced a Batten-berg from her bag and handed it to Chloe.

"We had best have a slice now before Margaret gets back" she winked. "Otherwise it'll be a hard push to even get a look in". Chloe gave her an unsure smile and walked back to the kitchen to make the tea.

May watched as Barbara and Victoria began to unpack

their bags. There was a collection of strange looking statues, small tasselled cloths and doilies piling up on the table. Victoria pulled an empty goldfish bowl from one of the bag but Barbara told her to put it back.

"That's for the room upstairs," She explained to Victoria.

"Why do you need a goldfish bowl?" May asked, causing both Barbara and Victoria to jump.

"Oh hello May," Barbara said, once she had composed herself. May felt a little guilty for not announcing her presence again.

"The goldfish bowl is a great tool for mystics such as myself. It's cheaper than a crystal ball and a hell of a lot easier to carry".

"Isn't it more fortune tellers who use crystal balls, not mediums?" May asked, though she had to admit that her knowledge of such things was small. It just seemed to her that a crystal ball would be more fitting at a carnival, than at a place of spiritual contact.

"As you mentioned earlier May," Barbara reminded her. "We're trying to create an atmosphere that will give the punters the impression that we are a genuine and professional outfit". Barbara pulled the goldfish bowl back out of the bag and looked at it for a moment. "We'll put it in the room and if it looks weird, or not the right style of weird, we won't use it". She shrugged and put it back in the bag.

"We could always put it the right way up and use it as a tip jar," Victoria suggested sarcastically.

May took the opportunity to ask Barbara a few things that had her concerned.

"Actually Barbara, I need to speak to you regarding the practicalities of hosting a séance," May explained. "I'm going to need a little tuition on how to speak to people, just as a real medium would". Barbara laughed but May didn't see what was so amusing about it.

"I do believe a ghost has just asked me to teach them how to act as if one with the supernatural. Don't worry yourself May, you'll do just fine. I plan to be in the room with you anyway, as a consultant if you like". May guessed that Barbara must have misunderstood her question.

"But don't I use special words and incantations? I can't just say: hello operator here, who can I put you through to? There's got to be some kind of etiquette to all this?".

"I could tell you what to say and how to act but it would soon become obvious that you were faking. They will come here ready to scrutinise your every word and gesture, though gesturing won't be an issue for you. Most of them will want to believe you but they still won't trust you as far as they can throw. At least not at first. You have to act naturally; your words must flow as if they were your own. Which is just why they should be. I can tell you a few phrases to set the mood but then it will have to be all you". Barbara explained, as she handed Victoria a large tasselled doily to hang on the mantelpiece. "As soon as you start reading from a script you'll lose them".

It started to make sense. May felt a little better about the whole charade. There was too much that was deceitful about their plan already and that didn't sit well with May. She understood that something's were better left unsaid, such as the fact that she was a ghost for a start, but it didn't make her feel any better about it. The fact that honesty would also play an integral part put at least some of her misgivings to rest.

"What about a physical form?" May asked. "They are going to expect me to have a physical presence. I can't just stand behind them and whisper in their ear. It would cause complete panic; I need some kind of body". Just then Chloe walked into the room carrying a tray with two cups and two slices of cake on it.

"I was thinking about that as well May". Chloe said, as she squeezed the tray on to the table. A couple of gargoyle shaped ornaments were knocked off onto the floor. They bounced slightly, the way cheap plastic always does.

"Actually I just remembered while I was in the kitchen, we've got an old tailor's dummy stuck up in the loft. I think that might serve our purpose". Victoria grabbed a teacup from the tray.

"Thank god I'm parched," She announced, to no one's interest but her own.

"I guess we could put a dress on it and a veil over it maybe. Dim the lights a bit" Barbara shrugged.

"We could explain that the lack of movement was due to her being in a deep spectral trance or something," Vicky suggested sarcastically as she sipped her tea.

"That's not a bad idea, not a bad idea at all". Barbara agreed. She was either oblivious to Victoria's sarcasm or had chosen to ignore it; May suspected the latter.

"If I'm sitting in on the séance, I can make sure no one gets too close." Barbara continued. "How big is the table exactly?"

"There's a small round one in there at the moment but there are a few others dotted around the house. Actually there's a long thin table in my room; I was using it as a desk," Chloe replied. Barbara snapped her fingers in the air like a magician. May half expected a rabbit to suddenly appear.

"Each end of a long table, dress it up, dim the lights. That might actually work!" Barbara said, enthusiastically. May wasn't entirely convinced.

"Didn't you just say that the clients would be inherently suspicious?" She pointed out. "It'll never work. They'll never fall for that!"

"Oh yes they will May!" Barbara explained. "They'll be hanging onto your every word. The room will be dark, not pitch black mind you. Just a little candle light I reckon; you can't go far wrong with candles in this game. They'll be analysing everything you say, the lack of gesturing will help. Their eyes will be every where except on you. They'll know you're there, they can hear you. It'll be the shadows in the corners and the flickering of the candles that they'll worry about the most".

"But what if they do stare at the dummy too closely?" May asked, she still wasn't convinced.

"Well if that happens, I'll fidget about. Draw their

attention away somehow. A few sudden movements here and there, that'll get there eyes twitching if nothing else" Barbara replied. May sighed and resigned herself to Barbara's expertise. She knew that she would be nervous of discovery regardless of any assurances she was given. She just wasn't a natural liar.

The living were busy and May felt useless again. She knew that any further vocal input on her behalf would probably be considered as interfering. She announced that she was leaving the room, it was only polite and ventured out into the kitchen. Gary and Penny were still in there, chatting and laughing childishly. May felt in the way there as well so decided to go outside and take a walk around the garden. She hoped that Mr Kibbles was outside as she hadn't seen him all day and she felt a need for one of his cuddles. Again she reprimanded herself for becoming soft but that didn't countermand her need for closeness.

Margaret and Deborah were just outside the front door as May passed through it; they were just about to knock. She announced her presence and Debra almost dropped her bag of multicoloured balls of wool. Margaret informed May about their meeting with Gary's son.

"He's agreed to visit sometime between six and half past, tomorrow evening," Margaret explained. "He was dubious at first but once I mentioned the bank account he became more excepting of us. He's not a bad lad May, I think he just needs the money at the moment. I don't think he believed us about actually speaking to his father but I would swear I saw hope in his eyes. He's a sweet boy May, I think you'll like him".

May left them by the door, still waiting for it to be answered and continued her stroll around to the side of the house. She was happy to see that Mr Kibbles was fine and trying to climb the bird table in the garden. He kept passing straight through the wooden stand but his lack of success didn't seem to lower his determination. May walked towards him with the mind to scoop him from his feet and hold him close.

Chapter Fourteen

It was six o'clock on Friday evening and they had everything prepared. Gary's son was due to arrive at any time.

May had examined the dummy that Chloe and Barbara had disguised. She had been surprised to discover that it looked rather effective, as long as you stood no closer than the opposite end of the table. With the curtains drawn and only the light of a few candles left to illuminate the room it would pass a casual inspection. They had dressed it in one of Penny's old black dresses, the one that she only ever wore to funerals. A cauliflower had been requisitioned from the kitchen cupboard, in lieu of a head. It had a thick black veil draped over it, courtesy of Barbara and was topped with a small black hat. The whole thing had been padded out here and there with cushion stuffing; they had definitely made an effort. The goldfish bowl was nowhere to be seen. May was thankful that her opinion had counted in that instance. The room was almost empty other than the long table and a few chairs. There was a tall, standing lamp by the window and every available surface had been covered with either black crepe paper or tasselled doyleys. May thought the room looked effective, if a bit noisy. The window was slightly open and a draft was brushing against the crepe paper and causing the tassels to flicker like impatient fingers. May made a mental note to get someone to close it before Gary's son arrived.

Everyone had congregated in the kitchen, May discovered when she came back down stairs. Chloe was leaning on the draining board again and the rest of the living were seated around the table. May took up her adopted position by the fridge, while Gary and Penny stood together in the far corner. They were holding hands again, May noticed. Gary looked nervous, which was understandable. After ten years of waiting the moment had finally arrived. He would see his son and, most importantly, have his wishes conveyed to him.

There was a bottle of wine on the table but it was, so far, unopened. Victoria had promised to stick to tea until after the first guest had departed. May understood just how a little wine might ease their nerves once the late arrivals turned up.

There was a soft tapping at the door and Chloe went to answer it, May followed close behind. The man standing on the doorstep was obviously Gary's son, the family resemblance was unmistakable. He was tall and smartly dressed. The dark grey suit fitted him well but he didn't seem comfortable wearing it. His tie was a little too loose around his neck and poorly knotted. It was obviously not his usual attire. May respected the fact that he had made such an effort to provide a smart appearance. She rarely took to people so readily but there was something to be admired about this young man. She could read him like a book and he hadn't even spoke a word as yet. He was a hard working boy with little wealth to his name, yet he had the willingness to present himself with as much pride as he could afford.

Chloe invited him in and directed him into the living room. Barbara's unique style of decoration seemed to take him by surprise. He politely refused the offer of a drink and Chloe left him sitting on the sofa while she went to fetch Barbara. May stayed in the living room and watched Gary's son as he nervously rubbed the palms of his hands together.

Barbara entered the room in a flurry of movement. She performed a half bow, half curtsy and another plastic gargoyle was brushed off the table by her sweeping arms. She was wearing a black dress with a dark red, tasselled scarf hung over her shoulders.

"Hello young man, my name is Madam Smith and I am

Madam Trump's assistant for this evening. I will be available to assist both you and her during the communication process".

"Hello, Madam Smith," Gary's son stuttered nervously. "My name is Martin Reed and I...um; I'm here to...um". He took a deep breath. "Can I really speak with my father? Right here, right now, tonight?"

"Well yes, sort of. You will be able to speak with him through Madam Trump and her extraordinary gift. Only she has the power to hear your father's words and she will convey them to you. She has the ability to become as one with the spirit world and will act as conduit between you and your dear departed father".

"Oh...that's ok, I guess". Martin said; he seemed a little disappointed.

"I will take you to Madam Trump as soon as she is ready". Barbara announced to Martin and gave May her cue to get ready upstairs.

May dashed out of the room and headed for the staircase. She glanced into the kitchen as she passed and gestured that Gary should follow her. May jogged up the stairs with Gary and Penny hot on her heels. They entered the séance room, that Chloe had allocated, through the closed door. May took up her position beside the makeshift dummy and the other two stood themselves in the corner by the standing lamp. The main light was switched off but there were two candle lanterns already lit and causing dancing shadows. They listened in silence for the creak of the stairs that would signal the approach of a physical being. It wasn't long before they heard approaching footsteps.

There was a tap on the door.

"Excuse me Madam Trump are you ready for us now?" Barbara called through the door. May didn't instantly recognise her name. I guess that's another thing I'm going to have to get used to, she thought.

"Yes, I am ready for you now," May announced. The door slowly opened and the hallway light, though dimmed slightly, still glared into the much darker room. Barbara waved Martin in first and then closed the door behind them; returning the room to it's previously lit condition. Barbara showed Martin to a chair that had been strategically positioned as far away from May as the table would allow. Once Martin seemed comfortable, Barbara took up her own seat by the far wall. May stood quietly watching until Barbara cleared her throat with a gentle cough to indicate that she should begin. The room was silent except for the sound of Martin's breathing.

"Welcome to my parlour," May said and instantly regretted it. It had sounded a lot better in her head.

"As you know, you have been invited here on the request of your late father, who sadly passed away over a decade ago". May was a little happier with the second statement. She looked over to Barbara to see if there was any evidence of opinion on her face. Barbara was enveloped in shadow, her expression hidden.

"I will now attempt to reconnect with him, please remain silent". Martin looked nervous, yet suspicious. Barbara really knew her stuff.

There were no flashing lights or creepy background music to feed the atmosphere. May didn't drift off in to any psychic trance and start mumbling strange incantations in an alien tongue. She just gestured for Gary to step forward and then she announced to Martin that his father was now in their presence. Martin's expression shifted but still reflected the same nervous suspicion as before.

As Gary spoke his eyes glistened and his voice wavered with mixed emotions.

"I'm sorry son. I never meant to leave you so suddenly and without even a chance to say goodbye. You have been the only thing on my mind since I died and I have spent the last ten years searching and hoping for a way to let you know just how much you mean to me".

"He says that he's is sorry for leaving you and he regrets that he never had the chance to say goodbye. You have been foremost on his mind and it has taken him this long to find a way to tell you how he feels". May relayed, with far less emotion.

"I have watched over you. I have celebrated your triumphs like only a proud father could but I have also witnessed your moments of hardship and sorrow. I felt helpless to aid or comfort you during these times and I feel guilty and incompetent because of it".

"He has tried to watch over you but has been helpless to aid you during times of hardship. For this he feels guilt and impotence".

"That was incompetence May!" Gary corrected her.

"Do you want my help or not, I'm doing the best I can!" May snapped.

"I'm sure you are and I really appreciate your help. It's just that...you got the words...never mind May, it's not important". Gary's protest crumbled under May's glare.

"If there is anything you would like to say to your father now is the time," May suggested. Martin seemed restless and unsure. He silently opened and closed his mouth a couple of times, before the words finally escaped.

"I'm sorry but I really don't believe in this stuff". He admitted in regretful defiance. "I don't even know why I'm here? I guess I was seduced by the promise of money but I'm finding it all too hard to believe. You say that you are actually talking with the spirit of my father? No sorry, it's just too far fetched. This whole thing is just too ridiculous for words". Martin stood up from his seat as if his own words had brought him courage. "Just look at this room!" He pointed at the candles and the black doilies, that hung from the mantelpiece like tasselled spider webs. "It's beyond ridiculous, its borderline tacky. I think we're just wasting each others time here".

"At least he didn't turn out to be gullible," Gary pointed out with a big prideful grin on his face. "He needs some kind of proof I guess, before he'll accept the truth. Give him the account details. Once he discovers that the money is real maybe the rest will become easier to swallow".

May wasn't at all happy. Neither Gary's conclusion nor Martin's accusations spelt wonders for her performance as a medium. She was supposed to inspire belief without proof and if she couldn't achieve that with Martin, how could she expect the paying customers to believe her. May remembered what Barbara had told her downstairs: act natural and be yourself.

"How dare you!" May yelled at Martin. "How dare you call me a liar! We invite you here, free of charge may I add and you accuse me of dishonesty. I'm here doing my best to help you and your father, yet all I get in return is suspicion and doubt. I gain nothing from this personally but still you accuse me of being a fraud!" Her voice echoed across the room. Her anger was far from fake but neither was it malicious. She didn't appreciate Martin's accusations but she wholly understood them. If only a week ago, someone had tried to tell her that they could speak with the dead, she would have taken a similar stance. She wouldn't have believed it was possible and she would not have been as polite about it either.

Matthew looked a little stunned; May's outburst has pushed him back into his chair.

"I'm sorry I didn't mean to cause offence. I'm sure you're a very honest and conscientious person," Martin said, while staring across the table at what he thought was May. He seemed to be trying to gauge a reaction from a dark figure, which was wholly created to mislead.

"But you still don't deny that you think I'm lying?" May snapped.

"Calm down May, you're scaring him," Gary said in an attempt to defend his son. May was having none of it.

"You can keep quiet as well! I'm trying to help the both of you".

"I'm sure you don't *think* you're lying to me," Martin offered. His voice was shaky and he spoke the last two words in slow motion, as if he regretted the sentence as soon as he had said it.

117

"So I'm crazy now? As well as a liar!" May snarled in reply. She was beginning to enjoy herself. This must be what it's like to be on The Colin Farley Show, she thought.

Penny stepped forward and pulled Gary aside by his shoulder.

"Stay out of it Gary, May knows what she's doing". May heard Penny say, as she led Gary back over to the standing lamp. May shot Penny a quick nod and a smile, now she only had Martin to concentrate on.

"What's your answer boy, haven't you got a tongue in your head?" May pressured for a response. She realised that she was getting her point across well enough and she didn't even have a tongue, not in the physical sense that is.

Martin seemed to struggle with a response. He fidgeted in his chair and opened his mouth several times but said nothing.

"Clearly you don't know your own mind," May told him in a firm but calmer voice. "Until you do, I suggest that we carry on with this séance. Minus any more wild accusations about who is deceiving who". Martin just nodded quietly; he seemed to be willing to agree to anything at this point.

"You need to open your mind son," May explained. "Imagine that your father is standing right here in front of you. Many years have passed since his death and you were but a young boy. Think carefully. What would you say to him, if you could see him, right here and right now?" The room fell silent as Martin bowed his head in thought. His breathing seemed a little laboured when he finally spoke.

"Why Dad?" He lifted his head and there were tears in his eyes.

May watched as Martin left the house. The evening had given him a little piece of paper with numbers written on it and a fresh perspective. He had a lot to do and think about but she expected to hear from him again soon. It had been a successful start; she allowed herself a moment of pride. After a little trust and belief had crept into the room, the séance had begun to gain momentum. A lot had been said between father and son, through May, and maybe some old wounds could now begin to heal.

The wine had been cracked open, almost simultaneously as the front door closed. May narrated the events of the séance and the living listened, while supping Dutch courage from wine glasses. It wouldn't be long before the late guests begun to arrive. Even after their experiences with May, Penny and Gary, the group was nervous. They would probably not even know the visitors were there but May couldn't guarantee that.

Chapter Fifteen

It was Mr Kibbles who signalled the arrival of the first of the departed visitors. He was curled up in the centre of the kitchen table surrounded by empty wine glasses. The people seated around him were unaware of his presence while they argued about who should nip out to the off-licence for another bottle. The wine that Victoria had brought with her had gone and they had also finished off the half a bottle of Ozo, which Chloe had found in the kitchen cupboard.

Mr Kibbles stood up suddenly and arched his back; his fur became spiky and rigid. He hissed and spat towards the kitchen door. With an almighty leap he dove towards the kitchen sink. He flew straight over it, through the window and into the garden beyond. Seconds later, the swift form of a black and white Jack Russell appeared through the inner wall and dashed after him. The dog was closely followed by a short, stocky middle aged man. He was dressed in a three piece, tweed suit. His trousers barely reached below his knees but his long, grey socks bridged the gap between them and his polished, buckled shoes. It was a style of clothing that May had not seen in many years. It was a fashion from beyond even her lifetime.

"Hello is that your dog?" May asked, as the new arrival quickly looked about the room.

"Good grief yes, my apologies". He said in a voice that seemed to make his every word sound like a quote from Shakespeare. "Where the devil did he go? He was just fine and dandy before he took to a sudden charging. Such like a mad thing he was, much out of character I must say".

"I believe he was chasing my cat," May replied.

Margaret and the rest of the living, looked up briefly at hearing May's voice but they soon fell back into their previous debate.

"But you're just so good at choosing wine Victoria and

you know a bargain when you see one," Barbara pleaded.

"Again my apologies. I find this rather mortifying, usually such a gentle animal is Trevor. May I excuse his behaviour as a vice of his breed, cats' effect him in such a way though more controlled is his usual manner. Worry not he has no history of catching one and not a lash of wisdom to what ends would be met should he win such quarry ".

"There's no need for apologies, I'm not at all worried in the slightest about my cat," May said. "I just hope your dog makes it back in one piece".

Gary stepped forward and offered out his hand.

"Mr Tailor isn't it?" Gary said.

"You're most correct Mr Reed".

"Call me Gary and I really wouldn't worry about the animals". Gary shook Mr Tailor's hand. "It's not like they can cause each other any harm now is it?"

"I'm sure there is wisdom in you're words and I am agreeable enough to answer to George".

"Very well George. I would like to introduce Miss Penny Saunders". Penny attempted a curtsy as Gary continued his introductions. "And this is Miss May Trump, the very person I spoke to you about". George stepped up to May and bowed before her majestically. May found it a little flattering but mainly disturbing.

"Can it be true? Are you such a spirit which communes with those with life still remaining?"

Victoria slowly stood up from the table; she seemed a little unstable on her feet.

"Alright you lazy lot!" She slurred. "I'll go but I'm getting the good stuff. None of your cheap plonk, I'm buying something French". Chloe offered her support, in more than one way and they both staggered for the door.

"Take care you two," May called. She watched as they walked together with arms linked, she wasn't sure who was supporting who.

"Will do May," Chloe replied, with a faint slur.

"And see if you can get some more of that Ooze,"

Margaret added. "That went down a treat that did".

George stumbled backwards a step but managed to keep his footing.

"Astounding!" He cried. "Such an incredible display of talent! Are all those privy to your gift or merely the sensitive among them?"

"Everyone can hear me, it would seem".

"Everyone seems what?" Barbara asked. May had to keep reminding herself that the living could only hear her side of the conversation.

"Seems to be able to hear me speak Barbara," May explained. "We have a new guest. Someone who might be interested in our new communication service". Barbara looked around the room.

"Um...hello," she said hesitantly. "I'm Barbara. I guess you can hear me even though I can't hear you. I'm helping with the...the physical stuff I guess".

"Remarkable!" George cried.

"He can hear you just fine Barbara," May explained. "We're going into the living room now, to discuss things. I'll call if I need you".

"Alright May, we'll try to behave ourselves in here". Barbara smiled nervously.

May led George into the living room, Penny and Gary followed behind. George took a seat on the sofa and remarked on the eccentric décor. May sat in the arm chair opposite, while Penny and Gary chose to remain standing.

"So what do you need from us?" May asked.

"Here we cross paths with a complication. My presence is as invited. Mr Reed, Gary my apologies, spoke highly of your special abilities. By way of him, well informed I became regarding the contact with his son that you endeavoured to perform. Of that communication, a pleasing result I hope?"

"It went well enough," May kept her reply limited. She didn't see what business it was of his. The jury was still out regarding Gary's son. May hoped that Martin would eventually come to terms with his experience and accept that he had indeed been in the presence of his father's spirit. Regardless of what little May could or could not predict about one client, it was hardy a matter for discussion with another.

George looked over at the other two ghosts present, as if in hope that they would be more forthcoming. Gary just nodded in agreement with May and Penny flashed a closed smile.

"The reluctance to impart such information is understandable," George shrugged before continuing. "Mr Reed was good enough to mention that there are plans afoot to hold many more of these séances. Understandably I am intrigued. The mere suggestion of free and open speech with the living would be enough to rile the most stagnant of spirits. Almost one hundred years dead I am, yet never before have I seen such an ability. There was word of another many years past and I regret never getting the opportunity to witness it directly. However, even though I truly believe that your gift could prove to be a vital resource and one that should have full advantage taken of it, I have a few concerns I must admit to bearing".

"Take advantage of me? How dare you suppose such a thing," May snapped. Nobody took advantage of her, she would never allow it. "If you think I'm just here to do your bidding, or anyone else's for that matter, then you're gravely mistaken".

"A misunderstanding has reared its head I believe," George said. "My words were not meant to suggest a curbing of your activities as such. Advice not instruction is that which I bring to this table. I fear how the living might react should certain facts regarding death reach their ears".

"Do you mean to say that you have no need of me, per say?" May leaned closer and George lent backwards in response. May was intrigued to know just what facts he had been referring to. "If you have no one who you wish me to contact, then you have accepted our invitation under false pretences Mr Tailor. I don't know what you're doing here and I'm not sure whether to let your presence here continue. You have already spoken of taking advantage of situations that are not of your concern, what other 'passive' advice should we expect from you?"

"Taking advantage of anyone, Miss Trump, is not in my nature". George held up his palms in a gesture of submission. "You are correct in your assumptions. Your ability would serve no personal need of mine. I merely wish to facilitate and aid in the minimisation of the risks involved in your current endeavours".

"Risks? What risks could there possibly be?" May was puzzled by the mere suggestion. "We're all dead, everything bad that could happen already has".

"If such words rang true my heart would no longer be a burden to carry," George's voice took on a solemn tone. "We are spirits far from free. Dark entities are abroad, whose attention may be drawn if actions, such as you intend, were to remain unfettered".

"So you're the George everyone's been warning me about!" Gary stepped forward and stood beside May's chair. There was a sudden anger and distrust in his voice. "They say that you speak of myth and legend as if it were the wolves at our door. I've been all over this world and the next yet I've neither seen nor heard from these entities you speak of. You just tell wild stories and try to breed fear in those who have nothing left to fear. This may come as a shock to you Mr Tailor but ghost stories don't work on ghosts!"

"Your own reputation precedes you also Mr Reed". George said matter-of-factly. May and Penny remained silent. May wanted to hear what Mr Tailor had to say. She had decided to leave to impromptu whines and groans to Gary, as he was performing them so well. She guessed that Penny held a similar thought in mind.

"I am not struck down by surprise to discover that the need for gossip is not a vice reserved purely for the living".

George continued in a calm, steady voice, between Gary's frequent huffs of disapproval. "Word of how you've travelled far and wide, in search of someone with such skills as that which Miss Trump possesses, does not constitute news to me. Much ground have you covered in the short ten years you've been dead but it is as a fraction of my century of experience. I am of a company of few, who can admit genuine memory of the last time they amassed in great numbers. Such an experience, I wish to never again endure. Something drew them to us and, even now, we are yet to discover exactly what had riled them so. My research leads my belief that dark emotions played their part in it. Fear, hate, jealousy and rage to name a few. Regardless of which theory you align yourself, they grouped together in such numbers that the very sky turned black in their presence. Ghosts of my generation and of times beyond, have either taken to the next realm, or have just been taken. Only the few of us who remain, keep watch for them and such things that may draw the attention of The Stalkers of Souls".

"What complete rubbish!" Gary sneered. "There are no such dark entities. Those who survived? Are you serious? We're already dead! You're just full of wild scare stories. The Soul Stalkers, are you kidding? Even the name sounds like something out of a fairy tale. There's just the living and the dead, that's all!"

"I assure you Mr Reed they are quite real," George stared Gary directly in the eye. "And prone to wander the earth much as we do. Over recent years, travelling alone or in small groups, preying on any soul who should wander through the dark alone has been their usual show of behaviour. Leaving no witnesses and thus, little proof other than the absence of their victims. Fear not, for avoidance is easily achieved through preparation and precaution".

"No proof and no witnesses, how very convenient for you". Gary said, as if spitting a foul taste from his mouth.

"A sad fact such as it is I agree Mr Reed. However, how many spirits have you met that still wander the earth fifty years beyond their death?"

"I will agree there's none that I can think of right at this moment, other than yourself". Gary replied. "I have always considered that those of us that are voluntarily earth bound are only here to tie up loose ends and maybe to create some closure to their lives. I myself have had little else on my mind since my death. I'm sure that once I see that my son is well and that he has no more need of me, I will move on to the next plain with little thought of returning". May couldn't help agreeing with him, it was very similar to her own plan.

"So you harbour the expectation that the activities of your Son, your grandchildren and possibly even your great grandchildren will interest you no longer?" George wore a knowing smirk as he spoke. May was beginning to realise that this wasn't the first time George had been in this particular ring. He must have fought for his beliefs on many occasions and the old ghost probably had more than a few tricks up his sleeve.

"Of my life, those I cared for are as we are, without need of breath. Yet the goings on of my family line still draws interest. Their blood, no matter how distantly, is still akin to my own. I transcend, like any other ghost and pay my respects to those who still fear the living sun. Those who have passed on with no intention of returning. They hide away in relative safety, unlike ourselves and those who still breathe the air that we hold so dear".

"I'm sorry but did you just say that the living are at risk from these things? These Soul Stalkers? As you call them". May interjected, while Gary threw his arms into the air.

"See what drivel the man speaks May!" Gary cried. Penny stepped forward and stood on the opposite side of May.

"Is my daughter at risk from these nightmarish things?" Penny asked in an unusually shrill voice. May suddenly realised that Penny's silence had been through engrossed belief; she was more gullible than May had given her credit for.

"Failing the proper precautions, yes. I will stand by my

belief that she is," George replied.

"I'm sorry May but we can't carry on with this," Penny raised her hands to her cheeks. "My god! What if we were never warned?"

Gary sidled around May's chair and pulled Penny in close. May could hear her sobbing into his chest.

"It's alright Penny," Gary whispered. "There is nothing to be scared of. There is nothing in this world or the next that can harm us. George's bogeymen are just a figment of his own warped imagination. Trust me; I would never let anything happen to you or those you hold dear".

"Do you see now what harm your delusions can cause!" Gary said, looking up at George. "You are more of a danger to us than any of your imaginary spectres. If it were up to me, I would have you slung out into the dark to wander alone. Then you would have your proof that the danger lives not out there but in here with all your gossip and lies". Gary turned his head back towards Penny. He whispered something that May couldn't understand but it seemed to stem Penny's tears.

George threw himself back into the sofa, folded his arms across his chest and drew a heavy sigh.

"It is to be expected," he groaned at May. "A spirit with a blinkered attitude is far from a novelty. Heed my words they will, eventually, though I hope before time is no longer an asset to us".

A man slipped into the room through the far wall. He was dressed in a multicoloured tank top, which he wore over a white, long sleeved shirt that sported an infectious flower pattern from collar to cuff. He clapped his hands together, as if to announce his presence. As he walked further into the room, his wildly, flared jeans flapped around his ankles, like parasols on a windy day.

"Well, well, well". His voice boomed into the room. "It looks like I've got here just in time. Is Old Man Tailor here giving you his doom and gloom speech?" He smiled and his brown curly beard spiked up around his mouth like a hedgehog. His hair was an unkempt mass of the same bushy, brown curls. George looked up at him and gave another heavy sigh.

"A pleasure as always Jeremy," George groaned more than greeted. He turned back to face May. "Another, which further than the end of his nose he will not see".

"Hello George," Jeremy boomed. "What are you doing here, this is hardly your thing now is it. On a cold dark night like tonight, I'd have thought you would be out there". He tipped his head and nodded towards the window. "Defending us from the forces of evil".

"Much amusement do you cause me," George replied sarcastically.

"Hello Gary, I'm not disturbing anything am I?" Jeremy said when he saw Gary and Penny's embrace. They parted from each other slowly, until all they held was each other hands.

"Not at all Jeremy. Welcome," Gary greeted, while Penny silently blushed. Gary introduced Jeremy to Penny and May. Jeremy offered Penny a slow nod, which was more like a bow but only from the neck up. He then turned to May and knelt down beside her armchair.

"So you're our window to the world," He said, looking up at May.

"I'm not your anything!" May growled, as she stared him in the eye. Jeremy stood back up swiftly and let loose a loud, bellowing laugh.

"I do like your attitude May. I'm rather excited about this whole affair. I've been a ghost for more than a few decades now, yet I've never met a dead medium before". His face straightened into a more serious expression. He brought his hands together, his fingers meshed and his thumbs touched his chest.

"I stand here before you May in awe, as I graciously request your assistance". May allowed herself a thin smile.

"Then take a seat young man" She replied. "And let us talk terms". Jeremy had already crouched halfway down, to sit next to George on the sofa, when he suddenly dropped heavily for the last few inches and partially disappeared into the framework and cushions.

"Terms?" He cried. "What Terms?"

"Terms of service of course. We're not doing all this out of the kindness of our hearts. All of this has been arranged for the sole purpose of commercial gain. There's no profit in charity and we are in need of a considerable amount of money".

"You do realise that you are talking to a ghost here? How am I supposed to get a hold of money? How do I get hold of anything? I'm intangible, as we all are. I had enough trouble getting a hold of cash when I was alive, I've got no hope now!" May turned towards Gary and gave him an accusingly glare. He had clearly not explained the concept of the service very well, May thought.

"Jeremy, I did tell you that there would be a price involved". Gary said in response to May's cold stare.

"Well yes but I hardly expected to have to bring my cheque book. We're ghosts for Fricks sake! What do we need with money? I had thought it would be something less tangible. Information, advice, emotional support even but never did I consider you meant hard cash"

"We don't expect you to pay directly," May explained. "We plan to secure the fee from those of the living who you wish to contact".

"Is that so advisable?" George said. "Intriguing it is but ethical? Not so much".

"What's it to you? You don't even want to use my ability. You just want to scare me into allowing you to censor me. If we're getting paid, I really don't care what the client wants me to convey. This is my gift, my business and I won't be told how to run it". May was in no mood to have her ethics questioned.

"That is the product of your own will Miss Trump. It is no charge of mine to usurp it, though the profit of such action leaves me in bewilderment" George said. "You can't take it with you when you're dead, is the phrase overshadowing my mind at this juncture".

"That's exactly my point!" Jeremy added. "Even if it does mean I'm agreeing with George about something".

"The money is not for her," Penny stepped forward and dragged Gary with her, as she refused to release her grip on his hand. "It's for my daughter. She needs the money to secure this house and her future. I've left her in a terrible financial mess and May has offered to help me sort it all out". Penny's eyes had begun to well up again. May appreciated her stepping in to support her; she knew that Penny wasn't comfortable with confrontation. .

"And a sudden realisation dawns". George smiled and stood up from the sofa. "Your motives have become clear to me. My assistance has been far from retracted. Your belief in The Stalkers of Souls may not be as sturdy as my own but unnecessary risks are still worth avoiding. I offer my assurance that my input will be as mere suggestion. To heed my warnings will stand to your judgment alone". May still didn't feel comfortable with accepting help from others; it just wasn't something she was used to. George clearly wasn't lying about the Soul Stalkers but that still didn't mean they existed. George believed every word he said on the subject, of that May was sure.

"Alright George, I'll listen but I make no promises. It'll take more than a few ghost stories to make me believe in the bogyman" Safe was better than sorry, she decided. There was still a lot she didn't understand about the spirit world and to alienate someone with George's level of experience was probably unwise, regardless of how warped his prospective might be.

"I guess I also see your point regarding the money. It's unconventional, well no it's completely conventional from a living persons perspective, it's just unconventional from ours. Let's see what can be arranged". Jeremy seemed to surrender to the idea.

"Well I think we've wasted enough time bickering," May pointed out and then cupped her mouth with her hands. "Barbara! We need a pen and paper and a willing hand to write with". She bellowed towards the door.

"Right then Jeremy, what do you need?" May asked in a much lower voice. The living room door swung open and Barbara burst in, waving a pen and notepad in the air. Deborah nervously crept in behind her.

"Are you still in here May?" Barbara called out.

"Yes we're all still here; now get ready to write this down". May instructed.

"Right then," Jeremy said. "I'd like you to speak with my daughter; she needs to know a few truths about me".

"Alright, what's her name and how do we contact her?" May asked: Barbara was waiting with the pen held at the ready.

"Her name is Julia Robinson and she lives at number twelve Bard's Lane. It's just off the main south road out of town". May relayed the details to Barbara, who scribbled them down in the notepad. So they finally had their first client, though May had expected a bigger turnout.

"Gary will let you know when we have contacted her and, if she agrees, when the séance will take place". Jeremy thanked May, Gary and Penny in turn. He said a brief goodbye to George and then stepped through the inner wall.

May was just about to tell Gary how disappointed she was that so few spirits had turned up, when Jeremy suddenly reappeared.

"You wouldn't believe the length of the queue out in the hallway!" he announced excitedly. "The line goes through the door and out into the garden, I've never seen so many ghosts all in one place".

"Then you had better show them in," May replied. So it was going to be a busy night after all.

Mr Kibbles suddenly appeared through the outer wall of the room. He walked up to May with his head held high, he seemed to be awash with pride. Trevor, the Jack Russell, crept along a short distance behind him. Mr Kibbles suddenly stopped and gave the dog an icy stare. Trevor scuttled backwards, almost tripping over his own tail as it curled up beneath him, and then gave out a small nervous whine.

Chapter Sixteen

It was yet another late start for May but she consoled herself on the fact that it was Sunday. If you can't get up late on a Sunday, she allowed her self the excuse, when can you? May sat on the edge of the bed and listened. The house was silent, which came as a pleasure after the racket of the night before. seventeen spirits had arrived at the house in response to Gary's enquiries. May had interviewed each and every sprit individually and her head had started pounding before she was even halfway through. Her throat still felt sore after all the cries for order, as the patience of those at the back of the queue grew thin. Deborah had jumped ten foot in the air every time May had been forced to yell at one disembodied head or another, as it poked through the living room wall with enquiries about how much longer it was all going to take. Barbara had started to complain about getting pains in her wrists, after the first of the notepads had been completely filled with all the relevant information. Deborah took over the note taking duties and had scribbled away in shorthand for the rest of the evening. The activity seemed to settle her nerves and there was less time wasted, now that May didn't have to keep pausing as Barbara struggled to keep up with the proceedings. May had been getting tired of all her requests to: 'hold on just a minute' and 'how do you spell that then?'

Some of the visitors had understood that there would be a need for preparation but others had shown disappointment at the lack of immediate action. A few had been expecting the séances to take place that very same night. May had explained, in no uncertain words, that she didn't run a while you wait service. This revelation had caused another barrage of questions and, after an unbearable amount of insistence, May had finally agreed to set a preliminary date for the first of the séances. They had until next Saturday night to prepare. It would ultimately depend on how the living clients took to the news; May had made that fact quite clear. She didn't expect the same level of belief as the spirits had shown her but there had been no subterfuge in their recruitment. May consoled herself with the knowledge that, even though there would be a few lies and omissions, the living would hear the truth for the most part.

Chloe and Victoria had returned with two bottles of red wine and a half bottle of Gin. May didn't understand why they had felt that they had needed quite that much alcohol. The raised voices and loud, howling laughter had begun shortly after. Even after Deborah had closed both the doors that stood between them, the noise was hardly muted.

It was still quiet, as May stepped out of her room. Chloe was probably in bed, nursing her throbbing head but May didn't begrudge her the chance to leave her problems aside for one night. May peered out of the landing window and saw that the sun was already riding high and blazing brightly. May began to realise that she hadn't really noticed the weather since her death. It looked like it was going to be a nice day and that fact lowered her mood a little. It was just another thing that death had excluded her from. Never again would she feel the warmth of the sun on her skin or a summer breeze as it stroked through her hair. It was not as if she had even appreciated such things when she was still alive. She added them to her list of lost opportunities; regret was an emotion that was becoming all too familiar to her now.

As May walked down the stairs, she heard a sudden loud grunt. She paused and listened. Another grunt, as if someone was suffering from pained exertion. After the third grunt, May recognised it as Penny's voice. May slowly followed the noise down the stairs. The noise was getting louder and higher pitched, Penny seemed to be in some distress. May followed the sound into the living room, where she found Penny crouched uncomfortably by the coffee table. Penny looked up at May; her face was

contorted with pain. Her eyes were flooded by tears; May
rushed over to her and knelt by her side. Every time Penny
tried to stand she cried out in pain and folded back into a
tight crouch.

"It's the pull of the angels, it's getting much worse,"
Penny cried and bowed her head. "I can't fight it anymore!"
May grabbed Penny's cheeks with both palms, pulled her
head around to face her and looked her squarely in the
eyes.

"Now concentrate girl, don't let it beat you!" May yelled
at the stricken woman. Penny looked back at her, tired and
helpless. May released her face and then grabbed her
shoulders firmly. With all her strength, May shook Penny
vigorously.

"Don't give up girl, push it away!" May cried. Penny's
head dipped back and forth, like a nodding dog. Her eyes
rattled from side to side, like a confused puppet and then
she suddenly settled into a sharp, forward facing stare. May
let go of Penny's shoulders as her piecing eyes met her
own. May felt the flood of power seconds before she heard
the evidence of it. It washed over her like a tidal wave of icy
water. May didn't feel as if the force had physically moved
her but she did feel like an army of thousands had marched
heavily across her grave. The coffee table bounced up and
down on the floor, making a loud banging noise. Two
empty wine glasses, left behind from the night before, flew
off the table and smashed against the far wall. The living
room door burst open and slammed against the wall to the
sound of splintering wood. Penny's eyes grew dark and
misty; her pupils lost definition and became a whirl of dark
shades. Moments later everything stopped as suddenly as it
had begun. Penny's eyelids snapped shut and she slumped
into May's arms. A single silver candle stick, which had
been spinning on it's edge like a coin, finally tipped over to
it's side and the silence briefly returned.

May allowed Penny to slip gently to the floor. Her
consciousness had left her and she was perfectly still, other
than her shallow, pseudo breaths. May tried to stand but

the strength in her legs faltered and she fell back into a kneel. She lent over Penny and looked upon her still form helplessly. May rolled Penny on to her side and checked if her airway was clear. She was aware that it probably didn't matter in the slightest but it seemed like something she should do, it was better than just staring at her.

May could hear slow deliberate footsteps coming down the staircase. That'll be Chloe, May thought, she's been awoken by the noise and is now creeping down here to investigate. She's carrying some kind of blunt instrument, I've no doubt. Penny's eyelids flickered; she was beginning to come around. May helped her into a sitting position, she seemed dazed and confused.

"How are you feeling?" May whispered. Penny rubbed her forehead and tried to stifle a yawn.

"I think I'm alright," she replied. "I feel very tired and I ache all over. It feels like I've just ran a marathon and now I'm just waiting for the cramp to set in". Penny smiled nervously and May took it as a sign that she would be alright.

"Well what the frick just happened?" May asked.

"I'm not really sure," Penny replied. She looked at the state of them room and added with surprise in her voice. "Did I do that?"

Chloe appeared at the open doorway holding a large table lamp in front of her, as if it were a claymore. Her grip on the stem was so tight that the knuckles of both her hands had turned white. She looked anxious and ready to strike at the slightest hint of movement.

"It's alright Chloe! It's all OK," May called out. Chloe jumped at the sound of May's voice and almost tripped on the lamp's trailing power cord.

"This is OK is it?" she asked, as she scanned the devastation around her. She was clearly unimpressed.

"Your Mum has just let off some steam, it would seem," May explained. "I don't know why or how but she seems to be just fine now". Chloe seemed to relax a little; she released her grip and let the table lamp slip onto the floor by her feet.

"What have you been up to Mother?" She scolded light heartedly.

May helped Penny back to her feet and led her over to the sofa. As Penny sat down, Chloe begun to clear up the debris.

"I'd have got the sharp end of your tongue if I'd done something like this". She mused, as she picked up a shard of broken glass with her fingertips.

"You mind you don't cut yourself!" May warned, as she watched Chloe deposit the glass into the bare palm of her free hand. Chloe nodded and smiled falsely in response, as if she were a child being told not to sit so close to the television set. May turned her attention back to Penny.

"What did you experience before you fainted?" Penny shrugged; her movement was sharp and twitchy.

"It's been slowly getting worse, getting stronger. I figured that, as I could still disregard it without much effort, it wasn't worth mentioning to anyone. This time though, it was different. It was so sudden and so powerful, I felt like a balloon being inflated to the point of bursting". Penny explained, her teeth chattered slightly, as if she was suffering from a deep chill. "I was barely holding on when you came in. I was fighting it with all my strength but I could still feel it winning. I was afraid that I would suddenly fold into myself and vanish. I thought I would never see my Chloe ever again". Penny looked up to see Chloe cautiously walking out of the room; she had a pile of broken glass in her cupped hands.

"What has she got there?" Penny asked and then realised. "What is she thinking? She's going to cut herself if she's not careful!" Penny motioned to stand but May gently held her down.

"She's being careful," May pointed out. "She's not being very practical or particularly safe but she's being cautious at least. Save your strength Penny, Chloe's a big girl".

"I guess you're right," Penny agreed reluctantly.

"I know I'm right!" May said. "Continue with what you were saying; you thought you might vanish".

"Oh yes," Penny said. "I was about to vanish or burst, or something. That was when you grabbed my shoulders and shouted some of the strength back into me. I tried May, I really tried. I pushed back as hard as I could. I think I saw stars and then it felt like I exploded. That was about it, the next thing I saw was you leaning over me". She paused and then look May directly in the eye. "I'm scared May, I think it was them! I think it was George's Soul Stalkers".

May was concerned by this. She wasn't worried about George's, so called, evil spirits. At least not regarding Penny's episode, for want of a better word. She was concerned for Penny and how deeply she seemed to have fallen for George's fantasies. There was another explanation, May was convinced of that much and she was pretty sure it didn't involve angels either.

"You shouldn't take any notice of what he says, "May advised. "George is scared of his own shadow, well at least that seems to be the general opinion. Not one of the spirits, which came here last night, believed in his wild stories, so neither should we". May said to herself as much as to Penny. If death had taught her anything, it was to keep an open mind. May kept her own misgivings silent.

"However," she added as the thought occurred. "He has been around for over one hundred years. He might offer a reasonable explanation. We would just have to be careful not to take everything he says as gospel".

"Maybe you're right," Penny agreed half-heartedly. May knew that she was just being amiable in an attempt to avoid an argument. It would take more than a few words to ease her fears.

"So then, what are you two conspiring about?" Chloe walked into the room carrying an old cylinder vacuum cleaner. "I hope it doesn't involve any more broken glass".

"We were thinking about going out, May replied. "We think we might know someone who could tell us why your mum blew her top earlier. We don't intent to break anything else but I've given up predicting likely outcomes of late. The strangest things happen when you're dead".

"So you're leaving me to cope alone with the old age delinquents," Chloe complained, as she unwound the power cord of the vacuum cleaner. May didn't entirely understand Chloe's reluctance; she had seemed quite comfortable in their company last night. She guessed it was the hangover talking, even though she showed little sign of having one.

"If you really need us to stay?" May offered, though couldn't she see the point of it. When there were other things they could be doing, to stay would be a waste of her and Penny's time. The plan for the day was mainly letter writing and phone calls, not the best occupation for a ghost. May assumed that she could dictate or even handle some of the calls, if someone else dialled the phone for her but surely it would be easier to leave such work to the living.

"No I guess not, not really". Chloe admitted, as she plugged the vacuum cleaner into a wall socket. The machine roared into life with a loud whining noise. Chloe hurriedly stamped on the off switch on top of the cylinder, as she cradled her forehead with her right hand. "I just don't know if I can handle them today, not with this headache? I guess they'll be feeling much the same though, so maybe they'll be better behaved today. I'll just have to keep the coffee flowing and hope for the best. I felt like the only adult in the room come the end of the night".

May and Penny left the house to the drone of the vacuum cleaner as Chloe sought out the smaller glass fragments with the hose. Penny knew the way to George's regular haunt, Gary had taken her there once before. May had to admit that she wasn't much of a fan of churches or graveyards but she could see how George would find it homely. With his sombre attitude and apocalyptic obsessions, he must really lighten the mood of the place. You have to give him some credit, May thought; he had

139

tried to offer up his gloomy tales with a smile. The added drawback of which was: it came across as if he enjoyed telling people that they were all doomed. Morbid fanatic or oracle, which ever he turned out to be, he may still hold the answers we need.

The church was only a ten minute walk, as the crow flies. May followed Penny straight through the wall at the back of the garden. She soon realised that they were taking the same route as the proverbial blackbird. They wandered, on a direct and unwavering course, through anything and everything in their path. May wasn't impressed. She didn't feel comfortable in the slightest, striding through the homes of strangers. She rushed after Penny, who had picked up quite a pace and called out for her to stop. At one point, May found alone herself in a bathroom with an almost naked man. He had nothing on except one blue sock and a green necktie. May didn't know where to look, as she scuttled though one wall or another. She finally caught up with Penny, who had stopped still and was staring at something.

"Slow down for frick's sake!" May puffed, purely out of habit, as she drew up to Penny's side. She glanced around; they were in somebody's bedroom. The walls were painted lilac; the wardrobe was white veneer and the bed...

"Oh my word!" May gasped; the bed was occupied. May grabbed Penny roughly by the arm and dragged her through the wall and into the room beyond.

"Oy!" Penny yowled, as May released her grip. May stared at her disapprovingly and tutted. She was lost for words; at least no pleasant ones came to mind. Penny shrugged defiantly, before marching off through the far wall. May followed behind, with the conviction to never take a short cut again.

The church was probably the largest detached building in the town and by far the tallest. The town hall came a close second but even that would look dwarfed if it were to stand next to the church's main clock tower. The squared structure stood twenty foot tall and was crested by battlement style roof terrace. The main body of the church stretched out in front of the tower for one hundred and twenty foot. The moss covered slate roof perched twenty foot from the ground. Arched windows adorned the grey stone walls at regular intervals, some with bright stained glass where others were clear or frosted. The church was surrounded by the town's only graveyard, which was large enough to cope well with the demands upon it. The two ghosts entered through the large wrought iron gate and began to wander amongst the gravestones. George was no where to be seen and neither was anyone else. They didn't have a clear view of the entire churchyard but what they could see seemed devoid of life. May felt a little uncomfortable, as she knew her own body was destined to slowly rot away in this place. As they walked slowly between the graves, May noticed that they were probably in the oldest section of the cemetery; the freshest grave she could see must have been more than fifty years old. Most of the graves there seemed forgotten and uncared for but a few showed signs of recent visits. The flowers laid may have been as dead as the bodies beneath but the fact that they were there showed that someone still remembered.

George suddenly stood up into view from behind a large headstone. Penny physically jumped and then blushed red. May was startled by George's sudden appearance but managed to hide the fact from the others.

"Greetings of the day ladies!" George announced; he seemed surprised to see them. "I didn't scare you, did I?"

"No not at all," May lied.

"You scared me!" Penny said as she placed her palm on her chest, as if to monitor her heart beat.

"Do accept my deepest apologies young lady. I am also surprised to see you here," George explained. "I was expecting someone else". He looked around the graveyard, as if searching for something and then turned back to face May and Penny. If he saw anything amiss, he gave no obvious reaction to it. May stepped closer to the head stone, which George had been hiding behind and began to read the words carved into it.

"You did give me an awful fright," Penny exaggerated. She fanned her face with her hand, as if she was about to swoon.

"Here lies George Sebastian Tailor," May read aloud. "A husband and father who is sadly missed by all, 1879 to 1915".George smiled.

"Ah! Very astute May," George smiled. "I see no detail gets passed you. Yes this is my grave, my resting place if you like. I find comfort here in times of need. I used to come here to watch as my family tended the grave but as the years have passed, they themselves succumbed to death. I met with them again before they drifted off to the other plain. Nowadays it just suffices as a meeting place. I do try to be approachable and I make it easy for people to find me. I am not usually very far from where my name is carved in stone, not for any length of time. Though your endeavours might drag me away for longer than I am used to May. Not that it matters; I rarely get visitors theses days". George sighed; he looked saddened by the thought. He shook himself and the smile reappeared.

"However, Today I have more guests than my time allows". He cried, as if motivating himself. "Not that I want to rush you but what do you need from me today? I have a prior arrangement planned and believe me, the lady has no time for tardiness".

"Oh! A lady is it?" Penny asked, in a tone of romantic suggestion. May gave her a look of disapproval.

"I'm just asking!" Penny defended herself.

"That is of my concern alone," George explained. "I can afford little time to this right now, so how can I help?" May took it to mean that it was none of their business and rightly so, she thought.

Penny described events of that morning. George nodded and waved his hand, to indicate that Penny should continue every time she paused. There was a lot of unnecessary detail in Penny's story but May kept silent knowing that any comment she made would just cause more delay. She could see George was eager for Penny to make her point.

"This is very important, were you upset or angry at any time prior to these events?" George asked.

"I was upset," Penny replied. "Frustrated even but I wouldn't say I was angry".

"I see," George stepped backwards and leaned causally against his own headstone. He cupped his chin in his hand and sighed.

"I see what?" May asked. George suddenly snapped his fingers.

"I think we have a budding poltergeist on our hands here? She's showing the classic symptoms. It would seem that you have quite a talented household". He explained.

"Poltergeist? Do you mean I can move stuff?" Penny asked. She looked worried and confused, which wasn't unusual for her.

"Yes, that is the main function of such a spirit". George explained. "You have a telekinetic force within you that must be controlled and then slowly released. What you experienced earlier this morning was... how do I put this? It's like an emergency pressure release valve. You need to learn how to gently expel the energy over time before it reaches such critical levels. It's generally why Poltergeist's get such a bad press from the living. They tend to draw a lot of attention to themselves when they blow their top, so to speak". Penny still looked confused. May, on the other hand, understood the concept and was intrigued.

"I guess that explains Victoria's wine glass the other night?" She suggested.

"Hold on one moment!" Penny stated, she held up her hand, as if directing traffic. "I've read about poltergeists. Aren't they supposed to cling to young psychologically stressed minds? Or something like that".

"I have heard that the living have made such assumptions but there is little proof". George replied. "I can't say I'm an expert but you do still stay rather close to your daughter. I gather she's going through a particularly stressful time at the moment?"

"Oh yes of course," Penny realised. She looked saddened by the thought but then her outlook seemed to suddenly brighten. "Well that's all going to change, I'll see to that myself!" May was worried about Penny's sudden new hope.

"You're not planning anything are you?" she asked. "What with this new ability you've got".

"What are you referring to May? I was talking about the whole séance thing". Penny replied.

"Oh...Oh nothing!" May lied, as she wondered if it was even possible for a poltergeist to rob a bank.

"I would love to help you improve your control but as I have said, I have a rather important appointment with someone and they are most likely waiting for you to leave, before revealing themselves. Maybe another day, if you would allow it?" George suggested.

After a short round of thank you and goodbye, Penny and May slowly picked their way back out of the graveyard. May glanced back and saw the dark silhouette of a woman weaving between the gravestones towards George. There was something familiar about the way she moved. Arms straight and swinging like pendulums, more of a march than a walk. It was not unlike May's own natural gait.

Penny suddenly grabbed May's arm. She yanked her gaze away from George and the approaching woman. She half led and half dragged May around to the other side of the church where the graves had more recently been dug. May started to complain but fell silent when she suddenly realised where they were.

There was a fresh mound only a few rows from the church and it was yet to receive a headstone. The flowers that had been laid were only a few days old but the petals had already started to turn brown around the edges. May knelt at the graveside with Penny, she felt her chest tighten and a heavy lump formed in her throat. The closest flowers were a small bunch of once white carnations; there was a note attached.

"Goodbye Mum I miss you. All my love forever, Chloe". May read aloud and then stretched her arm around Penny's shoulders. Her eyes welled up and she cried intangible tears.

Chapter Seventeen

There was always post on a Monday morning, Margaret realised as she recovered a few letters and a newspaper from the doormat. She was dressed in her light blue, frilly dressing gown and matching slippers. She could hear the kettle begin to boil; it was her usual routine on a weekday. She liked to read whatever fell through her letter box with a cup of tea and a bowl of one over sweetened breakfast cereal or another. She placed the correspondence on her breakfast tray and filled her small tea pot with steaming water. With everything ready, she carried the tray through the living room and into her small conservatory. It had been a retirement present from Alf. He knew how she liked to sit with a view of the garden. The cold morning air played havoc with her joints so the heated conservatory was a perfect compromise. Alf had left early that morning for a golf competition, which was being held a good four hours drive away. He always liked to get away early to avoid the traffic. His old Ford Cortina needed a free run just to warm up and would generally breakdown if it hit traffic with a cold engine. Margaret had told him on many occasions to trade it in for something more reliable but Alf had always refused. He said that the day his car was on the scrap heap, so would he be.

Margaret settled down on her favourite chair. She set the breakfast tray down on the matching table, next to her small portable television which she only used during breakfast or when Alf was watching golf on the big screen in the living room. She had opted for bamboo effect garden furniture in the conservatory, with large blue cushions tied on to the whickered frames. It was her way of trying to fool herself into believing that she was on a Caribbean beach holiday. Alf had agreed to take her away to such a place as long as she could find one with a golf course close by. Margaret didn't investigate any further, it was an unacceptable condition. She wanted to spend a holiday with her husband, not sitting on the beach with all the other golf widows. He had even suggested that they brought her friend May along, so she wasn't lonely while he was out on the course. She had met that remark with stern disapproval.

Margaret poured her tea and began flicking through the letters. Disappointingly, the first was a gas bill. She put it to one side and opened another; it was a letter explaining how she had won a grand prize and needed to phone a high toll number to find out what it was. She screwed it up into a ball and tossed it into a small whickered bin. Looking back at the pile in her hands, she was greeted with a bright picture of a Spanish beach front. It was a post card from her friend and cousin Enid. She turned it over and read about how the weather was great and how the people were all so friendly. There was a short sentence about how cheap it was in comparison with home and how much they wished she was with them. The last comment was an obvious lie, it wasn't as if they had invited her. Regardless of that fact, she was glad they were having a nice holiday. She wasn't disappointment at being left behind, she was thankful for it. She would have hated to have missed all the exciting events at the Saunders household. A jug of Margarita and seafood paella just didn't compare.

Margaret was still upset by May's death. She still felt confused at the thought that she was also still around to talk to. It was very unlike her though, Margaret mused, freely offering her help to that Chloe and her dead mother. I have never seen May Trump offer anything for free. Maybe death had changed her in ways that life never could. She seemed more vulnerable and less eager to condemn, which were qualities that Margaret had always admired. She had always wished that she had more strength of character and wasn't so easily pushed around by the wishes and plans of others. May would have never put up with half of what Margaret got talked into doing. She could never find it in her heart to say no. May would have seen them off with a severe tongue lashing and felt not a hint of remorse for her actions either. May was different now, Margaret could feel it. It was as if she was going through some kind of reverse Scrooge transformation. Maybe it was the situation with the Saunders household or maybe it was seeing that elusive cat of hers again. Margaret had never, in all the years she had known May, actually seen Mr Kibbles for herself. She had heard May speak of him on many occasions but he had always seemed to be out when she arrived. Margaret never even saw a sign of him. There were never loose cat hairs about her house, fur balls or signs of scratching. May had always been house-proud and Margaret had always assumed that she had cleaned away any cat related mess before she had arrived. Sometimes she just wondered whether Mr Kibbles even existed at all. She had once asked May just how Mr Kibbles had died but she always skirted the question. It was as if she didn't even know herself.

Margaret decided that none of it was important to her now. She really didn't care if Mr Kibbles was real or just a figment of May's imagination. If he gave her comfort who was she to argue. All that mattered now was that May was her closest friend and she had died but appeared to be doing well on it.

Margaret picked up the final letter, it looked rather official. It was enclosed in a brown envelope that displayed Margaret's name and address through a clear plastic window. Margaret tore it open and unfolded the page inside. The paper was headed with Fredrickson and Fredrickson Probate Solicitors. Margaret read it through and discovered it was about May's house and money and how she had died intestate. She had left no will and all her worldly possessions could end up as property of the state, if an heir couldn't be found. They admitted to discovering records that named Margaret as known to the deceased and were requesting any useful information she might have regarding May Elizabeth Trump. They had included a phone number in the contact details and Margaret decided to call them a little later in the day. As far as she knew May had no relatives but she made plans to inform them about the orphanage she had attended, there might still be records stored there? Margaret sipped her tea and then pulled her bowl of "Honey Crunch Star Shapes" closer. She used the remote control to switch on the television. The screen blinked and The Colin Farley show appeared. Ah! Margaret thought, a little normality for a change.

Chapter Eighteen

May sat alone at a small circular table. A shot glass of whiskey was half empty in front of her. She had never seen the saloon so empty and, with the morning light, so clearly. She hadn't before noticed the carpet of sawdust scattered across the floor. There were burgundy drapes by the windows, hanging from long brass poles. There were great wrought iron chandeliers hanging from the ceiling and on the far wall were stairs, she had never noticed the stairs? Even in the poor light of the evening and with the distractions of the crowds, she hadn't realised that the building had a second floor. May was beginning to wonder what else there was about this realm that had passed her notice.

She looked around the saloon. Only a few patrons supped at tiny glasses while a sombre tune was being played on the old piano. Greg, the bar tender, was polishing glasses and only Old Man Ferris held up the bar, muttering undecipherable gibberish at anyone within earshot. Greg nodded at him with false interest. Greg looked to be in his late thirties, while Ferris held the appearance of a man made out of old shoe leather; he was almost mummified with age.

May had never stayed in this realm for this long before. As the morning sun had risen over the dry plains surrounding the town it seemed to have lost most of its inhabitants. Much of the movement on the street outside was just the passing of tumble weeds.

She empted her whiskey glass and it filled her with the usual warmth. She left the table and took the empty glass to the bar. Ferris glanced up at her and mumbled something incoherent. May replied with a stale smile. She placed the glass on the bar and Greg reacted by picking up a whisky bottle and pulling out the cork.

"No thank you Greg," May said as she covered the glass with her palm. "Where is everyone?" Greg took another shot glass from under the bar and filled it for himself. Ferris pushed his glass forward and Greg topped him up before replacing the cork.

"It's always quiet here at this time of day," Greg replied. "Most folks scatter when the sun comes up. There's a lot more to see out there May, more than just this dreary old town".

"It's hardly dreary Greg," May said. "I find it all rather stimulating and it's not the whiskey talking either".

"I expect you do feel that way now but wait until you've spent a century here". Greg pointed out and May was again reminded how looks could be deceiving after death.

"You've been here that long?"

"Give or take," Greg shrugged and then emptied his glass in one gulp.

"Why hang around if you hate it so much? Why not venture out, if there's so much more outside?" Ferris mumbled something and Greg refilled both glasses.

"Well someone has to keep an eye on him," Greg nodded towards Ferris. "Besides I've been there, done it, seen it and brought nothing to show for it either". Greg wore a false smile and shrugged again. "I find it easier just to stay here now; easier and safer".

"Safer! What do you mean by safer?" May wondered if Greg was related to George in any way. It was beginning to seem as if all the dead people she met were obsessed with health and safety issues. She was all for the concept of taking care to protect life and limb but she no longer had either to worry about.

"You do know about *them*?" Greg gave May a quizzical look. Ferris banged his empty glass on the bar, his eyes had grown wider. May guessed that he was worried about something but could only sense it through his eyes and how urgently he seemed to need a drink. There were too many wrinkles on his face already, to tell if he was frowning or not.

"I've heard about there being some kind of dark entities

wandering about the living realm but to be truthful, I struggled to believe it. I was told there was safety in this realm from such things, so you can't be referring to the same *them*?"

"I'm afraid to say that I am," Greg replied, as he topped up the old man's glass. "They are the same in either realm but there's something about the sun here that seems to hold them at bay". Ferris mumbled something that May didn't understand.

"I know! I was going to mention it to her," Greg snapped at the old man. "They wander the plains after dark. They tend to stay away from the more heavily populated areas, like towns and cities. There's not been a reported sighting for over seventy years but the dead have long memories. I have never seen one myself but the same could be said for most. Ferris saw one real close up though and he's never been the same since. He hangs around here day and night now. Ever since that night he won't even trust the sun to protect him". May uncovered her glass and pushed it towards Greg, another shot couldn't hurt.

"I still don't understand," May admitted, as Greg filled her glass. "I was told that spirits came here to escape from The Stalkers of Souls". Ferris spluttered and banged his empty glass on the bar again.

"He says you shouldn't speak their name," Greg translated as his refilled the old man's glass yet again. "He thinks that speaking the name that *we* have given them, I'm sure it's not what they call themselves, in some way summons them to us. He's a paranoid nutcase at the best of times, so don't worry about it May. Whenever he starts talking like this I tend to stem the flow of whiskey". Greg corked the bottle and slipped it under the bar.

"You can be safe here or anywhere for that matter, if there is a large enough concentration of spirits. They don't seem to attack large groups. Some believe that we emit something similar to whatever it is in the sunlight here which keeps them at bay. They say that it is so weak within us individually, that it takes a number of us together to create the desired effect". May took a large gulp of whiskey. She found it a little unnerving to realise that you were not the biggest fish in the sea and had to travel in flocks to stay safe from predators.

"That's all very good," May said, as she placed her empty glass on the bar. "But what I still can't figure out is: just what harm they can do to us? We are already dead aren't we? What more do we have to fear?"

"To be completely honest we have no idea," Greg admitted. "Once taken, no one ever returns to tell the tale and I mean no one. As I have said: I have never seen one but I do notice when a spirit leaves and never again sets foot in this place. Regular patrons, who I used to serve every night for decades, are never seen again".

"And this all happened over seventy years ago?"

"No!" Greg replied. "This is what happens now! It's been seventy years since they since they came at us in force. Hundreds of them dropped down from the sky like a flock of birds; there was no group too large for them that night. Few were ever seen again, Ferris being one of the lucky ones I guess. We only have his words and the words of the other lucky few, as evidence of all this. Obviously that was on top of how our numbers had so suddenly been greatly diminished. It didn't even happen here, nothing of such a large scale has ever happened in this realm. I guess that's why so many spirits took up permanent residence here afterwards. There very presence helped to make this realm safer and it has taken this many years to regain our former population". Greg shrugged and pulled the whisky bottle out again. "I don't mean to worry you May, you're safe here as long as you don't stay out after dark. Make sure you get to a town or a city before the sun sets, keep out of the deepest shade and you'll come to no harm. More whisky?" Greg tilted the bottle towards May's glass.

May shook her head, she had a lot to think about and whisky would only cloud her mind. George had been right about some things, yet strangely emissive about others. Why hadn't he mentioned that the stalkers transverse both realms. Had he actually lied and said that this realm was safe? May mused, or had I just assumed the fact. She looked across the saloon towards the doorway and it's waist high, token doors. She could see that the sun was still riding high; night was still many hours away. Greg had mention cities; she could hardly imagine what such places would be like. Great monolithic structures looming over dusty deserted streets. Broken windows and the distant sound of shuffling feet, was how May had always envisioned a city of the dead. She was intrigued to discover just how wrong she could be; at least she hoped she was wrong. She thanked Greg and nodded to Ferris, who hardly seemed notice her as he repeatedly banged his empty glass on the bar.

"Be careful," Greg called after her as she headed for the door. His voice barely audible over the racket Ferris was making with his empty whiskey glass.

"And remember to seek out others before it gets dark".

The street outside was still deserted. May strode purposefully towards the edge of the town, evading the occasional speeding tumble weed. There was no wind to propel the rolling vegetation but May decided not to concern herself with the fact. She had more than enough to ponder over for the time being. There was nothing in sight but dusty dry fields, once May reached the edge of the town. She could see nothing taller than cacti all the way to the horizon. It looks like it'll be a long way to travel anywhere, May thought as she took in the view. Even with so many hours of sunlight left, a walking pace would hardly get me anywhere. She could see how easily someone could find themselves alone as the night set in. Suddenly something occurred to her: If I ran, for how long could I run for? She hadn't felt tired since her death. Her body didn't ache like it used to, in fact she hadn't felt a single pain since leaving her body. May considered the theory: I am a ghost and as a ghost I have no physical form to speak of. Which would suggest that I have no muscles for which to tire and no need to suck in great lungfuls of air because I have no lungs. Physical activity shouldn't have the same effect on me now, neither in a positive or negative way. I should be able to run as fast as I can, for as long as I want and yet feel nothing from it. She tested her theory by setting off at a slow jog towards the horizon. She felt no effort in her movements so quickened her pace. Now at a faster jog, a canter by horse's standards, May began to cover ground surprisingly fast. May glanced back towards the town; it had already grown small in the distance. She was surprised not to see a dust cloud in her wake, as she broke out into a run. She didn't feel the wind in her face, or any kind of friction for that matter. There was nothing to hold her back or slow her down. Even though she was now running as hard and as fast as she could, she continued to accelerate. May started to realise that she was being carried along by her own momentum.

She slowed her pace back down to a walk but her speed remained unchanged. She stopped completely still and was startled to discover herself gliding on the balls of her feet. She was still travelling across the dusty landscape at the speed of a running horse but she was also standing perfectly still. Her feet were impossibly close but not quite touching the ground.

She had already travelled a fair distance, yet she still couldn't see anything but open land stretching out before her. How far away were the other settlements? May asked herself. And why is there so much dead space between? She started move her legs again. A brisk walk, a jog. She slowly increased her pace back into a run. She accelerated until the ground beneath her began to ripple like water. The horizon seemed to grow ever closer, though she knew that it was just a speed born illusion.

The landscape around her suddenly changed. The grey dust became lush green fields and trees began appearing so quickly, that it was as if they were sprouting up through the very ground before her. She had to swerve to avoid a few, as they suddenly appeared in her path. The fields soon gave

way to meadows and the previously level ground began to
erupt in small hills and ditches. As the ground beneath her
dipped, May glided through the air above it. She felt herself
gradually loose height until her feet were almost touching
the ground again. Almost immediately the ground began to
rise again. She felt herself tilt backwards as she ran up the
side of a hill. She was still accelerating when she reached
the top and then launched high into the air. The ground
dropped sharply away from her, she was flying.

Beneath her the land opened out into a wide valley. A
vast forest covered most of the ground and a fast running
river cut through the tightly packed trees. May felt
exhilarated as she soared across the sky. She felt a freedom
like no other, all the way until she looked directly down. A
carpet of bushy green lay below her. From so high above it
looked like a huge soft blanket but May knew that gnarled
and age hardened branches lie in wait beneath. She felt her
heart rise up into her throat, as her ascent reach its peak
and she begun to fall. It was a slow, diagonal descent at
first but her angle gradually sharpened. In her panic she
flapped her arms like a bird, feeling both embarrassed and
disappointed at its lack of effect. She continued to fall
towards the treetops below. For a moment May sensed a
brief moment of hope. Her current angle lined her up
perfectly with the wide rushing river. A wetter but wholly
softer landing met with May's approval. She closed her
eyes and braced herself. Her angle dipped again and she
felt leaves slapping at her ankles. Her foot hooked onto a
branch and she fell, face down, into the foliage. For a
moment May was engulfed in a cloud of leaves. She could
hear the branches creaking, as they bent with the force of
her impact. May gradually stopped falling until, for a
fraction of a second, she laid perfectly still on a bed of
leaves. She had barely realised how painless the whole
event had been before the branches sprang back to their
former positions. May was catapulted back into to air,
somersaulting end over end, before plummeting back into
the treetops. This time there was no blanket of leaves to

cushion her fall. Small thin branches snapped away. Thicker branches span her around into a twisting tumble; leaves flew in all directions. Hitting branch after branch, painlessly, May finally exited the foliage and hit the soft earth below. She performed and unintentional forward roll and came to a rest spread eagled between two tree trunks.

May sat up, embarrassed but unhurt. A fall such as that should have killed her but she was beyond the risk of death. The heavy foliage above blocked out most of the sunlight and placed the area in thick shadow. Only a few pin pricks of light made it all the way through to the ground; it was a dark place. May scrambled to her feet. Any hint of exhilaration or embarrassment was gone; all she could feel was anxiety and fear.

The trees stretched ahead of her into a featureless shadow. May turned around and was relieved to see that the edge of the forest was only about fifty yards behind her. She could just make out the grassy bank of the river. A little less anxious, she turned her back on the river and stared into the shadows. She felt compelled to walk deeper into the forest but she held her ground and just gazed. It was subtle at first but slowly the shadows began to shift. They merged into each other. Gradually and almost methodically, they swamped over the tiny pinpricks of light, extinguishing their glow. The whole mass of shadow crawled along the forest floor towards May. It moved like liquid. An oil slick of shadow; a flood of sticky darkness. May began to slowly step backwards, as if a sudden movement would hasten its approach. Her breath became as mist and the leaves on the trees began to crackle as they became brittle with frost. She increased the speed of her backwards gait. With each footstep the darkness moved closer. May realised that it was slowly gaining ground. She suddenly turned and ran towards the river and the light. Dark shadowy fingers reached for her either side as she hop scotched from one small patch of light to another. She felt an icy cold sting, as the shadows brushed against her skin.

She leapt across the last patch of dark and fell into the bright sunshine, feeling the last of the chill grasping at her heals. She rolled over on the soft grass of the river bank and looked back into the forest. The darkness between the trees subsided and all became still again.

May sat still on the damp grass, her heart was pounding. She was aware that it was just a psychosomatic reaction. She had no heart as such, not anymore. Some might say that she never did but a few, those that mattered, knew otherwise. May knew fear but this was variation that she was unaccustomed to. She have lived her life in the fear of rejection, which was why she had never allowed anyone to come close enough to eventually push her away. The reason she had attached herself to the Saunders family was still unclear to her but she had her suspicions. Penny was harmless, as far as May was concerned. She was in a constant state of vulnerability and, between them both, May believed that she would be more likely the one to do the rejecting. Chloe, on the other hand, was a special case. May didn't understand the connection she had with Penny's daughter but as she ran through the forest, fearing for her life for want of a better word, it was Chloe who was foremost in her mind. May hadn't realised until that moment, just how much stock she had put into the young girl's welfare.

The river was overlooked by the forest for as far as May could see. There was not a single break in the trees and May wasn't too keen on re-entering the shade. She set off at a brisk walking pace along the river bank. She was travelling in the same direction as the flow of the river. The gentle spray of the rushing water occasionally brushed against her as began to pick up momentum. She kept one eye on the edge of the forest closest to her. May was relying on the assumption that the wide river between her and the rest of the forest would be enough to keep her safe from anything that lurked in the shadows there. She broke into a run and it wasn't long before she was moving faster than the river flowed. The feel of the spray lessened, as if it couldn't keep up with her increasing pace. Gradually the trees either side began to thin in number and the river narrowed. She was covering miles in a matter of seconds. The river became a stream and only a few trees lined her path in what had become a wide open meadow. The ground began to rise sharply again, as she reached the edge of the valley. Not wanting to make the same mistake twice, May reduced her pace to a slow walk and then stood still. Her speed didn't change but at least she had stopped accelerating. Even the uphill gradient didn't slow her down, she was beginning to worry. She tried to dig her heels into the earth but found no purchase. A bizarre thought crossed her mind and she started to walk backwards. It seemed to be working, she was slowing down. May performed, what she would refer to as, a referee trot and gradually her speed more manageable. She finally reached to top of the hill at little more than a walking pace and a couple of backward steps left her stationary.

The view was far from what May had expected. The grass ended a few feet in front of her, with grey concrete beyond. Tall buildings looked down upon her as if questioning her presence. May slowly walked towards them. The concrete became pavement and roads, which stretched off in all directions. Office buildings, thirty stories high, loomed each side of her as she followed the road ahead. She walked slowly and her speed remained unchanged, she had no momentum here. The streets looked deserted and the buildings lacked any discernable character. They varied a little in size but the same square grey style remained uniform among them. It was a soulless place; she had found her city of the dead. May listened out for the sound of shuffling feet.

All remained quiet as she wandered along the deserted street. A little further ahead the road reached a junction that stretched left and right. Her surroundings seemed to change. The tall, grey buildings were replaced by smaller, red brick structures. There were gardens with flowers and small stone mythical creatures within them. May stood at the junction and looked up and down the road. It seemed brighter here now and felt warmer. There were people in the street. An old man was pruning a rose bush in one of the gardens and a small group of children were kicking a football in the road. As May walked down the street, people smiled and waved at her as they passed. The football came hurtling towards her and she surprised even herself by catching it. What surprised her more was her reaction to it. She didn't yell and she didn't confiscate to ball as she would have done at one time. May just gently threw the ball back to the children and smiled. The children giggled and waved before continuing their game. May walked on, feeling as if she were wearing someone else's shoes. She should have been spitting feathers but instead she felt like whistling.

Further down the street there was a gap in the houses filled by a small parade of shops. A bookstore and a shop called Martha's Bizarre flanked a café, a greasy spoon as May liked to call them. The sign above it said Sid's Diner and May wondered what sort of man would open a café after he had died. This set her off thinking about Greg back at the saloon. Why are these people still working when the clearly don't need to? Martha's Bizarre was almost a personality description, for someone who chooses to run a shop in the afterlife. May was sure there was good reason. How many centuries could I get through without having something to occupy myself with? May also wanted to know where all the books and whiskey came from as well. I'll ask Greg, she promised herself.

May watched as a man and a woman entered the café together, while another man tried to exit. There were a few polite gestures as they passed by each other at the narrow doorway. May stepped up to the window and looked inside. There eight people, including the newly arrived couple. Three rows of four tables ran up and down the café.

They were the awkward built in bench style. Single structure tables that her friend Margaret always had trouble squeezing into. The smell of burnt cooking oil and cheap sausages wafted out and May was lured in to the cafe.

May took a seat on a vacant table by one of the walls. She picked up the menu and flicked through it. There was everything she would have expected from a similar place in the living realm. Everything seemed to be served fried except the toast but she assumed that would be drowned in butter.

"Are you ready to order?" May looked up and a large man in a grease stained apron stood over her. He smiled at her and offered out his hand.

"My name is Sid and welcome to my little eatery". May shook his hand.

"Trump, May Trump. Nice to meet you".

"Not *the* May Trump? The one than can talk to those on the other side. The medium, the dead medium?"

"I guess so?" May was surprised that he had heard of her. She didn't feel entirely comfortable about it either. "How do you know me?"

"Everyone knows about you Madam Trump. News travels fast around here, especially good news! It's got to have been the best part of a century since there's been someone like you around, someone with abilities such as yours. You're the talk of the town. There's spirits around here that haven't left this realm for centuries, which are considering crossing back over for a chance to be heard". He clapped his hands together and grinned. "Where are my manners? Is there anything I can get you? It's on the house! Well everything's on the house around here but you get my meaning".

"I'll just have a coffee thank you". May didn't like what she was hearing but she couldn't fault Gary's promoting techniques.

"Right you are but just call if you want anything else". He said and then and then added as he walked away. "May Elizabeth Trump, right here in my café. Just wait until Dora hears about this, she'll have a fit!"

Chapter Nineteen

Penny was practising but she was making little progress. She was alone in the darkened living room. It was daytime outside but the heavy curtains were still drawn. She had seen them move a couple of times and had attributed it to her own doing, until she had realised it was just a draft from a slightly open window.

So far her day had not gone completely to plan. She had hoped that she would be throwing things through the air on just a whim of thought by now. Even with the accusation of being a poltergeist supporting her endeavours, she was still suffering no creditable results. It occurred to her that she might just void of technique. She had no idea if the concentrated, wink-less stare method was even the right way to approach it. There was nobody around who could tutor her on the finer arts of cup spinning or plate throwing. It wasn't as if there was even a book on the subject that she could study. She considered seeking out George again but the thought of entering the graveyard alone sent a chill up her spine. Penny was aware that her fear of graves was pointless and habitual but, while her body was still fresh in the ground, she wouldn't even consider going on her own.

Chloe had returned to college that morning, not that she would have been the ideal company for such an outing. May was spending some time in the other realm. The house seemed colder, darker somehow, when she wasn't there. Penny had grown to look upon May as almost a mother figure, someone to take charge; Penny had never been a take charge kind of person. Gary had promised to come around later in the day but had not specified an exact time. He had gone in search of Eric, the plumber. Penny had been rather shocked at his initial accusation; Gary had spoken with more wrath in his voice than she was comfortable with. He had overheard Chloe speaking to one of May's old ladies. It might have been Margaret but Gary hadn't been sure. He had started ranting about how Eric was up to something sinister. He couldn't accept Eric's charitable actions for what they were, act of kindness from a man who had once sought her affections. Penny hadn't felt the same way about him. He had always been nice to her but she just didn't think of him in a romantic sense. She had explained everything to Gary but he hadn't listened. Words like: removing evidence from the scene of a crime and suspicious behaviour, had sprung to his lips. Eric was guilty until proven innocent, as far as Gary was concerned. Penny appreciated his gesture, in some ways it showed that he cared but it also left her worried.

She was surprised that he wasn't spending more time with his son. He may well be keeping an eye on Martin but he hadn't mentioned anything about it to her. He has been very busy, Penny excused, gathering interest for the séances. She liked him, she liked him a lot. There was something about him that made her feel safe and something that made her feel young; it was a feeling that scared her. There was a momentum building in the relationship that she wasn't totally at ease with. He was helping them with a motivation that was beyond his obligation. Part of her was grateful but another part still showed the scars from a previous doomed relationship.

She had been only young when she had met Chloe's father for the first time, young and very naïve. Eighteen years old with her life stretching ahead of her and dreams far beyond her station. She was from a family that always lived just above the bread line; luxuries were things that happened to other people. The house had to be maintained, it had been drummed into her ever since she was a small child. Too many of the great family houses had turned to rack and ruin over the years, he father had always told her but not this one. This house is our family's heritage. It's our past and your future, so look after it. He had listened to the same speech from his father before him. Every single bit of spare cash went into the house, from fixing the guttering to curing the dry rot. The running joke was that her younger sister was called Anna because they couldn't afford more than one Penny.

Jonathan had arrived in the town one summer, in a hail of shining glory. He tore through the high street in his brand new silver MG convertible, wearing an expensive tan suit and aviator sunglasses. Most of the townsfolk didn't know what to make of him, with his flash clothes and even flasher behaviour. Penny and the rest of her generation, looked on him with awe. The boys fell in love with his car and saw him as a symbol of what they might achieve one day. The girls all fell in love with him instantly. He was suave, sophisticated and a world of difference compared to the selection of bachelors that the town usually had to offer. They were mainly farm hands, who spent most of their time smelling of manure. There was also Kevin, the butcher's son but he had a strange piercing stare and a disturbing facial twitch. One of Penny's friends once told her that she had seen him hard at work in the back of the butcher's shop. He held a meat cleaver in one hand and there was blood splattered all over his apron. Her friend had confessed to almost fainting when she came face to face with Kevin's sinister stare, as he wildly chopped away at a cow carcass.

Jonathan had made quite an impact. Young, handsome and obviously not short of a bob or two, he soon became in great demand. Penny had only admired him from afar. She had always been a little shy and besides, she was generally too busy for such things. She had a multitude of cleaning jobs at the time, doing all she could to bring money into the family home. They had met by accident and within a few weeks a second accident had occurred. She had fallen in love with him and he had declared his love for her, one night behind the coconut shy at the annual summer fair. A few weeks later Jonathon had disappeared in a whirl of accusations. Half a dozen people, including the local bank manager, turned up at her door with complaints regarding sour deals and missing investments. Jonathon was a con merchant, a swindler. Her father had said she was well shot of him but he hadn't known she was pregnant at the time. She had been left, quite literally, holding the baby.

Penny had been heart broken and it still hurt even now, whenever she thought about it. Not only had he left her without an explanation or even a goodbye, he had abandoned his unborn child. He had forsaken Chloe and that infuriated Penny. He never came back, he never called, he never wrote. She had decided long ago that it was because he never cared, for neither her nor Chloe. Penny had thought that she had put this particular ghost to rest many years ago but old feelings bubbled back to the surface as if it had all just happened yesterday. Her muscles became tense and her eyes widened as the hurt and frustration, buried so deep for so long, burnt a fresh hole into her heart. She pulled at her own hair with both hands and screamed, and the coffee table flew across the room and shattered against the wall.

Chapter Twenty

It was still dark when May woke up, back in the living realm. The small alarm clock on the bedside table showed her that it was approaching five. Her position on the bed remained unchanged from since she departed but someone had changed the sheets while she had been gone. She climbed off the bed and stood up. She rubbed the life back into her face, symbolically and noticed the faint smell of furniture polish as she left the room.

Penny was sitting at the kitchen table when May walked in. There was an empty cup slowly sliding back and forth between her hands.

"Where have you been?" Penny exclaimed as she looked up.

"Good morning to you to!" May replied both surprised and annoyed. "You know perfectly well where I've been. I told you I'd be spending the day in the spiritual realm".

"One day you said! You've been gone almost a week. You do know its Saturday today?"

"What are you waffling on about? It's only Tuesday!" May recounted the past two nights in her head to double check. Penny was obviously mistaken, it must be all the stress she's been under.

"You've been gone for over five days May," Penny insisted. "The séances start tonight, everything's ready except for you". May was beginning to worry about Penny, she was clearly confused. May had spent Sunday night in the old town and last night in the city of the dead. She could remember it all perfectly. After the café she had wandered around for a few hours, sightseeing, before venturing into a jazz and swing club as the night drew in. It wasn't her first choice but it was crowded and therefore safe. Even so, it had turned out to be quite an interesting evening.

"This is really not funny Penny!"

"I'm not trying to be funny May! We've had all kinds of

167

spirits out there looking for you. Margaret's been having kittens. They were here yesterday spring cleaning, Margaret and her friends. Why did you stay out there for so long?"

"I didn't! I was only gone two nights". May pointed to the cup that was now stationary between Penny's hands. "When did you learn to do that?" Penny looked down at the cup and smiled.

"I've been practising. As I keep telling you: you've been gone all week. George came around and helped me to better control it. I could only manage sporadic movements before then, whenever I got a bit emotional. Now I have a little control, limited though it is but I can move small objects. I can't do anything too complicated mind you; I can't write a letter or dial a phone. I've tried but all I get is streaky lines and wrong numbers".

"And you've managed all that in just two nights?"

"You've been gone all week!"

It slowly dawned on May. Penny seemed so certain, so convinced but so was she.

"There must be some kind of time dilation between the two plains?" It was the only answer she could come up with. It would also explain why I keep getting up late, she realised.

"Sorry?" Penny looked confused. "Some kind of what?"

"Have you ever noticed that when you leave the other realm in the early hours of the morning, you wake up here on the wrong side of breakfast?"

"I get up late sometimes but doesn't everyone? In fact I have been waking up late quite often, now that I think about it". Penny frowned. "Are you saying what I think you're saying? Could we be time travellers? I do hope so; I've always wanted to go back to Edwardian times. She gazed up at the ceiling dreamily, "Jane Austin makes it sound so romantic".

"I'm saying no such thing girl. I'm talking about time moving at a different speed in one place to another. I seem to be losing four or five hours every night and it's not the whisky causing it either. Time is moving faster in the other realm compared to this. Twice as fast I believe or something of that nature, I've not done the math to be sure".

"I've never really looked at it that way," Penny admitted. She seemed a little disappointed. "I don't usually keep track of time when I'm dreaming, or realm-ing, or whatever it is? I guess it makes a kind of sense, though I much prefer my idea". Penny looked up at the ceiling again, doe eyed and distant. "Whatever you say Mr Darcy".

"What else have I missed?" May asked, drawing Penny out of her day dream.

"I don't know all the details as such; I've been busy with this". Penny made the cup move again. "What I do know, however, is that it's all due to kick off at seven o'clock this evening. There will be all kinds of people, dead and alive, descending on us by then". May checked the kitchen clock, she still had fourteen hours to prepare. She had hoped for a lot more but that had been as much about nerves as it had been about preparation.

"How many are coming exactly, do we even know?"

"I've got no idea!" Penny shrugged. "But the last I heard there were eight séances booked. I reckon we'll be getting a lot of spectators as well. Oh! And George wants to speak to you before tonight. He said something about steering you away from dangerous subjects". She shrugged again. "Whatever that means?"

"Well I've got a few questions for him! And I had better like the answers".

May was well aware of George's concerns. She had learnt a great deal over the past two days. She still remembered the sting of cold shadows, she could hardly forget it and a lot had been said at the jazz club. She had found it remarkably easy to talk to people about her experience in the forest, after a vodka martini or three. May had surprised even herself with her capacity to drink; she had hardly touched the stuff when she was alive. There was always a half bottle of brandy in her kitchen cupboard, for medicinal purposes only of course. Some people had listened but others had waved their hands and walked away at the first mention of *THEM*. May had stood corrected at one point, when she had described it as a close encounter. A man, with more dead years than living under his belt, had highlighted her error, with more than a little conviction.

"You felt not the touch of the stalkers young lady!" Which May felt was a little strange coming from a man who looked half her age.

"You would not be here if it were so".

Mr Kibbles suddenly skipped through the kitchen window and jumped onto the table. He rubbed up against May's arm and purred. It would seem that he had missed her as well.

Chapter Twenty One

It was already late in the afternoon by the time George finally arrived. Trevor, his lively Jack Russell, leapt after Mr Kibbles as soon as they had entered the house. The terrier obviously suffered from a short memory. It was either that or he was a glutton for punishment. May was sure that it would soon all end in whimpers. She silently directed George into the living room, through the closed door. She intended to keep their conversation private; she saw no sense in worrying the others quite yet. She had purposefully refrained from telling Penny about what had happened to her in the spirit realm. There would be no profit in scaring her unduly.

May had last seen Chloe in the kitchen studying. She was trying to catch up on all the college work that she had missed in the past few days. Penny and Gary had sought their own privacy upstairs. Penny had referred to it as: a milestone conversation.

George took a seat on the sofa while May sat on one of the arm chairs opposite him. The coffee table was missing; she also noticed that there was a large dent in the far wall. The paint was cracked and the plaster had crumbled. She made a mental note to seek out an explanation.

"So George! You wanted to see me," May said.
"That much is indeed true," George nodded as he spoke. "And your recent absence has left me rather concerned. I feared foul play had befallen you?"
"I was quite safe in the other realm. Nothing bad could possibly happen to me there, could it George?"
"In relative terms I would hasten to agree".
"In relative terms?"
"Justly so. Evidence would suggest there's truth in such a statement". May was losing her patience, subtlety was getting her nowhere.

"Why the hell didn't you warn me about the other realm? You lead me to believe it was safe but I very nearly bought the farm out there".

"An outrageous suggestion May! I would cry warning in my slumber, had I still the need. Neither should I speak false on such matters. I venture towards belief; I'm no pedlar of lies".

"Yet you failed to mention that the stalkers reside in both realms".

"An oversight perhaps, if your words speak true; not that I distrust them of course. I suffered a siege of doubt last we met, a fitting distraction wouldn't you say and it would not be beyond me to err. The stalkers are of neither world yet, beyond the touch of sunlight, they have the freedom of both. The sunlight of this realm is of no matter to them which is a mourn worthy fact to heed. Only when flocked together like livestock, can we hope to fend them here"

"What about the time difference? You never told me about that either. You mentioned nothing regarding the fact that time moves faster over there".

"Did I not? Well it's hardly a noteworthy circumstance. It has little consequence for those of a settled spirit. Only such as I, who flitter from each to another, should hold concern of it".

"I lost the best part of a week! I now have this séance thrust upon me with no time left to prepare".

"You've hardly been blessed by a settled spirit May, a modicum of inconvenience is not unexpected in your case. I suspect that I belittled the effect with yourself in mind. I take it that no such concern has befallen you before now. Only the passing of an extended leave has drawn your wit towards the variation". May felt impelled to agree with him. If it wasn't for her two day stint, she would never have realised.

"What's the point of it?" May couldn't imagine purpose it served, unless it was a tool for the impatient. Why wait for two weeks, when the time could pass in just one. May never understood the concept of looking forward to something. An upcoming event was exactly that, upcoming.

There was nothing to be gained by pining for that which will eventually pass regardless.

"The purpose of this effect has been a source of bafflement for many inquisitive souls over the years. None can truly say of its function. My belief is that segregation is in its aim, the point of which still lies beyond my understanding. Those who wander this realm act with much precaution while in the next. A day and night is sufficient of most errands, to linger further would pose the threat of displacement. Life moves at an inconsiderate pace. To blithely stand aside from it, is to risk a return to foreign shores. Time suffers hindered movement for those who have forsaken this realm. Souls who still hold the belief that the world has ceased to turn and that life is still much the same as their mind recalls it. I endeavour to set free their view of reality but my efforts feel akin to flogging a horse".

"Don't you mean flogging a dead horse?"

"On the contrary May! I mean to indicate a comparable action by the phrase. I would find no difficulty in flogging a *dead* horse and would suffer more reaction for my efforts. My advice seems forever met with ignorance and suspicion, regardless of the realm in which my quarry might dwell".

May saw the truth in his words. Most of the spirits she had spoken to about George admitted to doubting him. They ignored his insights, yet failed to replace them with their own assumptions or ideas.

"Well I'm willing to listen now," May said. "But I want to know everything, no more omissions".

"Then the truth you shall have May. However everything I say will be tinged by experience, assumption and theory. No evidence or carving of stone exists to show proof of these words but I stand by them as if they were as fact. Those who agree stand likewise and those who condemn offer little basis for their doubt. The Stalkers of Souls have eluded sight in either realm regardless of our efforts to bring forth proof of them. Where the tales of their deeds continue in the other realm, word of their endeavours here ceased many years ago. Their capacity to exist in this realm has no need of clarification, for we have seen them; I have seen them. It is a thing to which memory shall never fade. Seventy years back, I was not as I stand before you today. I was unhindered by concern. I felt such liberty as only the dead can set claim to. I made an exhibition of this world and stood familiar of all its offerings. But after so many years a spectator, such trappings become commonplace. When a thing so vibrantly new reared its head I felt impelled to pursue it. I was across the globe when my attention was first drawn and it was no mere evening stroll to venture towards it. Hindsight stakes claim to my tardiness as my saviour. To have been present at the onset would have meant an unimaginable doom. As I had stood for all events since my passing, I again stood a mere witness to the experience of others".

"What are you blathering on about?" May was struggling to make sense of his words.

"You my dear May! I was drawn towards you, at least another such as you. Many are drawn to a power such as yours. The promise of connection, the promise that things previously left unsaid could yet again touch a living ear. The mere rumour of such a thing could draw the attention of a thousand souls, from either realm".

"That's good though, isn't it? Safety in numbers, that's what every body keeps telling me".

"I would be inclined to agree, if the circumstances were not so charged. A large gathering, such as I witnessed that night, should imply a haven of sorts. It is a puzzlement that I have pondered for more years than memory can measure and it has led me to only one potential conclusion. Charged emotion, dark emotion draws them to us. The promise of connection funnels many spirits towards a single soul, like water down an ever narrowing pipe. Impatience and jealousy would grow strong in such a circumstance. The many competing for the attention of only one, it would take a mere spark to light a fire of dissent among them. This is my assumption of that which alerts them but not of that which they truly crave. An occasion where a large group could become unruly is hardly an occurrence of note, yet they fail to attend such events. Nothing before or since has drawn them in such numbers but I believe I know that which dictates their actions. The one ingredient that marked that fateful gathering from all others was that one unique soul. They came for the one who shared a power such as yours May and I am fearful that they will yet come for you".

May hadn't expected that and it didn't fill her with much confidence. She was grateful for George's honesty. It was all based on assumption and guesswork but if he believed it all so ardently? May didn't want to agree with him. She didn't want to put stock in a faith that left her with so few choices.

"If what you say is true then it would be wise to cancel the séances and avoid using my gift altogether".

"I would be inclined to agree, if only to starve their advances. If my assumptions are correct, abstinence would merely hinder their ability to discover you, it would not deter them from the chase". They're coming to get you, May thought. There's nothing you can do but hide but they will still find you. My body has already left me and now they wish to take what little remains. George's words made sense to May but there was still that use of the word assumption. She was sure of his devotion to his theories but even then, there seemed to be a small sliver of doubt buried deep with in him. She thought of how Penny would take the news if she cancelled everything they had been working towards. It would mean letting a lot of people down and May wasn't used to that in the slightest. She prided herself on always keeping to her word and it was the promise she had made to Penny that guided her final decision on the matter.

"I don't think I'm going to fall for your tall tales today George. I don't doubt that you saw something frightful many years ago but it has nothing to do with me. You can waste your time making wild assumptions and spinning fantastical yarns as much as you like but not with me. I've got a busy night ahead and I'd rather if you weren't any where near me. I'm nervous enough as it is without you trying to silence my every word with your paranoid delusions". There was no doubt in May's mind that the entities, that George referred to as The Stalker of Souls, actually existed. She knew that there were dark forces at work but she also knew that people were reliant on her. So what if they were coming for her, she wouldn't run and she wouldn't hide. Nobody pushed May Elizabeth Trump around. She was stubborn, pigheaded and ever so slightly brave.

Chapter Twenty Two

It was just before seven in the evening and clients had already begun to arrive. The living were closely followed by their dead counterparts, who appeared to have crept along behind them during their journey to Chloe's house. The entire Thursday Night Club were playing host with Chloe, while Penny and Gary made the spirits feel welcome. Tension filled the air as the ghosts were restless. Most had been waiting many years for an opportunity to contact their enduring relatives.

George was providing May with unwanted company. May was certain of his intentions; he had made no secret of them. Regardless of May's wishes, he would watch over the upcoming proceedings and offer his advice and guidance whenever he saw the need. May's complaints had been little more than gestures. She knew that if she had stoked more heat out of her argument she could have convinced him to leave but she was unsure of the wisdom in such an action. She wanted to give George the impression that his company remained unwelcome, when in fact his presence did afford her a little comfort. She was still trying to convince herself that continuing with this endeavour was the right way to go. She fought her fears with inventive ignorance. There wasn't any risk, no additional risk that is. The Stalkers of Souls acted with no set agenda. They were purely a random phenomenon. Opportunist assailants; way layers of unfortunate spirits. Such assumptions served her purpose and she forced herself to swallow them like so many dry crackers. Her true beliefs stood weak and alone against her stubbornness and her deep seated reluctance to break a promise. Emotion had little hold on her when pitched against principle.

May heard the sound of someone knocking on the door downstairs, shortly followed by the rumbling drone of overlapping voices.

"The game is afoot it would seem," George remarked. He stood in the corner of the room, near the door, readjusting his tie for what must have been the twentieth time. May sat behind the table with her head bowed down and her arms crossed against her chest. The doily style table cloth that Margaret had dyed black and given to Chloe earlier that afternoon held her attention. It looked familiar and May was almost certain it was hers, so she only managed a low sign in reply to George's statement.

"Maybe my wisdom will fall on ears less stubborn?" George suggested. Not likely, May thought, I'm sure this is the cloth I used to have in my dinning room. She remembered that she had once given Margaret a set of keys to her house, just in case of emergencies. There would be raised voices later that evening, May promised herself as she looked up towards George.

"Are you still here?" George shrugged in silent reply and continued playing with his tie.

The silence that followed only spanned a few minutes before a soft tapping came from the door.

"Hello, is everything OK in there?" It was Barbara's voice toned down to a whisper. "We are about ready down here. Shall I send the first one up?"

"Oh...oh yes, please do" May's response wasn't immediate. She had slipped into a brief daydream and Barbara's voice had seemed like a distant interloper. It had been more of a memory than a dream, about a time in her life where everything had seemed just right.

She had met someone, someone special. It had been a purely accidental introduction that had caused some embarrassment to the other party. May had complained and the gentleman had apologised in no uncertain words. In a matter of seconds May had found herself twisting her opinion from one of disdain to one of admiration. It was the first time May had discovered that a foolish action didn't always require the participation of a fool.

He was carrying too much and hurrying unnecessarily; he wasn't watching where he was going. May had seen him approaching as she walked in her usual confident stride, central on the path with arms straight and swinging like two great pendulums. The pavement was narrow and damp from the recent rain but she had faith that her sensible shoes had sufficient grip. As they grew closer their eyes met. It had been a fleeting connection but it had proved enough to put them both off balance. He had stumbled and the three cardboard boxes he was carrying shifted in his arms but he swiftly regained his footing. He had then moved closer to the kerb to allow for room to pass. May strode onwards, her footing was stable but her perception wavered. She had felt disturbed by an unfamiliar sensation, it had left her light headed and feeling vulnerable. With only a few metres between them, the man had dropped one foot into the road where it became sodden in stale puddle. May strode onwards with her arms still swinging. May remembered the moment in slow motion. She knew that time had passed at a constant rate but, no matter how she tried, her mind couldn't speed up the event. Her left arm had caught the edge of one of the boxes which flew upwards, clipping the man's chin as it span passed his head and into the road behind him. He had tittered backwards on his heels and reached out in desperation. His hand caught May's wrist as it swung back down to her waist. May had then screamed. She still felt embarrassed by her reaction, even now after so many years had passed. The man had fallen backwards into the road, in reaction to May's regretfully shrill cry but his grip on her wrist remained unbroken. She had tumbled down after him until they had both ended up in a heap on the puddle strewn road. The man laid flat on his back and May had fallen across his chest at an angle. The shouting had begun almost immediately as May had struggled back to her feet. The apologies had taken more than a moment to arrive and were preceded by a series of buts. Never the less they had still passed his lips before he could stand. May had admired him for having the courage to admit when he was wrong and the modesty to repent while still lying on his back in a muddy puddle. A short but uplifting companionship had developed and Barbara had just dragged May from the memory of it.

May sat up straight and fixed her eyes on the door. Her stomach began to turn and a nervous feeling rose through her throat. She steeled herself and swallowed her anxiety. The sound of Barbara's retreating footsteps had faded and May listened intently for their return. George was silent and his tie, though slightly crocked, was now perfectly still. She glanced over at him and lifted her finger to her lips in a gesture that he should remain that way.

The footsteps soon came, becoming louder as they approached. A soft tap on the door and a light cough preceded Barbara's well rehearsed announcement.

"Madam Trump seer of the other worldly, I have a visitor here who wishes an audience".

May hadn't liked the script the first time she had heard it and it hadn't grown on her any in the meantime.

"You may enter if your mind is open and your heart is true". May didn't much like her own script either, what there was of it. As Barbara has suggested, May would be working off the cuff for the most part but a few choice phrases had been thrust upon her. Barbara had ensured her that it would lend a little professionalism to the proceedings.

The door slowly creaked open. Less light entered the room compared to the test séance, because the light bulb in the hallway had been changed with one of a much lower wattage. Barbara led in the first guest and quickly closed the door behind them. Barbara couldn't be blamed, even though she often boasted about her physic powers. She couldn't be expected to know that she had just closed the door in the face of her guest's dead counterpart. The ghost merged through the door behind them and took up its place just behind May. It moved swiftly and, in the poor light, May couldn't distinguish much more than silhouette.

Barbara showed the guest to the chair at the opposite side of the table and it was only then, in the faint light of candles, that May could see her clearly. A woman in her early thirties sat before her. She wore a pink knitted jumper which sported a small silver broach that resembled a woodpecker in mid-peck. Her hair was a light mousey brown which could have been a dark blonde but under the flickering light May found it hard to tell for sure. Her hands were meshed together on the table and her eyes were straining to see May's dummy through the dimness. Barbara moved over to May's end of the table and bent down until her mouth was level with the Dummy's, make-shift cauliflower, head.

"Come on, get on with it" She whispered through the corner of her mouth.

"What brings you to my parlour on this dark night?" May said, glad of the prompt but instantly regretting the use of the word parlour. The woman smiled and pointed towards the window.

"The number 46 bus, it stops right outside". May sighed; it was going to be a long night.

"No dear, I meant why have you come to see me," May explained in a level tone while inside she was screaming the same abusive language she would normally reserve for the Colin Farley show.

"Oh sorry" The woman squeaked, May guessed that she was blushing but couldn't confirm it.

"Well you see I'm interested in this kind of spooky supernatural stuff so when that nice old lady came knocking on my door I was kinda cool, yeah, up for it" Her hands waved as she spoke and slapped back down on the table with every pause. "And it'll be nice to speak to me Nan I guess, not that I'm holding my hopes up too high." A pause, a slap on the table. "I mean no offence of course".

"Then I will begin" May said, "And I hope you will leave here with a little more faith as well as the answers you seek". May spat out the words realising that faith was something she herself had never shown freely or often. If she had been in the woman's shoes a week ago she would have been shouting accusations and switching on lights by now.

"But I've not got any questions," the woman protested but May chose to ignore her.

"Are there any spirits among us who wish to speak to this woman before me," May said and a voice issued from behind her.

"I don't mind dear, before or after is all the same to me". May had not yet seen the ghost clearly but still thought that the family resemblance was uncanny.

"I have a spirit coming through now who wishes to convey a message" May announced to the room. Barbara gave May a thumbs up gesture and George leaned forward in his chair. May gestured to the ghost behind her to step forward and speak. There was a short pause.

"Oh you mean me!" The ghost cried before stepping forward to stand parallel with May. May could see her now. The ghost had probably been about May's age when she had died and her clothing suggested that this had only happened within the past decade.

"OK then here goes," The ghost announced. "My name is Anne Thompson and I've been dead for 8 years, Two months and seven days". May half expected to hear an applause.

"I stand here today to tell my granddaughter and namesake a terrible family secret". May repeated Anne's statement word for word and there was a synchronised gasp from both Barbara and the still breathing Anne Thompson.

"I have held onto this knowledge ever since my own mother confessed to me on her deathbed. I missed my opportunity to pass this burden on to my daughter so I must now skip a generation and confess our family sin to my dear little Anne". May relayed the message bit by bit as the late Anne spoke. Barbara was almost leaning over young Anne, which was unnerving the already disturbed woman. She was clearly shaken but was still hanging onto May's every word.

"This has not been easy for me, holding on to this vile secret. The amount of times I've just wanted to cry out and tell the world about this, is...well it's like...um, well it's a lot so it is". Everyone in the room, alive and otherwise, was eager for the late Anne to finally get to the point. Even May was now curious but not to the same extent as Barbara, who was almost salivating at the prospect of some real juicy gossip.

"After all this time I'm really not sure how to say this" Late Anne admitted. May relayed the message, apologized to the room and then turned to face the dithering ghost.

"Would you please get on with it," May concentrated to keep her voice from being heard by the living people present but still managed to produce a commanding tone. "You agreed to this meeting and all it entails. Now get on with it, we have other people waiting down stairs". May was surprised that none of the, so far, patent spirits hadn't floated in to see what the hold up was.

"Yes you're right, of course you are," The Late Anne seemed to gain a little substance, her shape became more defined. She spoke of her family's embarrassment and May, who had the least interest, felt disappointed as she repeated the confession for the benefit of the living.

"Your Grandmother has asked me to inform you of the truth behind your Great, Great Uncle Harold".

"Not Uncle Harry" Young Anne complained, her hands began to dance again. "He was a guiding star, a role model for generations of our family. He was an explorer, you know. Africa, Asia, the Middle East. He roamed through jungles and crossed desserts, alone and with no more than the pack on his back and the boots on his feet. He was a hero and still is a hero, to me at least". Her hands slapped back on the table and she glowed with genetic pride.

"Well that's not entirely true" May relayed Late Anne's responses. "He didn't actually leave the country; he never owned a passport in his life".

"But the stories?"

"All lies"

"But all those old photographs you showed me?"

"Mostly taken at London zoo and Brighton beach"

"No... This can't be. What about the time a lion mauled his leg?"

"Never happened".

"But I saw the pictures, I saw the scars".

"That was no lion. The scars were from when a ferret got trapped down his trouser leg".

"Oh my," Young Anne looked truly dejected. "I even named my hamster after him. I'll never be able to look little Harry in the eyes again". Tears began to flow and May wasn't sure if they were for her uncle or her hamster.

Chapter Twenty Three

The morning brought with it a sense of renewal for May. The evening had been a long and arduous one but she almost glowed inside with a feeling of achievement. Questions had been answered for many of the visitors, most of who had left with a new perspective on life. The spirits, some of whom had been waiting this opportunity for decades, were more than gracious in their admiration and gratitude. May had felt like some kind of celebrity, surrounded by the grateful dead. She felt useful and productive, which covered most bullet points in her working life ethic. Financial reward, payment for services rendered, covered the rest and May was eager to find out just how much money had been accumulated. A queue of happy customers had passed through her parlour, for want of a better word, and only a couple of sceptical guests had left with their eyes still blinkered. If their payments metered equally with their gratitude, May wouldn't have to do very many repeat performances to raise a substantial amount of money.

May could hear the bustle coming from the kitchen before she had even reached the top of the stairs. Barbara's voice was prominent but May could hear Deborah's softer tone filtering into the pauses.

"What do you mean?" Barbara was clearly unhappy about something. "But there were eight of them here last night". As May descended towards the hallway she could hear Margaret's voice grunting in agreement.

"I've counted it twice Babs," Deborah tried to explain, "It's all there apart from the I.O.U from young Miss Thompson". May began to hurry a little; she didn't like what she was hearing.

"Oh yes, poor dear, struggling on the bread line that one," Margaret pointed out. "She said something to me about paying by instalments; a pound a week I think she said".

"Hold on a minute, a pound a week, we're not giving out H.P here," Barbara said. "What's that all about; commune with the dead now and pay later".

"It makes us sound like some kind of T.V shopping channel". Victoria's voice, May had guessed that she was in there somewhere.

May entered the kitchen and saw the Thursday Night Club all seated around the table. They each had a half empty cup in front of them and an unopened family pack of biscuits acted as a centre piece. Chloe wasn't there and neither were Penny and Gary. Mr Kibbles was by the window trying to catch the net curtains, which were caught in a draft and swaying slightly. May took up her usual position by the fridge before announcing her arrival.

"What's going on in here," May barked. "Where's Chloe?" All four heads of the T.N.C turned towards her but it was only Deborah who jumped in her seat.

"Good morning May," Margaret said without the slightest quiver, she was obviously getting used to May's disembodied voice.

"Chloe has gone back to college," Barbara offered, "but she says she's only doing a half day. She said we can stop here for a bit and straighten a few doilies if need be". Deborah had regained her composure.

"I don't think I'll ever get used to this," she admitted with a wry smile. "I guess you want to hear the bad news May, as it was you who did all the hard work". Then she added, "On the night that is". Deborah opened a little account book that she had brought with her. It was black and leather bound, it showed signs of age and frequent usage.

"Here we are," she said after she fingered through a few pages. "Eight guests arrived, three paid in advance and two left in a storm of slamming doors having paid nothing. Out of the final three: one paid in full, one paid a half charge and Anne Thompson wants to sign up for some kind of finance agreement".

"What do you mean by a half charge, besides, I thought it was all going to be cash upfront".

"It was May but nobody who came last night has money to spare for extravagances," Margaret pointed out. "Take Mr Wilson, he's only got his pension. He admitted to me that he won't be able to join his friends for their weekly dominoes game in the Hare and Trebuchet this week because of last night, and he only paid half".

"She's right May," Deborah agreed, "It's a small town and none too prosperous at the moment".

"This ain't the big city," Victoria piped up, "You won't find none of those yuppie types around here, believe me I've looked". She suddenly looked dejected.

"All a girl can expect around here is a meat pie and a matinee at the local picture house. I tart up my face and wear my best frock but where doe's it get me, no where near a candle lit Bucks Fizz I can tell you".

"I thought you didn't like candles!" Barbara said.

"No Babs, I just don't like your candles".

May was praising herself on another wise decision as she remembered how Margaret had once invited her to one of their Thursday night get-to-gethers. There wasn't any real risk of her going but she found it comforting that her unsociable attitude had served her well on occasion. Since her death she had discovered an unusual need for company which had made her doubt her life choices. May smiled; sometimes it was good to play the witch.

"Stop babbling the lot of you," May barked. Deborah jumped in her seat again as all heads turned towards the fridge.

"For a start Victoria you're no ordinary girl, not any more. You're an old girl and the sooner you realise that your courting days are behind you the better". Victoria placed both her hands, palms down, on the table and stood up from her chair.

"I'll have you know I've got hoards of men clambering over each other for my attention," Victoria protested. She seemed to take little offence with May's remarks but still showed a need to protect her own sense of honour.

"There's life in this old girl yet". May was, in a small way, beginning to like Victoria. She was a harlot in surgical stockings but she had a fire inside not unlike her own.

"It's hardly appropriate to discus life in front of a ghost like that," Margaret bellowed in May's defence. May hadn't even noticed the connection between Victoria's statement and her own situation. There's no life left in this old girl, May thought but there's still plenty of fire.

"Some people have no respect for the dead Marge," May said while watching Victoria squirm in her seat, clearly unable to muster any words that would cast her in a more favourable light. Margaret grunted in agreement. An expression, usually reserved for scolding young children, drew across her face and was aimed directly at Victoria.

"Bu...Bu...But I didn't mean," Victoria stuttered, "I...I wasn't making any". Her head drooped and she slowly sat back down.

"Sod it, whatever," she muttered under her breath.

"Barbara forget the candles they're spiritually redundant. If they help the living so be it but as far as the dead are concerned, they're pointless". Barbara opened her mouth as if to speak but remained silent as May continued.

"Right Deborah, if you've quite finished hopping about at my every word, how much money have we made? How many more of these séances do we need to perform before we hit target? So to speak". Deborah took a deep breath before consulting her little black book.

"I reckon we only need to do another ten or so". May was surprised, only another ten. That's not too bad, she thought. Deborah looked at he book again and nodded to herself

"Yes I'm sure we will have enough money to get the roof fixed after ten," she cracked a little smile.

"Ten just to get the roof fixed!" May exclaimed, "What about all the rest? If it was only about the roof you could have just held a whip round and saved all this bother".

"All in good time May," Deborah offered, her smile was beginning to droop at the corners. "We shouldn't rush things, its early days".

"Early days! This is only a temporary arrangement; I'm not planning to make a career out of this!" May started to pace around the kitchen, waving her hands in great unseen gestures. Deborah took the opportunity to hide in her book while Barbara looked over at Margaret and gave her a double upward palm shrug. Margaret returned the shrug and mouthed a silent "What!"

"You probably think that just because I'm dead I've got nothing better to do," May accused as she paced by the draining board, causing four heads to twist towards her with whip-lashing speed. "I've got plenty of things I could be getting on with. Being a ghost isn't just wandering around and shaking chains you know. There's so much been put aside for this".

"Are you pacing about again May?" Margaret asked as she rubbed her neck. "I think you made me pull something. I've told you before about angry pacing at your age; it can't be good for your blood pressure". Then she added in a quieter voice, as if merely thinking aloud, "Come to think of it you've not got any blood any more so I guess its alright now and I doubt you'll wear a hole in the carpet either". She formed a nervous grin, "Small blessings eh!"

"And you moan at me about respecting the dead," Victoria had found her voice again. May stopped pacing. She had made a promise that was turning out to be more of a commitment than she had first realised. It was still a promise, regardless of her own expectations. It was going to take a lot of time and patience. Time she had, patience was still a work in progress.

"Well I've known her a lot longer than you have," Margaret excused but then added after a pause, "Yes maybe you're right. Sorry May dear, you know how my mouth runs away with it's self".

"Never mind about it Marge," May said, her witches hat always appeared to slip off where Margaret was concerned. May could think bad things about her and feel justified but when it came down to speaking her mind in front of Margaret the censors worked overtime.

"OK how long for everything? How many séances before Chloe is set up for the next few years, at least until she's finished with her education and can support herself that is?" A silence followed May's speech; it was Deborah who finally broke it.

"That's not an easy one to answer I'm afraid," and she looked it. "There are too many variables to calculate for an exact time frame but I reckon it will run pretty much parallel, week by week, if you know what I mean".

"Week by week!" May barked, her hat was securely back on her head. "Are you saying it's going to take years?"

"Eh...well yes", Deborah stuttered a reply. May silently screamed in frustration. The atmosphere in the kitchen suddenly thickened and Mr Kibbles scooted from the room.

"I think it's time to open those biscuits," Margaret offered.

Chapter Twenty Four

The great iron gates were fused open by rust and time as he drove through. He kept the speed of his car down to a creep as he passed over the weed infested gravel. The grounds were vast and unkempt. Lines of trees guarded the long driveway on both sides; some were half toppled and seemed to be dead or dieing. His attention was drawn straight ahead as the building hove into view. Three stories high and about one hundred foot long. The orphanage must have looked majestic at one time, he thought. Years of neglect and abandonment had seen half its windows broken. Its walls showed signs of damp amongst the infestation of ivy. The stone was cracked and crumbling, like wrinkles on the face of an old man.

He saw Mr Jones's white Ford Escort van parked just outside the main entrance. He pulled in behind it and switched of his engine. He gathered up his paperwork, which was spread over the passenger seat and shovelled it back into his briefcase.

Richard Cole had worked for Jackson's for fifteen years. He had been only eighteen years old when he had first joined the company as an office junior and had spent the following two years mostly making coffee and photocopying. He watched and he learned until he became what he was now, the company's third best probate investigator.

Being only third best, in his boss's opinion, didn't worry Richard any. He was the company's youngest investigator by a clear ten years. Only experience, or the lack of it, held him on the runner up's plinth. Academically, he considered himself the better man but he had too much respect for the others to voice his opinion. He had taken on this particular project because it was so fresh on the list that he was sure that none of the competing companies had picked up on it yet. He was hoping for a fast turn around to impress his boss and maybe raise himself in his opinion.

Richard locked his car and walked towards the main entrance of the orphanage with his briefcase tucked securely under his arm. The three stone steps that led up to the large open doors showed fresh footprints in the dry dirt and dust. Richard climbed the steps and entered the building; he guessed that Mr Jones's was already inside waiting for him.

It was darker than he had expected, the only light was filtering in from the open doorway. Particles of dust infested the air around him as he walked carefully down the entrance hallway. The was an old iron wheelchair laying on it's side partially blocking his way and he fancied he saw it's upturned wheel move slightly in the poor light. There was wooden sign hanging from the ceiling by two short chains which indicated that the reception was further ahead. Richard gingerly continued forward and the light grew dimmer the further into the orphanage he went. He stopped dead and turned his head sharply left, causing his ear to face forward. There was a sound, a low rasping, he could have sworn he heard it. A moments silence then again the sound erupted, he could hear snoring. Richard faced forward again and continued walking. Peering ahead into the dimness he could just make out the shape of the main reception. A few metres closer and he saw the two booted feet resting on top of the curved wooden counter.

Mr Jones awoke on the first shoulder shake and almost fell off the swivel chair he had been sleeping on. Richard had tried shouting at first but the snoring only turned into snorts and splutters before returning to its regular gurgle. He had reluctantly resorted to the gentle shoulder shake. He had heard of people claiming for assault over less, which was why he panicked when Mr Jones flailed about in the chair to gain his balance.

"Hells bells Ricky, you trying to put me in an early grave

son?" Mr Jones stood up from the chair which snapped upright once relieved of the man's weight. He was in his mid sixties and had grown a little large around the waist over the past ten years or so. He often referred to it as his spare tyre and would tell stories of how he had been an amateur footballer in his youth.

"It started as soon as I quit playing" he was known to say, "I was a lean mean goal scoring machine before then".

"Sorry Mr Jones, I was trying to be gentle," Richard apologised. He looked at the man in front of him. He was wearing his usual blue dungarees over a grease stained tee-shirt that must have once been white, Richard had never seen him wearing anything else.

"Never mind boy," Mr Jones replied with a smile. "Now then, you'll be wanting to see the records room I reckon". Mr Jones pointed towards a room behind him.

"That's why I'm here," Richard replied but Mr Jones had already turned around and began walking into the room. Richard shrugged and then followed.

The records room was small, only a desk and four filing cabinets filled it leaving little space between. Mr Jones was already getting comfortable on the chair behind the small desk. He'll have his feet up and be snoring again soon, Richard thought.

"If whatever you're here for is here it'll be in here," Mr Jones said cryptically. "Help yourself and don't mind me". Richard placed his briefcase on the end of the desk and then pulled out a few sheets of paper.

"Who is it today?" Mr Jones asked; he had his head laid back and his eyes closed. "Anyone I know?" Richard shuffled the papers in his hands until they were in order.

"Miss May Elizabeth Trump," He read out loud from the top sheet. "Only died a week or so ago but I'm chasing this one early before any of the other firms get hold of it".

"Trump eh?" Mr Jones said. His feet were not yet on top of the desk but stretched out beneath. "Rings no bells with me that one son. I told you about how I was caretaker here back before it was closed down and all those kids were sent off to foster homes and such?"

"You have on many occasions," Richard replied as he flicked through the papers in his hand. He was trying to familiarise himself of key details before delving into the dusty file cabinets.

"So I don't need to tell you how I've seen a good many strange goings on between these walls do I. You know about it all by now do you? Our little talks we've had while scurrying around in old council buildings. There's been more going on than I can tell you in a few short sittings son, a good deal more". Mr Jones stretched out his arms and yawned, all the while his eyes remained closed. "I won't waste good snoozing time if you're not interested, though it could be connected with that case of yours. Wake me up when your finished son". Richard sighed and opened the closest filing cabinet, the metal draw squealed on its runners.

"There's some oil in the van if you need it," Mr Jones murmured as he folded his arms over his belly.

"No need thank you".

The draw was tightly packed with cardboard folders, each labelled with a name. He fingered through, blowing the dust from a few, trying to find the right name. Some of the folders were so full of papers that they were splitting down the sides; some had been roughly repaired with tape and staples. He had soon exhausted the first drawer and pulled out another. Mr Jones began to snore.

Richard moved on to the next cabinet and started rifling through the tightly packed files. He occasionally held his breath, as he pulled out a dusty file where the name looked suspiciously like the one he was searching for. After the dust had been cleared, it turned out to be another red herring. Undeterred he carried on searching. He rummaged through every cabinet and every drawer in the small room while Mr Jones's rumbling snore was the only thing that reminded him that he was not there alone.

Forty minutes later, while running through the first filing cabinet for a second time, Richard discovered the folder. It was so thin that Richard thought it was empty, when it first caught his eye. It was tightly wedged between two, full to bursting, file folders. He squeezed it out to the sound of tearing cardboard, as the two adjacent folders finally began split under the pressure of their overload of files. He blew the dust from the flimsy folder and there, scrawled in black ink, was the name May Elizabeth Trump. Richard carefully opened it and a solitary sheet of paper slipped out. It swooped between his legs and settled on the floor just under the desk. He looked back into the folder, it was now empty. It was a lot less than he had hoped for.

Richard slipped the folder back into the file cabinet long ways so that it protruded like a book mark. He used one hand to support himself on the desk while he bent down to pick up the solitary sheet of paper. The desk began to wobble as it took his weight. Mr Jones's snoring began to splutter like an engine running on fumes; spittle escaped his lips and began to trickle down his chin. Richard retrieved the paper and pushed himself back upright. Mr Jones yawned and then slowly opened one eye.
"Are you done yet son?" He asked as he wiped away the drool with the palm of his hand.
"Almost," Richard replied, as he laid the sheet of paper on the desk. Mr Jones sat upright in his chair; he had both eyes open now.
"What you got there then?"
"It's the only thing I could find regarding Miss Trump," Richard began reading out loud. "Orphan registration form. Name May Elizabeth Trump, Previous address unknown. Next of kin Mrs A. Collins, brackets, maternal aunt".
"Did you say Collins son, Mrs Collins?"
   "That's what it says here," Richard pointed at the sheet of paper on the desk.
   "Mrs Collins eh. Now that's a name I know. I'll always remember Annie Collins, she's not someone I'm ever likely

to forget son". Mr Jones looked up to the ceiling and crossed himself. "She put the fear of God in me and no mistake".

Chapter Twenty Five

May looked out of the bedroom window. Mr Kibbles was outside in the garden, trying to catch something alive. May couldn't see his latest prey but she was sure that it was unaware of the slinking ginger tom cat. The bushes in front of him rustled causing the cat to stop still. He began to wiggle his haunches, which May recognised as his usual prelude to pouncing. The bush rustled again and May could just make out the twitching nose of a field mouse. There was no doubt in her mind that Mr Kibbles had also seen it, as he didn't hesitate to act. With surprising speed and grace, he launched himself into the air. May watched in amusement, as he disappeared into the bush without a sound or disturbance any living thing should hear. To May's amazement the field mouse scurried out of the bush, as if its life depended on it and burrowed beneath the tripod base of bird table. Mr Kibbles burst out of the bush seconds later, wide eyed with his fur puffed out like a big ginger pompom. He stood still with his back arched and his tail swishing, his eyes were glued to the tall wooden bird table. It must be a coincidence, May thought. She considered the possibility: the mouse can't see Mr Kibbles it must have been spooked by something else, something living. She watched on, so mesmerised that she didn't hear Penny calling for her from downstairs.

Mr Kibbles began to circle the bird table, moving closer with each revolution. May couldn't see the mouse but she was sure it was still buried in the loose dirt. A sudden flash of brown darted through the short wooden legs. May watched as the mouse scurried across the lawn with Mr Kibbles hot on its tail. Drawing closer, Mr Kibbles leapt into the air and landed just to the right of his quarry. The mouse made a sharp left turn, directly away from the pursuing cat.

"A psychic field mouse?" May blurted aloud. She hadn't even considered that such a small creature could be blessed, or cursed, with such sight. Were there little mouse

séances going on under the floorboards in the dead of
night. May tossed the thought aside.

"You're going senile old girl having thoughts like that,"
She muttered to herself. The idea of mice in commune with
the dead made her feel ludicrous but it gave life to a
further thought. Where were all the dead mice? Where
were the ghosts of all the animals?

It hadn't occurred to her until then. Where were birds?
They die don't they? Where were their spirits? The rabbits,
the badgers and even the foxes? There were plenty of living
ones in the area. They had tipped her bins over on more
than one occasion, so why wasn't she seeing dead foxes.
Animals had spirits that roamed the earth after death, she
was sure of it, how else can you explain the existence of Mr
Kibbles. Where were all the others? What was so special
about Mr Kibbles? Then she remembered George's dog,
whose name she didn't care to remember, George's ghost
dog. There's nothing special about a scruffy ginger tom cat,
she decided, except to me. He had turned up at her door
looking friendly and almost familiar. She had let him in and
spent the next fourteen years lugging tins of 'Kibbles Cat
Chunks' home with the weekly shopping. He wasn't special,
he was just hers. Even so, where were all the others?

"There you are! I've been calling for ages". Penny's head
protruded through the bedroom door, it looked detached
and levitating. May drew herself away from the window
and watched Penny as she fully entered the room.

"People are already here! Victoria is entertaining them in
the lounge at the moment". Penny sighed. "She's been on
the sherry again, so I don't know how long it will be before
she offends someone". May put her thoughts to one side
and promised herself more time to ponder on the lack of
wild-death later. She could hear voices rising through the
floorboards, now that she was more locally focused.
Unfamiliar voices droned submissively around a loud
cackle. Victoria was in full flourish, May surmised, a second
bottle of wine was probably already open.

"Where's everyone else?"

"They're all down there, last I saw," Penny explained. "Margaret is helping Chloe in the kitchen and Barbara is pottering around, adjusting doilies and such. Deborah is in charge of greeting the guests but Victoria has muscled in and pushed her to one side. Deborah's protests are being drowned out to a mere squeak, it's frustrating to watch".

"Deborah is hardly the best choice of host, I must agree with that but Victoria spins the coin way too far the other way". May stepped up to the door.

"I guess I will have to go down there and sort it all out!" She barked as she passed through the door, Penny hurried after her.

"You can't go down there shouting orders all over the place".

"It's what needs doing," May started down the staircase, "Someone has to shake that bunch up and you don't have the voice for it".

"But what if one of the guests hears you? It'll be the shock of their lives, hearing a disembodied voice shouting the odds at a drunken pensioner". May stopped still, Penny had a point. Not only would it take a bucket load of explaining but, if they still hung around afterwards, they would surely recognise her voice at the séance. It would breed mistrust and no mistake, May realised. They would begin to suspect that they were being hoodwinked. This would be true, if only with a positive slant. They had come to speak with the dead through a living medium. May had accepted this deception as merely cutting out the middle man.

"How else do we sort this out?" May shrugged. Penny stood at the top of the stairs with one hand gently caressing the stress from her temple.

"I was hoping you would have an idea," she admitted. May didn't know what to do as her mind was still full of dead animals. She made an effort to clear her head but a fresh plan still failed to emerge.

Barbara's sudden arrival at the bottom of the stairs

promised the solution.

"Babs, what's going on down there?" May called, her voice was only just above a whisper. Barbara started to climb the stairs.

"Are you there May?" she asked as she scanned the top of the staircase. "I was just on my way up to see if you were ready for the first guest".

A door opened in the hallway below and Victoria staggered out. She clutched onto the door frame and shouted back into the room.

"You just stay right there handsome while I fetch another bottle". She waved her free hand at the doorway and stumbled across the hallway towards the kitchen. She glanced up at the staircase and leaned against the wall by the kitchen door.

"Hello Babs," She called, her voice was slurred. "Its all good down here; I've got them eating out of my hands I have". I hope she means figuratively, May thought as she watched Victoria use the door frame to swing herself into the kitchen.

"Hello girls, now where has that wine gone?" There was a loud crash, like the sound of a chair toppling over, followed by the tinkle of broken glass.

"I'll deal with this!" Barbara said; her voice was tinged with annoyance. "I'll send the first one up as soon as I can". Barbara headed back down the stairs. Chloe's voice crackled from the kitchen. May sensed a temper on the boil behind the tone. She didn't see Penny in that voice, someone else had lent Chloe that particular trait.

May took up her usual position at the table in the séance room. She could still hear raised voices filtering up through the floorboards. It was a mesh of shrill tones. No discernable words reached May's ears but the sense of anger was unmistakable. Victoria had gone too far, May realised. She had drunk more wine than usual, which was no easy task and allowed herself to lose what little control she would normally cling on to. May didn't know what had made Victoria stoop even further into, what she considered to be, the slippery slope of depravity but there was little chance of an acceptable excuse. She had been hitting on her clients. Her reputation could become tarnished; people would lose respect for her. Séances were supposed to be a sombre affair; there was no need for a warm up act. People came to her hoping to speak with their departed loved ones. They didn't expect to get chatted up by the oldest hussy in town.

The raised voices faded to a barely audible hum. The room was dark; the door was closed and the candles had yet to be lit. May felt the presence for only a moment before she heard the voice.

"How much longer is this all going to take?" The voice rasped. It was deep and coarse, like rubbing two pieces of sandpaper together; May felt it as much as heard it.

"I should be speaking to my ex-wife by now; at least that's what I was told". The voice came from the far corner of the room, close to the window. May turned to face the voice but she could only see a faint, shifting shadow that seemed to sway from side to side like a sapling in a gentle breeze.

"There has been a slight delay I'm afraid," May announced. The shadow began to gain clarity; a shape was slowly emerging. May felt a chill stretch the length of her spine, as she remembered the event in the other realm; the encounter in the forest. The shadow drew into its self; something was forming inside the swaying darkness. May took short, shallow breaths. Her mind span with visions of shadowy fingers clawing at her body and dragging her downwards. The still lingering fear of a waiting, darkened underworld mixed reality with dark imaginings. A silhouetted figure emerged from the swirling shadow. May's panicked mind saw talons of slick, oily mist reaching towards her. Sharpened claws glinted in a nonexistent light; an unknown fluid dripped from their points.

May released a guttural scream that seemed to tug at the pit of her stomach, as if to pull her innards out through her own, widely stretched, mouth. Hands suddenly gripped her shoulders and a blinding light encompassed the room. Voices filled the air around her as her eyes slowly adjusted.

"I gather that all is not well May?" It was George's voice, it was calm and compassionate. May turned her head to see George standing behind her; it was his hands on her shoulders.

"May dear, are you in here?" Margret stood in the doorway; her hand was still on the light switch. Barbara stood beside and a little behind her.

"We heard an almighty scream," Barbara said, "It's set the visitors off into a real tizzy".

"Get your hands off me!" May barked at George, who took a step backwards. His hands slithered off her shoulders. May was beginning to get her focus back. The room was still blurred and her heart was pumping faster than it should. Her reaction had been half conscious and half instinct. The physical contact felt unnatural to her, unexpected and unwanted.

"As you wish," George surrendered. "I intend only aid in my actions".

"Who's got their dirty mitts on you May," Margret shouted into the room. "I'll...I'll," she stuttered. She had clearly realised that anything that could touch May was way beyond her own limited control. "I'll get Babs to do something mystic," she threatened, pulling out a barely conceivable retaliation plan.

"It's alright Marge," May reassured. "Go and see to the guests and send the first one up as soon as you can".

"That's if they're still down there," Barbara piped up, "you gave them quite a fright. I wouldn't be surprised if they've run for the hills by now".

"Leave it alone Babs," Margret produced a box of matches from her pocket and handed them to Barbara.

"I was only saying! You didn't see the look on Harry Dermott's face when May let loose". Barbara took the matches and started lighting the various candles scattered around the room. May had forgotten about the candles but realised that Barbara was unlikely to do the same. Barbara lit the last candle and retreated from the room.

"Good luck May," Margret said as she switched the light off and closed the door.

May looked back towards the corner by the window; a tall figure returned her gaze.

"I'm sorry to have frightened you," it was the same rasping voice she had heard from the shifting shadow. The figure stepped closer and, as her eyes adjusted to the candlelight, May could see him more clearly. He looked down at her with half closed eyes as if straining to focus. His face was wrinkled and saggy like a basset hound, only a few grey hairs adorned his head. He looked to be almost seven foot tall and as thin as a dry twig. His grey suit, at least three sizes too big, hung off him like damp washing on a clothes line.

"I've hidden myself away from everything for so many years that my spirit had lost cohesion. It's been quite a struggle to resume my human form".

"What on earth were you thinking?" May stood up from her chair, "creeping up on a person like that. It's got to be rude or something similar to greet people without form. It must be like running around naked, in public, for all to see". May's stomach was still spinning but she allowed her self to believe it was due to social disgust rather than fear.

"I never thought of it that way. I guess all these years spent alone have taken their toll. I haven't had to present myself to anyone for such a long time". His shrug was barley visible under the draping suit. "It's almost as if the mess you first saw is the real me now. I guess I'm going to have to keep an eye on that from now on".

"A familiar voice, if I'm not mistaken?" George stepped around May and wagged his finger. The thin man squinted, until his eyes were merely slits. George stepped closer.

"Wilfred?" George said, "I do believe you're Wilfred Brown"

"Yes I am and who might you be?"

"George Sebastian Tailor, at your service. I accompanied a Mr Gary Reed, when he addressed to your grave regarding the service Miss Trump is offering here. Your voice merely issued from beneath the dirt. You failed to appear before us but your voice suffers from some distinction".

"Well that's what you get left with when you die of throat cancer. Even after death, I can't be rid of such reminders". May sat back down and watched as George shook Wilfred's hand, she half expected it to come away in his grasp.

"Alright you two," May said. "I don't expect any more scares tonight. I've got a lot of work to get through".

"It will be as you ask May," George agreed. "We will be as mute as the proverbial critter, unless such a need should arise that should require us to behave otherwise". He directed Wilfred back to the corner of the room, before retaking his previous position behind May.

A brief silence followed. May didn't like thinking of it as a ghostly silence but it was technically a true description. A soft tapping on the door broke it regardless.

"We seek the wisdom of the great seer of spirits, Madam Trump". Barbara was putting on her best circus voice. It sounded as if she was announcing the arrival of The Great Gonzo and his dancing fleas.

"You may enter," May replied with far less theatrics. The door slowly opened and the room became a little brighter. Barbara led a nervous looking man up to the table and motioned for him to sit. May figured that he was in his late forties, if he had been younger he must have been through some troubling times. His face was round and his skin blotchy. His hair was still in the process of going gray and thinning quite dramatically at the crown. He wore a tweed jacket that almost fitted. The arms showed wear that didn't coincide with his elbows; he was obviously a second user. His arms were resting on the table and his hands were so tightly clenched that his knuckles had turned white. He offered May's dummy a nervous smile.

"What brings you before me?" May asked with half hearted theatrics. Barbara nodded and stepped backwards towards the door.

"I was told that you had the power to let me speak with my mother, God rest her soul". The nervous man replied as Barbara pulled the door closed, dropping the room back into its previous gloomy state.

"Yes, what you heard is true," May explained. "My gift of sight will allow you to converse with your mother. This does not mean you can speak directly to her, however, I will act as a conduit between you". If your mother is present, May thought, no spirit had arrived with the man. She was beginning to wonder where it had got to and what could be more important to a ghost than the opportunity to communicate with those they had left behind.

"What is your name?" May asked, playing for a little time.

"My name is Harry Dermott and my mother's name is...was Janet, Janet Dermott". Harry pulled a tartan handkerchief from his jacket pocket and wiped away the specks of sweat, which had begun to form on his forehead.

"Very good," May acknowledged.

"Is she here? Is she here right now, in this room?" Harry asked and May couldn't help wishing that she was.

"It's not yet clear, whether your mother is among us or not". May walked the thin line between truth and lies. "My sight is blurred with shadows and smoke". She was still holding onto the truth; she could smell the candles burning. "I have hope that it will all become clear soon enough". George leant forward so that his mouth was, uncomfortably, close to May's ear.

"I could journey under floor," He suggested. "Of the many souls beneath our feet, one may shine a light on her location". May nodded in silent response.

"Very well, I will endeavour to be swift". George sank effortlessly through the floor, leaving May with jealous thoughts. I still can't do that!

"Is everything alright?" Wilfred asked, as he stepped out of the corner. May used the opportunity to fine tune the truth again.

"I have spirits around me wishing to speak," May

explained to Harry, "But your mother is not among them".
Harry brought out his handkerchief, wiped his forehead
again and then gave May's dummy a puzzled look.

"Let me get this right. Are you telling me that I can't
speak to my mother now?"

"I'm sorry to say this but if she's not here there's not a
whole lot I can do about it".

"If the ghost of my mother really existed, I have no doubt
that she would be here". Harry shook his fist at May, his
handkerchief still gripped between his fingers. It was as if
he was waving a small tartan flag at her, which diluted the
assertiveness of the gesture some what.

"I should expect she's been held up somewhere". May
held her temper as best she could. "I'm sure she would be
here if she could, she might just be running late". May spat
the words out with little grace. The sentiment was there
but her tone sounded far from genuine.

"That's one possibility I guess". Harry's nervous
disposition seemed to dissolve, slowly being upstaged by
anger and mistrust. "Another theory I have... is that
maybe...maybe you can't speak to my mother
because...because you don't have any special gifts". His
statement stuttered a little, before his nervousness finally
took a back seat and his speech gained momentum.
"Maybe you're just a fraud, a con artist, someone who's
just out there to take advantage of the lonely and grief
stricken. He stood sharply from his chair but his hands
remained, palm down, on the table. "Maybe...maybe you're
just a liar!"

"How dare you!" May stood up as well, not that Harry
could see and shook her fist. "You call me a fraud! Me, of
all people, a fraud?"

"Now I think we should all calm down," Barbara
suggested as she stepped towards the table.

"Calm down? Did you hear what he just called me? A liar,
me!"

"I just think that, maybe, there's been some kind of
misunderstanding here," Barbara said.

"I'm being taken for a fool here; I'm being conned," Harry

said, turning towards Barbara. "I don't know what part you're playing in this charade but you're just as guilty as your phoney medium over here". Harry pointed towards May's dummy, "See how she doesn't even move as she talks. No emotion, it's like she's reading from a script, it's all part of your elaborate scam!"

"I assure you its no scam," Wilfred offered from the far corner. It was a pointless gesture as May was the only one who could hear him.

"Believe me when I tell you, this is not a trick. Madam Trump really can speak to ghosts, in fact I reckon she finds it easier than talking to the living". Barbara used a calming tone but it didn't appear to be working.

"Believe you!" Harry sputtered. "How can I believe you when you don't offer any proof?" May strode around the table until she was standing, up close, behind Harry.

"You want proof?" She screamed directly into his right ear, "how's this for proof?" Harry spun around on the spot, his handkerchief slipped from his grasp as his hands slid away from the table.

"What the heck!" Harry cried as he stared into, what was from his perspective, empty space.

"Is this proof enough?" May had snuck behind him again. Harry turned back towards the table; his nervous expression was beginning to reform. He slowly backed towards the door. His head twitched from side to side as he searched for an explanation in the flickering shadows. He bumped into the door and, like a pair of spiders trying to escape a bath tub, his hands scurried around the wooden surface behind him. With his eyes fixed firmly ahead, his hand gripped the door handle. In one fluid movement he opened the door, slipped through into the light beyond and then slammed it shut behind him.

"That wasn't very fair May, now was it," Barbara said. Her hands were clasped to her hips but she showed a wry smile. "He won't be back, I'd bet money on it".

Chapter Twenty Six

George slipped through the door only moments after Harry had closed it.

"He moves with much haste," He said, using his thumb to gesture behind him.

"I'm sure he does," May acknowledged. "Did you find out anything?"

"Who are you talking to now?" Barbara asked.

"George, I told you about George?"

"George...George," Barbara pondered. "Oh yes, the harbinger on doom".

"That's hardly a fair description," George protested. "I must agree that it is a common misconception, however, I was not aware that the living shared in the delusion".

"What do you expect? All she's heard about you has come from me and I'm not one for sugar coating the truth. You hardly come across as the life of the party. You're every other word could be loosely translated as 'We're doomed!' It's almost as if you're the ghost of Frazier".

"Who?"

"Barbara, you had best be sending the next one up".

"Oh yes of course". Barbara replied, before stepping out of the room. May waited for the door to close.

"Did you find out anything downstairs?"

"Who's Frazier?"

"It's not important, where did Janet get to?"

"That much remains unclear. Of those within earshot, none could speak clear of her current location. An admission by Sandra Cummings, places her whereabouts three days back. News more recent was not on offer to me".

"Sandra Cummings?"

"Your paths have yet to cross I gather, though it matters not." He waved his hand dismissively and started pacing up and down. "I accompanied Mr Reed at the broach of your offer to Mrs Dermott and it appeared to appease her; she delivered an animated reaction. I fathom not, any reason that could alter her enthusiastic disposition to any remarkable degree. Such a deduction leaves me with little else to ponder on the matter. My grave suspicion draws me to conclude that she has been waylaid beyond her choice or control; she is now of the taken".

"Of the taken?"

"As grievous a truth as it is May, she has played as quarry for The Stalkers".

"What absolute drivel!" Wilfred stepped out of the corner, wagging his bony finger at George. "I'll have no talk of such fairytales around me. I've heard about you and your ghouls; your Dark Spirits. I've been warned about you and your tendency to blather about creepy figures who roam wild in the night. If it's not bad enough just being dead, you would like us to shiver at the sight of our own shadow".

"What knowledge of merit do you possess," George replied, "he who lay buried through choice. No news have you, not acquired through eavesdropping on those who pass you by".

"You only hear the truth when no one knows you're listening".

"The truth as only they believe for themselves. A blinkered truth and you are as the fool who follows".

"Stop bickering you two," May scolded. "It's not going to help anyone". May stepped in-between them and used both her arms in a gesture of holding them apart

"I merely act in defence of honour. I refuse to stand mute beneath such bombardment".

"In that case you can take it outside. I don't want to be listening to it. You're only here because I allow it. This is my séance, my show and my rules". May turned to face Wilfred, "and you can go with him, if you can't keep it buttoned!" She still hadn't forgiven him for scaring her earlier.

"That's hardly fair!"

"If you don't like it you can crawl back under the dirt where you came from!" May stared directly in his eyes, as much to try to convince herself that she held no fear of him, as to hammer her statement home.

"Ok...ok, alright," Wilfred held his hands at chest height. His palms were facing towards May, as if to indicate a white flag moment. "I certainly don't wish to cause any offence and I most definitely don't want to miss out on the opportunity tonight represents but I can't stand silent in the presence of this scare monger".

"Scare monger? What ludicrous..." George began in response but May quickly shot him down into silence with a sharp stare and stern finger gesture.

"Sshh your noise!" May hissed, before turning back to face Wilfred. "If you can't keep quiet, I must ask you to leave".

"Very well Miss Trump," Wilfred surrendered as he backed away towards the darkened corner. "Not a further word will I utter". He merged back into the shadows, "until it is my turn to address the living of course".

"That's all I ask". May walked back around to her usual place at the table, George followed close behind.

"Her absence is of The Stalkers work. This much is undeniable in my mind; neither is she the first to fall fail in recent times. They grow ever more active in the passing of a few moons and the cries for the lost add proof to this". May just sighed in response.

"I sense that doubt still endures within your thoughts and this brings grief to me. They make feast of the sceptical and flourish in pools of denial". May didn't openly acknowledge his words but she agreed with the reasoning behind them. She was a ghost and most of the living would deny her own existence because they didn't understand and were helpless to affect her; how was this any different? Here she was, a dead spirit drifting around the living realm acting sceptical about the things she doesn't understand, it was almost hypocritical. She used to say that it was naive to believe in such things. Now, she was beginning to realise, it was naive not to.

A soft tapping on the door drew May out of her thoughts.

210

She shook her head gently to focus herself on the task ahead. The evening had not started well; she hoped the next spirit turned up at least.

"We seek an audience with Madam Trump," Barbara's voice, from the other side of the door. "We wish to employ her gift of vision".

"Please enter," May replied, "with an honest heart and an open mind". It was another of Barbara's suggested phrases. The door crept open and a woman, not much younger than May had been before her death, followed Barbara into the room. Her hair was a dark blonde but it had obviously been dyed that colour. Grey strands mingled with the blonde, like so many weeds in a flower bed. Time had been kinder to her face than it had to May's but no amount of creams and potions could prevent every sign of age. Even in the poorly lit room, the thick layer of foundation failed to hide all the wrinkles. As the woman sat down at the table, May realised that she was possibly more than ten years her senior.

"Welcome to my... welcome," May greeted, unable to force herself to say 'parlour' again.

"Thank you," the lady smiled, "I've been told that someone from beyond the grave wishes to speak to me".

"That is correct," May didn't actually know; she hadn't been involved in the recruitment process. In fact, she realised, she wasn't involved in half of the preparation work. She made a mental note, to at least acknowledge the effort the others had put in. Even George had been giving Gary a helping hand with locating spirits with an interest in availing themselves of May's unique service. "If you could please tell me your name, it would help in locating the appropriate spirit".

"I know what her name is," Wilfred growled from the corner.

"Yes of course," The lady replied, unaware of Wilfred's statement. "My name is Cynthia Smythe". Wilfred stepped out of the shadows, his arms waving and his teeth clenched.

"That's not her name!" He barked, "She's Cynthia Brown,

My wife!"

"I think I have someone coming through now," May said to Cynthia. Wilfred stood next to his wife and leaned over her.

"You even discarded my name. Smythe? Why the heck to you call yourself Smythe? That's not even your maiden name". He looked up at May, "I want you to tell her, from me, that she's an evil cow and I wish she was dead. Just so I can tell her in person just how frickin' much I hate her".

"Are you sure you want me to say that? She is your wife after all, there's no need to start this séance off with insults".

"No need!" Wilfred growled with his teeth bared like a rabid dog, "this evil cow frickin' murdered me!"

"Are you talking to me?" Cynthia asked; she looked puzzled.

"No, not you". May waved dismissively at Cynthia, even though she knew the woman couldn't see her.

"Are you sure? Have you got any evidence?" May whispered, trying to keep her voice down so that Cynthia couldn't hear.

"Of course I'm sure. How could I not be sure? I was there when it happened," Wilfred explained.

May forced herself to blink a few times, her vision had become blurred and the room appeared darker. The candles had burned only halfway down their length and the flames where still as bright as they were when first lit. A few glances around the room made her realise that it wasn't her eyes that were losing focus, it was Wilfred.

"Why won't you tell her? It's the only reason I came here. She needs to know I know. Others need to know. You can't let her get away with it. She needs to be punished. I need justice; I need retribution!" His features were foggy and his form had become wispy around the edges, as if he was surrounded by heat haze.

"Hello...Madam Trump?" Cynthia called out across the table. Barbara stepped forward and stood just behind her.

"I'm sure it's all ok, she must in a mystical trance of some kind". Barbara waved her hands above her head, out of Cynthia's sight. "Madam Trump is everything alright? Are you ok May?"

"I think so... I mean yes...everything is as it should be," but May wasn't convinced her statement was true.

"See there's nothing to worry about," Barbara reassured Cynthia. "It's probably just a bit of ectoplasm blocking up the ether".

"All is not well!" George cried as he stepped out from behind May. His eyes had grown wide and he gestured with stiff movement. "Rage brews within him! Wilfred has become as a lighthouse to The Stalkers; they will be upon us with haste!"

"You now, is it?" Wilfred's form was turning into a swirl of black and red. Fingers of smoke stretched away from him, tiny particles of light began to twinkle in the air around him. "I need justice; I don't need you!" A finger of smoke darted towards George, its tip was glowing red. Like an arrow of smoke, it hit George squarely in the chest. He was thrown from his feet and flew backwards, disappearing through the wall. May looked on, stunned and unable to move. The fear returned and held her in place. She felt the coldness; she felt their approach.

Wilfred's form had become no more than a thick cloud. Tendrils of smoke snaked across the room, touching the walls, the ceiling and anything else that stood in their path. The smoke retracted a few inches on each contact, like the stalked eyes of a snail, before reaching out again and slithering along the surfaces as if tangible. One tendril stroked Barbara's shoulder; she shivered and took a step backwards.

"Oh my," She said, "a cold spot". The tendril wavered in mid air before drifting away from her towards the nearest wall. Another finger of smoke brushed against a candle causing the flame to splutter and die.

"If you won't give me justice," Wilfred yelled. "I shall take it for myself". His cloud drifted closer to Cynthia, who was still waiting patiently for May's next response. New tendrils emerged, which quickly snaked towards his unsuspecting widow.

   May struggled to shake the fear which held her in place. She felt weak and useless, where was this inner strength that Margret had so often spoke of? There was something coming and she felt powerless to prevent it. Another candle went out.

   The smoke began to encompass Cynthia's neck. She lifted her jacket collar as she felt a chill.
   "I think I've found a cold spot as well," She said.
   "Why are we getting cold spots May?" Barbara asked. May opened her mouth to reply but could only summon a squeak as she watched the twisting smoke tighten around Cynthia's neck.
   "Is it just me or is it getting a bit close in here?" Cynthia brought her hand to her chest and swallowed hard. Barbara took a step backwards and reached out for the light switch. There was a sudden flash of light and a loud pop, as the bulb blew out. The room fell back into darkness but the noise had given May the jolt she needed; she could move again.

   "Get out!" She cried. "Get out right now!" There seemed little hesitation in her movement as Barbara grabbed Cynthia by the shoulder.
   "Come on! I don't know what's going on but we've got to leave". Cynthia slowly craned her head around, all the colour had drained from her face and her eyes were bulging in their sockets. Her mouth opened and closed like a fish out of water, she seemed to struggle with every shallow breath.
   "I can't move my legs!" She wheezed.

   May looked down and could see how the smoke had wrapped its self around Cynthia's ankles. She didn't know if there was anything she could do about it, she didn't know if she could even touch the smoke but she felt her strength returning and couldn't stand idle any longer. May took a step closer towards the spiralling mist. She reached out for the nearest Smokey tendril but as she lent closer she heard a low, guttural growl. May hesitated; her fingers were just a few inches from the cloud of sparkling smoke. Out of the corner of her eye she could see Barbara frantically pulling at the, now unconscious, Cynthia. May stared ahead at the red and black cloud and watched as the centre of the mass began to funnel towards her. Suddenly the growl became a howling as Trevor, teeth bared and wide eyed, flew out of the smoke towards her. He landed at her feet and instantly spun back around. Growling and snarling, he leaped back into the Smokey cloud. The sound of barking and gnashing teeth came from Wilfred's mist. The smoke began to recede back into the main cloud. It pulled away from the walls and the ceiling. It tugged at Cynthia as it tried to draw her unresponsive form with it but Barbara's grip was stronger; the tendrils slowly released their hold. Now that all resistance had gone, Barbara pulled Cynthia from her chair with such a force that she tripped over backwards and fell to the floor, pulling Cynthia on top of her.

The cloud pulsated and began to drift across the room towards the far wall. May strained her eyes and fancied she could see Trevor as he twisted about inside. The barking and snarling continued as the cloud moved. Sparks began to shoot across the surface of the smoke, linking one tiny crackle of light to another. The cloud pulsated faster and faster until in resembled a huge blackened heart. May edged along the table watching and listening, not knowing what the cloud would do next. The snarling turned to growling. There was a sudden yelp followed by a whimper and then there was only silence. Wilfred's cloud abruptly exploded. Thousands of tiny flecks, like burnt paper, drifted through the air. May watched them float towards the floor; it was as if a party balloon full of confetti had just burst. Then she saw Trevor, he was lying motionless on the floor.

Barbara climbed to her feet and pulled open the door.

"Help!" She cried through the open doorway. "Help, anyone!" She grabbed Cynthia's arms and dragged her out into the light of the landing.

May took a single, precarious step towards Trevor's limp body but something caught her eye that prevented her from taking another. She looked towards the corner of the room, near the window. A shadow seeped into the room like a pool of water. Thick, black and shimmering like an oil slick; it washed across the floor and walls like a slow moving tide. The chill hit May as if she had just fell into a frozen lake. Her fingers became numb as she backed away towards the door. She glanced towards Trevor but ,to her surprise, the dog was no longer in sight. The slick of shadow pooled purposefully towards where Trevor had lain. May felt as if she was going unnoticed as the wet darkness flowed passed her feet. She felt cold hands suddenly grab at her ankles and, before she could react, she found herself standing between Gary and George on Chloe's kitchen table.

Chapter Twenty Seven

Number 217 Kings Road was a small terraced house with a bright red door. Richard Cole sat in his car. He had managed to find a parking space directly opposite the house. His briefcase was open on the passenger seat as he checked, for the third time, that he had all the correct paperwork to hand. He was feeling confident that he had this case all wrapped up. All I have to do is knock on the door, lay on a bit of charm and get the paperwork signed, he told himself. Three days work and a nice neat case solved. The company gets its cut, I get a nice little commission and, if I'm lucky, a pat on the back from the boss. Job well done and any praise well deserved.

Miss May Trump. Her only recorded relative was a Mrs Annie Collins, deceased, who was married to Mr Sidney Collins, also deceased. Richard had dug deeper within the census and discovered Mr and Mrs Collins had one child, Mrs Rosie Gallagher. He had found no record of Rosie's death but he had discovered her last know address. He was confident that Rosie, or maybe even her forty five year old son, still lived at number 217 Kings Road.

The loud tapping on the passenger side window made Richard jump in his seat. His briefcase slipped off the passenger seat and its contents spilled into the foot-well. A grey haired man stared at him through the glass. Richard reached over and wound down the window.

"I didn't mean to startle you," the man apologised. He was in his mid sixties, as far as Richard could tell and wore a silver, puffed out coat. It had a fur lined hood, which stuck out from the back of his neck like a huge open pocket. Richard couldn't help thinking that it would have looked more suitable on someone a quarter of his age.

"That's ok," Richard replied, "I was miles away. What seems to be the problem?"

"I just wanted to warn you," the man explained as he

leaned in through the window. "I wouldn't leave your car here for very long. There have been at least six cars broken into on this street alone during the past couple of weeks. I live just along the way and it's the rarest of days not to see broken glass on the pavement".

"Thanks for the advice," Richard replied, eager to start picking up the pile of paperwork on the floor but unwilling to take his eyes of the strange old man leaning through his window.

"You're welcome," the man began to retreat away from the car, "and don't go leaving that bag in plain sight either. They'll grab hold of that quicker than a ferret up a trouser leg".

"Thanks again," Richard said as the man begun to walk away. Richard watched him through the wing mirror as he begun to wind the window back up. The man hadn't got more than two car lengths away when he appeared to stumble.

"See what I mean!" The man yelled, as he regained his footing, "more broken glass!"

Richard picked up his paperwork and shuffled it back into order. He wasn't worried about his car, not to any real degree. It was getting old. He had brought it new eight or maybe nine years ago and even then it hadn't been anything flashy. It did the job he asked of it and had, so far, proved reliable. It was a little basic: manual windows, no airbags, no air con, no sun roof, cloth seats and a cassette player. He had wondered when he had first brought the car: why a cassette player? Compact discs had been widely available for years, so why had the car manufacturer fitted a cassette player. He didn't own any cassettes; he didn't even know anyone who still owned any cassettes. It was lucky the radio worked because the only music he owned was on C.D. Richard knew that he would be lost without his car, he needed it for work but he didn't think anyone would be desperate enough to steal it.

Richard locked his car and then, with his briefcase tucked

under his arm, looked through all the windows to check that nothing of value was left in plain sight. He was across the road and standing in front of the bright red door when he remembered that there was nothing of value in his car anyway.

The doorbell was attached to the doorframe with sticky tape. It was off-white plastic and played 'God save the Queen' when Richard pressed the button. It sounded as if it had been recorded in an oil barrel and Richard wasn't sure if that was due to damage or design. He waited for a couple of minutes and was just about to press the bell a second time when he heard the sound of movement coming from the other side of the door. Footsteps followed by coughing and finally dead bolts being drawn back.

The door opened only an inch and Richard heard the security chain as it took the strain.

"Who is it?" A woman's voice asked through the crack in the door. Richard tried to peer through but it was too dark inside the house.

"My name is Richard Cole; I'm a representative of J.P.I, Jackson's Probate Investigations"

"What is it you're selling?"

"I'm not selling anything, as such, I'm..."

"I'm not interested in buying anything anyway," the voice cut Richard off in mid speech. "What are you bothering me for then? If you're not trying to sell me anything, as such, eh?"

"I'm a probate investigator," Richard tried to explain. He hoped that a little charm and reasoning would penetrate through the mostly closed door. "I believe that you are a possible heir to an unclaimed estate"

"An estate eh? That's interesting." The voice paused and the door moved slightly. "No...No thanks. What would I do with an estate? I can't even drive!"

"Sorry I seemed to have explained that wrong," Richard apologised. He was well aware that the mistake was not his but he also knew that a little humility could go a long way in situations like this. "I mean to say inheritance, money, you may be entitled to some money"

"Now money is something I can use. Inheritance, doesn't that mean someone has died?"

"Yes, I'm afraid it does". Richard was beginning to lose his patience but he made an effort not to allow it to show in his voice. "This would be a lot easier if you would open the door"

"I'm sure it would be but I didn't get to where I am today by opening doors to just any Tom, Dick or Harry. It's not safe out there; there are a lot of strange people about. Did you know we've had six cars broken into, in the past two weeks, on this street alone?"

"Yes I heard," Richard sighed.

"Not that it effects me in any way, I don't drive you see".

"Yes, as you've mentioned".

"Oh yes, so I did. That's just like me, anyhow, who died?"

"Miss May Trump," Richard opened his briefcase and pulled out a file. He wasn't comfortable having to discuss the case while standing in the street. He was used to people inviting him in, especially when the prospect of money was mentioned. He was used to comfortable surroundings with a hot cup of tea and maybe a biscuit.

"Never heard of her," the voice behind the door admitted.

"She's a distant relation on your mother's side," Richard explained.

"Have you told my mother, she never mentioned her and I only just saw her yesterday" Richard began to hear alarm bells.

"You are Mrs Gallagher, Mrs Rosie Gallagher?"

"No of course I'm not," the voice replied. Richard could sense a little anger in the tone. "I'm Sadie Jenkins, just as it says on the label under the bell!" Richard took a quick glance at the door bell.

"There's no label under your bell"

"What? The thieving little..." The door slammed shut and Richard could hear the chain rattle as Sadie unhooked it. The door swung wide open and Richard could, at last, see who it was he had been talking to. Sadie was in her early thirties and was only as tall as Richard's shoulders. He looked down at the top of her mousey, brown head. Her hair was tied back in a ponytail, held in place by a fluffy pink band. She looked up at him and he saw her sad blue eyes, which she used to give him a hard, cold stare. Richard smiled without realising and he met her stare with puppy dog eyes.

"What are you looking at?" She growled at him, before tilting her head out of the door to examine the doorbell. Richard was finding it hard to speak so he just widened his smile in response.

"Whatever," Sadie snapped and then said, as if speaking to only herself, "I must remember to put a label on that doorbell"

"Morning Sadie," the voice came from Richard's left and he turned his head towards it. A middle aged woman, somewhere in her forties, stood in the doorway of the next house. She wore a red, floral apron over her clothes which was freshly stained with flour and, what Richard hoped was, jam. "Who's your gentleman caller?"

"Morning Heather," Sadie greeted, in a much kinder voice than she had used with Richard. "I'm not entirely sure who this guy is. He's been going on about how he wants to give me cars and money but I think he's confused me with someone else"

"That's not entirely correct," Richard protested, as his voice finally returned to him "I'm a probate investigator and I' m trying to trace the heir to an unclaimed inheritance"

"That's interesting," Heather said as she lent against her door frame. "Who's the dear departed then?"

"My Mum's cousin, or some such" Sadie said, as she too leaned against the door frame. They must have looked like a pair of bookends from across the road.

"I don't think I got that bit right either," Richard admitted. "I was under the impression that Sadie, I mean Miss Jenkins, was somebody else. Mrs Rosie Gallagher in fact"

"Rosie Gallagher, little old Rosie?" Heather's face brightened and grew a broad grin. "Little old Rosie Gallagher, now she was a hoot! The laughs we had on these two doorsteps, she used to say the funniest things. She had your house Sadie, before you moved in of course, just her and her boy". Her smile drooped slightly at the corners."
It's just a pity how the boy turned out though. Rotten little devil he was and we don't know were he got it from either. Rosie was a sweet soul and that boy wanted for nothing, you just can't help some people. He'd have the teeth out of your mouth, if you kept it open long enough and if he could make a few quid out of them. Sneaky, nasty and selfish, Rosie done well to get shot of him when she did" Her smile perked back up again and she looked Richard in the eye. "How is dear old Rosie, nowadays?"

"I couldn't tell you, I came here to find her myself," Richard explained.

"Oh right, well you won't find her around here" Heather announced, shaking her head. "She emigrated to Spain three or four years back".

Richard realised why he had been unable to find anything more about Rosie in the census, other than the address on Kings Road. She would be registered in Spain now. Any records, including a possible death certificate, would be held in Spain.

"I was beginning to realise that myself," Richard agreed.

"So all that talk about money and cars was for the benefit of a person who isn't even in the same country as us," Sadie pointed out. Then Richard saw her smile for the first time.

"I guess so," Richard said through his own smile.

"How are you going to find her now?" Heather asked.

"I can probably trace her through the internet now that I know she's an ex-pat," Richard replied. "I still need to trace her son as well. Is there anything more you can tell me about him?"

"I know plenty about that rotter," Heather said, "but not out here. I've got a cake in the oven that needs checking on, besides that I sure you wouldn't say no to a cuppa".

"That sounds good to me," Richard agreed. He had never been left standing on the doorstep for such a long time before. He was usually across the fresh hold at the first mention of inheritance. This was not going as easily as he had first thought.

"Ok then, don't be shy, go on through" Heather stood aside to allow Richard to enter her house. "Come on then, you to," she told Sadie. "He is your gentleman caller after all"

Richard thanked Heather for her time and hospitality before stepping back outside. Two hours, three cups of tea and a slice of raspberry sponge cake had past since Heather had first invited him in. He was armed with a lot of fresh information, some of which would be useful regarding the case but the rest was mostly unconnected gossip. It had been rather productive, Richard decided, I have another potential lead to follow and the phone number of a gorgeous girl, who can be quite sweet once she let her guard down. Sadie had warmed to him after a little while. Maybe it was because she felt safer with Heather close by and the fact that they were in far more comfortable surroundings than before. Richard would have liked to have given his charm and confidence the credit but she seemed to be impervious to them both.

The night was drawing in as walked across the road; there was almost a skip to his stride. He stepped up to his car, with his keys already in his hand and then felt something crunch under his shoes. Richard looked at the broken, driver's side window and sighed. It wasn't even as if he hadn't been warned. Six cars broken into, in the past two weeks, in this street alone. Richard, pointlessly, unlocked the door and pulled it open. I guess I' m number seven, he thought as he brushed the glass off the seat. He looked up and groaned out loud, his radio cassette player was missing.

Chapter Twenty Eight

May felt disorientated as she climbed off the table. She found herself surrounded by concerned faces, some of which she recognised while others were strangers to her.

Every single the ghost in the house had congregated in Chloe's kitchen. It was packed wall to wall with spirits, yet the room was deathly silent. May could just about see Penny; she was almost pinned up against the far wall by the crowd. She seemed to be cradling something in her arms but May couldn't see what it was through the mass of souls. Gary and George were still on the table but were now crouched down low and looking up at the ceiling. They reminded May of the old Duck and Cover posters that she had seen as a child. It was as if they were waiting for a bomb to be dropped.

May wanted to say something but was afraid to break the silence. She looked at the faces around her and realised that they were all tilted upwards as well. Their faces looked pale, even for ghosts, and their eyes were open wide and unblinking. May followed their gaze and felt renewed dread as she saw a puddle of black, shimmering liquid like shadow hovering above her. It rippled and swirled like an upturned whirlpool and May felt it beckoning to her, inviting her to let go and fall upwards into its seemingly endless depths.

May felt a hand on her shoulder as George tried to silently comfort her. She would have usually pulled away from him and given him the sharp end of her tongue but at that moment she didn't. It wasn't fear that held her temper, even though she hated to admit it, she felt reassured by his presence. It felt as if his touch was anchoring her to the floor, preventing her from drifting into the darkness above. Had she been alone, May was unsure how she would have reacted to the bewildering feeling that was beginning to overwhelm her. The fear made her shy away from the darkness but something else drew her towards it. The temptation to let go felt somehow familiar, it almost felt like a sense of belonging. It was as if the darkness marked a path that she was meant to travel; a passage home.

The shadow lingered for what seemed like hours, May was afraid that it was just waiting for her and would never leave until she finally released herself into its swirling maw. Gradually the darkness began to slowly shrink and recede into the ceiling, like water through an open plug hole. Eventually it became no more that a small dark stain and even that faded away in a few short minutes.

There was a communal sigh as the last sign of the darkness finally vanished. May felt George's hand release her shoulder. She turned and looked up at him.

"Fortune smiles, for we have been granted a reprieve it would seem," George said, looking down at her. Gary was clambering off the table behind him. May watched him push through the crowd towards the far wall, where Penny was still standing.

"Behold the proof of my many warnings," George pointed out. There was less pride in his voice than May would have expected.

"Was that really them this time?" May asked, even though she felt the truth of it for herself.

"Never before has there been so little space between us, yet against the presence of a single foe, we have prevailed" George spoke quietly and slowly, as if he was explaining it to himself as much as to May. "One alone was drawn to us by the rage Wilfred mustered. A scout of their kind I suspect; I fear more are yet to follow".

The room began to clear under a drone of whispered voices and George climbed off the table as space on the floor became available.

"I'm sorry I doubted you," May said, even though her scepticism had been as much for show as due to disbelief.

"Your words lighten my heart May, though the retraction of others would yet please me greater. My name have they sullied and my reputation guttered, by their naive and fearful words. I long to hear the recanting of each and every accusation but I fear we have little time for such indulgence. A change in attitude is sure to be seen, though my current thoughts are with Trevor; I must ascertain his state of wellbeing". May merely nodded in response, she couldn't think of what else to say. She wasn't used to being wrong, even if it was only partially and it had left her lost for suitable words. She had last seen Trevor slumped on the floor of the room upstairs and, even though she was unsure what harm a ghost dog could actually come to, she didn't expect that George would find him unscathed.

The thinning crowd parted, creating a narrow passage which Penny and Gary squeezed through to get closer to May and George. May could now see that it was Trevor that Penny held in her arms; he was still limp and motionless.

"Are you alright May," Penny asked as she approached. Her voice sounded calm but May could see the fear that still lingered in her eyes.

"I'm fine I think," May replied. George stepped forward and took Trevor from Penny's arms. He cradled the dog like a baby as he checked him over.

"It is as I had hoped," George said in a quiet voice. "No harm has befallen him". May looked down at Trevor's limp, motionless body; he seemed far from unharmed.

"How can you tell?" May asked. "There would be no sign of life either way. He was dead to begin with, so how can you tell that he hasn't fallen even beyond that? Whatever that would mean? Whatever does exist, if anything at all, beyond being dead?"

"We have not been christened by this event," George explained, as he gently laid Trevor onto the table. "We are many years' dead and have seen much come to pass. Wilfred's sour spirit, though rare, was beneath unique. Anger and vengeance had so consumed him that little else remained. Faced with the object of his ire, deep seated as it was, control became as a mere dream to him, as did his original self. Emotion usurped all thought and reason, leaving only his rage to command his form and action. Such an unfettered condition afforded him with a grasp of telekinesis and with it the power to cause effect to both the living and the dead". He glanced up at Penny. "Wilfred was no poltergeist, fear not a similar fate. Born of fear and hate was his power, dark and leash-less as it was. Against such manifestations Trevor had fought before and has soon enough recovered".

"But what of them? The Soul Stalkers, has he ever fought against them and recovered as readily?" May asked.

"Not at all and no mere fraction toward it either," George replied. "No closer than tonight have we approached their kind. From afar has been our sole experience until now. He has no more felt their touch than have I".

"How can you be so sure?"

"His mere presence among us should be proof enough of that".

"Why did he fight? How did he fight when Wilfred was no more than a cloud of charged emotion?" May asked. Even the opportune appearance of the dog confused her. Why had Trevor suddenly attacked Wilfred? For an animal who seemed to cower at the mere sight of Mr Kibbles he had shown little reluctance when he confronted an entity that consisted of mostly rage.

"He is a dog," George simply replied. "A dead dog I grant you but still a dog all the same. He is blessed with an uncomplicated mind. He suffers no complex thoughts as we do. Much as any animal, he lacks the basic wit to analyze all he sees or hears. Instinct and emotion are his governors. He surely sensed the rage in Wilfred and reacted in kind. Many years each others companion have we been and a strong loyalty between us has bloomed. I guess that he feels an emotion not unlike love towards me as I do for him. Such an unclouded emotion in an animal may be employed to counteract rage, as is my theory. A positive emotion should go some way to neutralise a negative one, stealing its power and sapping its strength until it becomes formless and inert. Alas it is a street of two directions. As in this case, Trevor's own strength has been depleted, though not too soon I'm grateful. Akin to a battle between fire and ice, one must falter before the other. Trevor stood as victor in this instance, as is usually the case. A human spirit will tend toward retreat as they feel their strength wane but an animal will fight on until the bitter end". He looked down at Trevor and gently stroked the dog's head. "And don't feel sorrow for Wilfred's soul. He has become a mere wisp of his former self. His strength will eventually return and, with hope, as will his senses".

"Are all the animals are like this?" May asked as she remembered her thoughts, regarding the seeming lack of wild death. "Have you seen others acting in the same manner? Have you seen many animal spirits at all?"

"Of both counts I indeed have," George replied, turning back to face her. "I stood witness to a battle between one other and a spirit of dark emotion. Much time has passed since but the presence of a Stalker was said to be witnessed shortly there after. An other dog it was, a Labrador if my memory serves. A companion of a human soul, of that I'm certain. If truth be told, I have never seen an animal alone, or any wild spirits. I have always thought them timid, having taken the fear of humans with them to the grave".

It seemed far too convenient an assumption, as far as May was concerned. She couldn't believe that the only reason that she hadn't seen any wild death was purely because they were avoiding her. If what George said was true, that they were merely acting as they had when they were still alive, then death had brought to them a far better understanding of the art of concealment. Even the most timid of animals couldn't stay hidden at all times. Sooner or later they must venture out, in search of food at the least. May knew perfectly well that the dead had no need for food but, as George had pointed out, even the ghost of an animal was mainly guided by pure instinct. May herself knew that a hot sweet tea was unnecessary and beyond her grasp but that didn't prevent her from craving for one.

Half of the ghosts had left the kitchen and those who remained had gathered around the table; they were listening in to the conversation between George and May. One of which stepped forward, it was Jeremy.

"I guess we all owe you an apology," Jeremy smiled

228

nervously at George. "It seems that you were right all along".

"I would gladly gloat if time would allow it," George replied. "Sadly that is not the case. Much time has slipped by, wasted by closed minds and now there is little left for which to prepare. Their return is inevitable; they have sensed the existence of many souls ripe for the plucking. I know not why they will come; I know only that come they will".

Chapter Twenty Nine

She opened her eyes and immediately closed them again. The light was too bright for her eyes and she was beginning to feel a painful throbbing in her head. This wasn't a new experience for Victoria. It was far from the first time she had suffered from a hang over but it didn't stop her from making her usual promise to herself.

"I' m never drinking again," she said, as she had before on more occasions than she cared to remember. She followed with a groan, as her headache rose in intensity; it felt as if her head was pulsating like a toad's chin.

Victoria gingerly opened her eyes again, this time the light didn't hurt quite as much but it still made her wince. She looked around and realised that she was lying on an unfamiliar bed in a room that she didn't recognise. It was not the first time this had happened to her either but she had to admit to herself that it had been a long time since the last. She tried to sit up but the throbbing reached a crescendo which forced her back down. She stared at the ceiling and tried to make sense of what little she remembered from the night before.

It had been another one of those séance night things, which Barbara kept getting so infused about, at that young girl Chloe's house. That must be where I am, Victoria guessed, at least I hope so. There had been people knocking at the front door and she remembered Deborah being asked to play host. That had not been a good idea, she remembered thinking that much. I would have made a far better choice, far more out spoken and far more entertaining. She had followed Deborah as she invited the guests into the house. That was when she had first seen him. I almost dropped the wine bottle, she recalled.

It must have been over thirty years the last time I had seen Bob but he still had that cute dimple on his chin. It was the only thing about him that hadn't aged so disgracefully, she realised. So what if he was old, grey and as wrinkly as basset hound, so was she after scraping the foundation off at the end of the day. He still had that dimple and it reminded her of how he was, back when they were young, free and a lot more agile. Unlike the wine bottle, the years had dropped away from her and she had felt giddy each time he had looked in her direction. It wasn't the wine making her legs go numb, she assured herself and Bob had always made my knees knock together.

She had watched Deborah flit around the room, offering people tea and coffee in her usual quiet and polite manner. Using her secretarial skill set, Victoria assumed, I bet you spent more time with a sugar bowl in your hand than a pen back when you were still working. She had kept the derogatory and slightly envious thought to herself. When Victoria had once tried working in an office environment, back in her youth, things had not gone so well. Her outlandish behaviour had been misconstrued as flirting, coupled with the fact that she never managed to get much work done, her clerical career had ended quite quickly. They were a bunch of boring kill joys. They wouldn't know a good laugh even if it slapped them about the face with a wet kipper. I've got too much personality for them to handle, it was like trying to work in a room full of dead people. Victoria suddenly realised just how little things change.

"Tea, you offer them tea!" Victoria remembered saying. She had two glasses in one hand and held her wine bottle up in the air in the other.

"Is there none among you who would like something a little stronger, something with a little more substance?" She pointed at Bob with the wine bottle. "I know you like a little drop of the good stuff Bob or at least you used to"

"Many things have changed since we last met Vicky," Bob stood up from the armchair he had managed to claim earlier. He's gained a bit of weight around the middle, Victoria had noticed, I bet he can't run around a football pitch like he used to.

"Pour me a glass and we can celebrate the things that have not," Bob laughed loud and Santa like. His head tilted back and his mouth stretched so wide across his face that it was as if someone had just unzipped his head open. Victoria passed the two glasses over to Bob and unscrewed the wine bottle.

"Robert Jones, you haven't changed a bit"

Things were a little fuzzier after that. She had vague memories of fetching more wine and talking brashly and loud. Flashes of what seemed like quieter, more personal conversations with Bob. Oh dear! Victoria suddenly remembered, I put my arms around him and sat on his knee.

The bed room door swung open, dragging her back into the present.

"Come on, get out of bed," Barbara barked from the doorway. "There's a cup of black coffee waiting for you downstairs". Victoria forced herself to a sitting position.

"Not so loud Babs!" She groaned. "My head feels like it's got a woodpecker trapped inside it"

The coffee helped and so did the pain killers, which Margret had dug out from the bottom of her handbag. Victoria sat at the kitchen table with her hands cupping the hot mug of coffee. Margret, Barbara and Deborah also sat around the table facing her. Chloe was leaning against the kitchen sink with a look of disproval on her face.

"We've got quite a mess to sort out now," Barbara stated and Margret and Deborah nodded in unison.

"You do all over react at times," Victoria defended herself, "I was only a little drunk. Come on now, what harm could it have caused?" Victoria still wasn't sure exactly what had occurred on the night before. Her memory was still patchy and blurred but she did recall hearing sirens at one point. Well that can't be a good sign, she thought, how did I cause that to happen?

"For once Victoria," Margret announced, "you're not to blame. Well at least the main issue wasn't your doing".

"Then why wake me if I'm not to blame?" Victoria protested, even though she was beginning to feel better now than she would have if she had just stayed in bed, dehydrated and in pain.

"Don't you remember the ambulance?" Deborah asked in surprise.

"She barely remembers her name I'm guessing," Margret suggested.

"Never mind all that for now," Barbara said. "The important thing is that Cynthia is going to be just fine and the doctor said that she should be able to go home in a day or two".

"What on earth was going on upstairs?" Chloe asked, clearly not amused at the situation. "All I heard was that she collapsed during the séance and, for some reason, you felt impelled to drag her unconscious body all the way across the landing to the top of the stairs. I'm just thankful you stopped there. Who knows what state she'd be in if you had bumped her down the staircase. I could get sued over this! If Cynthia gets it in her mind to. You've seen the adverts on television, I'd end up losing everything!"

"May told me to get her out of the room and she sounded rather urgent about it," Barbara explained. "This was after Cynthia had collapsed of course"

May Trump, Victoria thought, she's that disembodied voice I keep hearing. I'm never getting used to that! Margret's friend, recently deceased and no less bossy for it either. I guessed she would be involved and what about how she keeps standing in front the fridge! How are we supposed get at the milk when we need it?

"What has May got to say about it now?" Chloe asked.

"I've no idea," Barbara admitted. "I've not heard from her this morning. I heard her talking to someone in here last night but I was too busy phoning for the ambulance to hear exactly what was said. I've not heard a peep from her since".

"Yes! How about in here last night," Margret said. "How cold *was* it in here? I only popped in here for a quick chocolate biscuit and it was so cold my fingers felt numb. You could see nothing through the window either, it had completely misted up. I didn't hear no talking though. It was spooky quiet; if you know what I mean, creepy even".

"Something strange was going on last night," Barbara said. "I just don't know what. I'm hoping we'll hear from May soon but I can't sense any thing from the other side at the moment".

"Do give it a break!" Victoria said. "The only way you can sense the presence of a ghost is exactly same way we can, by hearing them talk". She had never held much stock in Barbara's psychic powers. She had only ever turned up on a Thursday evening for the company and the occasional chance of a tipple.

"You're a one for talking madam," Margret said, "I bet you can barely sense what day it is". Victoria was about to complain but then she realised that Margaret had a point, on that particular morning at least.

"Regardless of whatever happened last night," Deborah pointed out," all is not lost. I managed to reschedule most of the clients. Understandably, Cynthia's dramatic exit put a few people off the whole idea. One in particular told me that it just wasn't worth the risk; he wanted to talk to the dead not become one".

"There's no such risk as that, is there?" Margaret asked. Victoria could see that she was getting a little worried; it reminded her of the time she had told her that the government was thinking about making sponge cakes illegal.

"I thought that Cynthia just had a funny turn or something," Margret said. "I'm guessing that these séances can be a little unnerving and I definitely know May can sometimes be unsuitable for the faint hearted but there's surely nothing more sinister that that going on".

"She has no backbone that one," Victoria added. "Cynthia has never been a big fan of surprises, not since her the death of her first husband that is. She's always been jumpy, even after all those rumours had died down".

"I remember that now," Barbra said. "Everyone was talking about it. They went on for quite a long while. It was a good month after he had passed on, if I remember rightly".

"What were the rumours about?" Chloe asked.

"Well Wilfred wasn't a well man," Victoria said. "The Cancer had a good hold on him but he was a fighter. He held on a lot longer than the quacks at the hospital said he would. Some people said that he was lingering on due to something unnatural, even Barbara was accused of having a hand in it at one point".

"It was nothing to do with me!" Barbara piped up. "I told them then and I'm telling you now, I had no hand in it. It's not like I even have that kind of psychic power. I mean, all that spiritual healing rubbish is just not my bag. I'm a seer, a conduit between the living and the afterlife. I can: commune with the dead, predict the future and read your mind, only if I wanted to that is. Curing the physical body with just the power of the mind! Now that's what I call hocous pocous clap trap".

"Calm down Babs," Margret said. "Nobody here is accusing you of having any real psychic powers". Victoria couldn't help laughing. She had a dirty laugh that was a cross between a cackle and a giggle; she sounded like a turbulent witch.

"Yes I can," Barbara replied with pride.

"Can you really read peoples minds?" Chloe asked but was drowned out by Victoria's loud cackling.

"Nicely put Marge," Victoria said and then paused to get her breath back. "Now then! Getting back to the rumours about Wilfred and Cynthia. People have said that they heard Cynthia complaining that Wilfred was lingering on a bit longer than she liked. It was common knowledge, in certain social circles, that Cynthia had been spending a lot of time with a Mr Smythe. All the while Wilfred was cooped up in bed with the home help". Victoria looked up at four shocked faces. Deborah had her notebook open on the table and was writing furiously.

"That didn't come out right did it," Victoria acknowledged. "Wilfred was cooped up in bed, alone. The home help, a lovely lady who's also a member of The Hare and Trebuchet woman's dominoes team, was just in their home, helping I guess".

I didn't know you were a dominoes player Vicky?"
Margret said, after she had narrowed her eyes and closed
her mouth.

"Oh yes every Tuesday at The Hare and Trebuchet,"
Victoria replied. "It's a great way of meeting men".
Although it's not a way of meeting great men in my
experience, Victoria added in silent thought.

"But what of Cynthia and Wilfred?" Chloe asked
impatiently.

"Well the rumours I heard were that Wilfred's cancer was
aggressive and terminal," Victoria continued. "It should
have killed him many months earlier but he battled for his
life with his every breath. It was said that Cynthia had
grown impatient and had helped hurry things along a bit.
There was no proof of course but that didn't stop the
tongues wagging all over town. Anyone with an open ear
could hear all the loud but whispery, stories being told on
every street corner and over every garden hedge. Stories of
how Cynthia was putting weed killer in his food or rat
poison in his cocoa were the most popular topics of
conversation. Stories that bounced back and forth,
between friends and neighbours, for quite a while before
and after Wilfred's death".

"That's terrible," Chloe cried. "Cynthia must have felt
awful. Hearing all those accusations and after just losing
her husband".

"It's only terrible if it's not true," Victoria pointed out.

"And I'm guessing that you had nothing at all to do with
these rumours Vicky?" Barbara asked accusingly.

"That's right Babs," Victoria replied. "I had nothing to do
with it". It was a lie but even though she had no doubt that
she would have gotten away with it, Victoria couldn't keep
her face straight. She didn't find it amusing, far from it.
There was very little that she had done in her life that she
had later regretted but whenever she recalled her
involvement in those rumours, her heart had always been
struck cold.

"Well I didn't start them at least, "Victoria said fighting
off the nervous smile. "I may have passed them on to a few

people but everyone was talking about it back then. I'm not proud about it, not in any shape or form but I don't blame myself for any of it either!" It was another lie but this one she kept to herself.

"Ha! Finally the truth is revealed," Barbara exclaimed. "I have always known that you were involved in one way or another. Some of those stories had your name written all over them".

"Look here Babs!" Victoria was happier fighting then pondering over past mistakes. I'll fight my corner on this, she steeled herself, even if I am in the wrong. "I may have dressed up a few things in the telling but in essence I only retold what I had overheard in the post office queue. I didn't spread anything that wasn't already free flowing".

"He who is without sin," Deborah said quietly and without even looking up from her notebook.

"Do what?" Margaret said as she turned in her chair to face Deborah.

"You said that out loud," Victoria pointed out. "You do realise that you said that out loud, don't you?" Deborah slowly closed her notebook and gently placed her pen on top of it.

"The first time I heard about these rumours was during one of our weekly get-togethers," she said as she raised her head to face the others. "We were all there as usual and we were all involved in the conversation. We are all guilty of spreading the rumours. We discussed Cynthia and Wilfred's personal problems at great length and we all put our penny's worth in".

"I don't remember that," Margaret said. "Are you sure I was there?"

"Oh yes I'm quite sure," Deborah said as she bent down and brought her handbag up from under the table. She began to rummage through it until she pulled out another notebook. It was identical to the one on the table, if a little more dog-eared around the edges. She flicked through the pages.

"Ah there it is," she said as she opened the book fully and began to read. "Barbara said that Cynthia was probably using poison, while Victoria had surmised that she was hiding Wilfred's medication. Margaret got rather upset, see dear you were there, when it was suggested that Cynthia may have ruined a fresh cream sponge cake by lacing it with rat poison".

"Hold on one minute," Barbara said. "You wrote it all down; you took notes?" Deborah smiled and closed the notebook.

"Yes dear," she replied. "It's what I do".

Chapter Thirty

Richard sat in his car. The results of his latest search through the census was scattered across the passenger seat next to him. The Squirrel Nut Pickers played 'Put a Lid on it', through his newly fitted CD player. The volume was turned down low; it was nothing more than background noise. He had begrudged buying it but he hated driving in silence. On top of how much it had cost to get the window repaired, he was beginning to worry that his expenses were going to out weigh his commission, if he ever got to the bottom of the Trump case that is.

The C.D abruptly stopped and the radio automatically cut in, as a local news station began to broadcast the hourly headlines. It was one of the features that Richard was just going to have to get used to, at least until he worked out how to turn it off. The breaking news was about how the police were questioning a sixty year old man, at the local station, in connection with a recent spate of car crimes.
"I turn now to our crime correspondent, David Symonds, reporting live from the scene".
"Thank you Gordon, I'm here outside the Dresden Street police station. I can see a man; he appears to be in his mid sixties and wearing a silver, hooded jacket. He's being lead out of a police van by two officers; he's wearing handcuffs. Now he's shouting something at the officers but I can't quite make out what he's saying. I going to get closer and see if he is willing talk to us". Richard could hear the sound of hurried footsteps.
"Hello Sir, do you know why the police have brought you here?"
"I warned them all!" Richard found the voice familiar but he couldn't place where he had heard it before. "I told them all first, I gave them all a fair chance!"
"You warned who Sir?"
"Please stand back sir," Richard assumed it was the voice of one of the police officers. "No questions at this time please

Sir!"

"They are the guilty ones for not heeding my words". It was the familiar voice again, which was quickly followed by the sound of a scuffle. A few grunts and a scrapping noise, like shoes being dragged along concrete. The radio suddenly fell silent.

"I'm sorry but it would seem we are having some technical difficulties," Gordon cut back in from the studio. "Hopefully we will be able to speak to David again soon. Meanwhile in other news: the church bring and buy sale has achieved a record result this month…" Richard switched the radio off and his Squirrel Nut Pickers C.D started to play 'Hell'.

Richard picked up the paperwork from the passenger seat and began to flick through the pages. He had managed to trace Rosie Gallagher through the latest Spanish census and further investigation had sadly revealed that she had died of natural causes more than two years ago. Richard had begun to worry at that point. He was afraid that the trail had gone cold again, that was until he was able to secure a copy of her death certificate. When he had discovered that her son had been recorded as her next of kin and his full name was printed clearly on the limp photocopy, he had regained fresh hope. The solution to the case may yet be still within his grasp.

Jonathon Gallagher was easy enough to track down through the local census. He was even still registered at an address within the town. It had seemed a little too easy to Richard. He delved deeper and searched through births, deaths and marriages. He expected a result through births and not been disappointed. Marriages turned up empty, which left him with a desperate hope that deaths did the same.

Richard had cursed his own suspicion when he discovered the record of Jonathon Gallagher's death. It didn't surprise him though and neither did the cause. What little Richard had uncovered about the man had been neither complimentary nor affectionate. He had built a mental picture of a heartless swindler who would have and probably had, scammed his own mother for whatever he could get. It had made perfect sense to Richard, that such a man would meet such a sticky end. Jonathon Gallagher's final entry in this life had been as the victim of a violent crime.

Richard was left with nothing but the address of a dead man. It wasn't quite the end of the line but he felt like as if there was a brick wall waiting for him just around the corner. There was little else he could do and giving up, after all the work he had already put in, wouldn't help him get his foot onto the next rung of the ladder. It was a last ditch attempt to solve the Trump case and walk back into the office with his head held high. He slipped the paperwork into his briefcase and climbed out of his car. He starred across the street at what he knew to be an empty house. The chance of finding a fresh link, another branch to the Trump family tree was slim but it was still a chance. It was another straight road with terrace houses running down both sides, like one long, continuous building. The only obvious difference between it and The King's road was the apparent lack of broken glass on the pavement. Richard crossed over the road and stepped up the door of the house adjacent to the late Mr Gallagher's. Cold calling the neighbouring properties was just a stab in the dark, Richard thought. It took him a moment to notice the morbid connection between his thought and Mr Gallagher's untimely death.

There was no bell so Richard rattled the letterbox. A few moments later the door swung open and a half dressed man starred at him suspiciously.
"Who are you?" The Man grumbled. He looked half asleep, as if he had just rolled out of bed. His grey hair was sticking up at every angle and his bare stomach over hung his pale blue pyjama bottoms as if it was jelly escaping from a bowl.
"Hello Sir," Richard replied, his polite and professional

voice. "I'm sorry to disturb you. I would just like to ask you a few questions about your previous neighbour: Mr Gallagher".

"Johnny? Are you talking about Johnny?" The Man asked; the guardedness in his eyes seemed to fade a little.

   "I believe so Sir, Mr Jonathon Gallagher".

"You do know he's dead don't you? I knew him well, the poor Bugger. Terrible what happens if you wander around at night these days".

"I'm sorry for your loss Sir". Richard's brick wall was still no where in sight. "Would you mind if I ask a few questions regarding the late Mr Gallagher?"

"Oh no, not at all," The Man replied. Richard watched the man's entire demeanour relax in front of him and gave the credit to his own, well rehearsed, doorstep etiquette. "However, I do tend to get a real dry mouth when I do a lot of talking. What with me being down to my last can of Applerott and all". He grinned knowingly at Richard, who put his pride back into his pocket and drew out his wallet. Richard offered The Man what he figured would be more than enough money for a few cans of the locally brewed, triple strength cider. The Man's smile dropped and he gestured for more money. Richard didn't see him grin again until he had put double the amount in his open, waiting palm.

"Thank you very much you're very kind," The Man said as he clenched his fist tight around the money.

"You're welcome Sir," Richard lied. "So then, what do you know about Mr Gallagher?"

   "Oh yes, I knew him well. We had some great laughs we did. Funny fellow was Old Johnny, full of stories he was, full of japes and jokes. We spent many a night talking over a crate of booze. I'm talking about long talks from early evening to the small hours. I've always been a good listener and I've got an opinion of most things, as long as I keep whiskers wet that is. A dry mouth tends to clam me up, as you now know, so Old Johnny always made sure there was plenty to drink on such nights. I've been missing him you know; it's been getting pretty dry this past month".

"I'm sure it has," Richard nodded and pointed at The Man's clenched fist. "But that lot should keep you going for a while. Did Mr Gallagher have any family that you know of?"

"He did have his Old Mum but she passed away a couple of years back. Other than that I don't know. There's just his kid I guess".

"He had a child! Do you know how I might get in contact with them?" Richard still couldn't see his brick wall, in fact there didn't even seem to be a corner for it to hide behind.

"Who me? No I never met the girl. But then again, strictly speaking, neither did he. He didn't get on with the mother's folks, he told me. He said that it all happened when a deal went sour and he was forced to leave under no uncertain terms. He barely escaped a lynching that day, by all accounts. He's neither spoken to mother nor child since, as far as I'm aware".

"So he never saw his daughter, ever?" Richard felt disappointed but he also began to feel a little sorry for the late Mr Gallagher. He may have been a selfish and compassionless scam artist but to never get to see your child, your own flesh and blood, must have been soul wrenching. He must have had a soul at least.

"He saw her alright, he just never met her. She's why he moved over this way. He used to live way up north from here but then upped sticks to be closer to her as soon as he heard that he had become a dad. He used to watch her and follow her about sometimes, nothing creepy or sinister though. He just wanted to keep an eye on her, make sure she's safe if you like. He was a good guy was Old Johnny, he got himself into a few scrapes now and again but he was a good guy for the most part".

"Did he tell you her name?" Richard asked; he had little hope of getting an answer. "Maybe even her mother's name?" Even just a surname would be something to go on.

"Oh yes of course he told me their names. We talked at lot, me and Johnny, I told you that much already".

"That's great!" Richard said as he fumbled with his briefcase and pulled out a blank sheet of paper and a pen. "What are their names?"

"Let me see now". The Man glanced at his feet and cupped his chin with his free hand. "I'll remember, just give me a moment". He began to stroke the bristles on his chin while Richard silently cursed at what he saw as another brief glimpse of hope slipping beyond his grasp.

"I'm sorry". The Man released his chin. "I'm really not very good with names. Johnny used to refer to his kid as 'his little angel' for the most part anyway. I only heard him mention her actual, proper name a couple of times and that was a good while back now".

"What about the mother's name? Do you remember anything about that?"

"I don't know," then The Man's eyes brightened and he raised his finger to point into the air. "You know what! I do remember something. Johnny told me the whole story but only one thing sticks in mind for sure. I found it funny. It made me laugh out loud at the time. He said that he had only come to this town for the money he could make on a deal. A real good earner he had called it but then he had met this girl and, as I mentioned before, it all turned out sour. I remember him saying that it had all been about the money, in more ways than one". The Man grinned, as if he had just won some kind of game show.

"And that's it, that's all you can remember? It's hardly useful is it?"

"It's the best I've got," The man said and then he winked at Richard. "Maybe if I had a little more incentive it might jog my memory some?" Richard sighed and pulled his wallet back out of his pocket.

"In for a penny in for a pound," he groaned as he pulled his wallet open.

"That was it!" The Man snapped his fingers. "I remember it all now!"

Chapter Thirty One

The house was a lot less crowded. The visiting ghosts had slowly dissipated until only a small group remained: May, Penny, Gary, Jeremy and George. Trevor had finally awoken, to the relief of many around him but the resulting cheer had scared both him and Mr Kibbles from the room.

George had tried his best to answer the tirade of questions thrust upon him but in the confined space of the kitchen all of their voices had merged into a single low pitched drone. May was surprised how the mergence of all the: who's, what's, when's and where's, sounded much like a long drawn-out wooing noise.

George had climbed back onto the table and had made an attempt to engage the crowd. He had stood up as tall as he could and waved his arms around while yelling until his voice sounded hoarse. All eyes had turned upon him but the drone drowned out his own words. The essence of his speech must have reached a few of the closer ears, as a fresh murmur had gradually washed through the crowd like a slow moving wave. The announcement that he would answer everyone's questions at the cemetery later in the day, or a variation of the truth, seemed to finally reach all present. As May watched them leave, she guessed that some would head directly to the cemetery in order to get to the head of the queue. It was a sale philosophy the she had witnessed before and had treated with much distain.

"Now that they've all gone, I'm going to see if Trevor is alright". Penny announced. "The poor pooch looked scared out of his wits when he bolted through that wall".

"Let me know if you see Mr Kibbles," May asked after Penny just as she stepped through the same wall.

"We will do!" Gary replied, as he raced after Penny.

"You must accompany me to the cemetery May," George suggested. "I have knowledge of an adamant spirit which demands of you an audience".

"Demands! They can demand all they want. I will be there when it suits me and no other. I also wish to speak to this spirit and bring them down a station or two to boot but I must to speak with our living folk first". She was beginning to realise that Chloe and the Thursday Night Club were still blissfully unaware of what had so recently occurred.

George and Jeremy bade her a farewell that was tinged with warnings.

"That which does not concern them should be kept beyond their knowledge". They slipped through the wall and May found herself alone, thinking of how little the door was getting used of late. She glanced at the clock: it was just past 3am. She settled herself into a chair; there would be a few hours wait until they would arrive. A brief visit to the other realm couldn't hurt, she thought as she allowed herself to drift away. An hour and no dawdling, she promised herself but the transition didn't come. She fell into a living sleep, a sleep of lonely and troubled dreams.

From her usual vantage point in front of the fridge, May looked down at The Thursday Night Club as they talked and bickered around the kitchen table. She kept silent, unwilling to announce her presence just yet. She had awoken from a sleep she was no longer used to and it had left her feeling a little dozy. She felt confused by her failure to transcend into the spirit realm and was overwhelmed by a craving for a cup of hot sweet tea.

Deborah was complaining that she was spending more time holding a pen than a knitting needle nowadays. She spoke of her concern about unfinished cardigans and upcoming birthdays, as if there was little more important at large.

"Why don't you skip a few days," Margaret suggested. "We'll hold the fort here. Have a few days at home to get them finished, if it means that much to you?"

"I agree," Victoria added. "You should go home at take all

your notebooks with you! At least that way we can speak freely without the fear of being quoted word for word in five years time".

"They're both right Deborah, in their own way," Barbara agreed. "Everyone loves to receive your knitted delights on their birthday. I still cherish that crystal ball cosy you made me last year".

May watched as Chloe walked into the room, bleary eyed and wearing her bright yellow dressing gown. She stepped up to the kettle and switched it on as if there was nobody else in the room.

"Good morning Sweetie," Margaret said. Chloe spun around on the spot. She grabbed hold of the edge of the sink, as her slippers lived up to their name.

"What are you lot still doing here?" She yelled, as she regained her balance.

"We have been home and back dear," Deborah offered.

"We helped ourselves to tea," Barbara added. "I hope you don't mind".

"Tea? No...no of course not, I wondered why the kettle was warm. You've been home and back again? Don't you people ever sleep?"

"Not so well nowadays," Victoria admitted, "Unless I've had a skin full that is".

"Oh we sleep well enough," Margaret said. She stretched out her arms and pointed at the air around her in a gesture that encompassed everything. "Especially as I've been skipping my afternoon naps ever since all this palaver started. You do realise that it's so close to noon now that I had to check my watch before I gave you a morning greeting".

"Oh dear, is it? I've been up half the night studying. I'm really getting behind on my course work". Chloe mimicked Margaret's outstretched gesture; her voice was tinged with sarcastic frustration. "What with all this palaver going on!"

"I know just what you mean dear," Deborah agreed. "Lots of things are getting put behind because of it".

May could sense the sarcasm and growing irritation in Chloe's voice, even if Deborah didn't. It was a selfish reaction from Chloe but May understood the cause. They were only trying to help, for one reason or another, but sometimes it was just nice to spend a little time alone in your own home. It must have been bad enough waking up to find four old ladies invading your kitchen, without the knowledge that spectral eyes were on you at all hours of the day and night. There had to be another way for Chloe to keep possession of this house. If Deborah's calculations were correct, Chloe could end up saving her home at the expense of her own sanity.

The ghosts had to go; she had to go. May knew that time was growing short and staying within the living realm was becoming dangerous. All she really wanted to do is drift back into the sprit realm and never return but she still had a promise to keep. She knew that Penny would stay here no matter what the danger. Until her daughter was settled and secure she would never leave her side. May's own moral code would never allow her to slip away and leave her to battle it out alone. She didn't know if The Soul Stalkers could even affect the living but she was sure of what fate would lie in store for Penny should she desert her.

"We're only here to help," Margaret said in a calm, quiet voice. "I expect it's getting more than a little annoying having us oldies turning up at your doorstep everyday but you did agree to this. You invited us into your home and you still need our help. You even gave us a set of keys. None of us were sober at the time but you still gave us an open invitation to come and go as we pleased. If you want to amend the arrangement, please do by all means but you need to let us know. You need to tell us what it is you want". Margaret glanced over at Barbara and smiled." Not all of us are psychic".

"Of course you're right," Chloe relented. All hint of sarcasm left her voice. "I'm sorry if I was a bit short with you but this whole affair is beginning to wear me down".

"No need for apologies," Margaret replied, still smiling. "Finish making your coffee and come and sit with us; we have much to discus".

May watched as Chloe smiled, nodded and turned around to start making coffee. She had always admired Margaret's ability to soothe anger with nothing more than a calm voice and the right choice of words, though she wouldn't have always so readily admitted it. In her place, May would have spat all the wrong things back at Chloe and turned the whole thing into heated argument that would have left them with only hurt feelings and wasted time to show for it.

Chloe took her coffee over to the table and pulled up a chair. She cupped her hands around the hot coffee mug and smiled gingerly at each of the others in turn, they smiled back. Deborah opened her notebook and Victoria sighed.

"Ok then," Margaret said. "We had better make arrangements for the next séance".

"You're not wrong Marge," Barbara agreed. "We've got people already booked in on top of the over run from last night. May's going to be in for one busy night, if we ever hear from her again that is".

"She'll be here," Margaret said with unmistakable belief. "She always turns up when you need her".

"Just like the proverbial bad penny!" Victoria piped up. Margaret shot her such a dirty look that, for a brief moment, made her face seem to change into something almost inhuman.

"I'll have none of that kind of talk Victoria! May has never let me down. She never shies away from what needs to be done. She'll be here alright!"

May acted on Margaret's statement as if it was her cue to speak. It had given her a warm feeling to hear her friend defend her with such respect and admiration. She felt as if she would be letting her down if she didn't announce her presence there and then.

"And here I am," May called out. "Thank you Marge and as for you Victoria, I'm beginning to think that you and I are way overdue a little talk."

"What's that supposed to mean?" Victoria spat her reply but received no reaction from it.

"Where have you been May?" Margaret asked. She looked relieved to hear her voice but also a little annoyed at her absence.

"That's what I'm here to tell you," May replied. "Much has happened. There's more been going on than any of you can sense but first I must ask something of all of you".

"Anything May," Margaret swore. "Anything you need".

"I need you to stop! It's over; there are to be no more séances".

An hour had passed since her conversation with Chloe and The Thursday Night Club. May had left them to ponder over all she had told them about Wilfred's ghosts and the arrival of a Soul Stalker. George won't approve, she thought, he'll probably say that I've told them too much about the affairs of the dead. She didn't care; it wasn't George that she was afraid of.

Chapter Thirty Two

Penny was scared. She didn't know exactly why she was scared but the events of the other night still haunted her. She had heard George explain about The Souls Stalkers, what ever they really were, but she still didn't understand the threat they posed. Gary had tried to explain but all the rumours he had disregarded over the years had never really sunk into his memory. He had given her a patchy account of how spirits had disappeared and were never seen again. The details were vague and the entire account stank of Chinese whispers. Even when she had approached other ghosts for answers she was met with the same outcome. Names and places changed with each telling but the soul of the stories were all the same. They appear without warning; one touch and you're gone. There was nothing else anyone could tell her. No one could answer her questions: Why did they come? How did they make you disappear? Where do you end up? And most importantly: Can they affect the living? Is my daughter safe?

She had tried to find George but he was in such great demand now, that he seemed to have gone into hiding. She wasn't even convinced that he had the answers she sought but he was the closest thing to an expert as far as she was aware. Many other ghosts had obviously come to the same conclusion because the graveyard was heaving with spirits.

Penny slowly made her way through the headstones towards George's grave, there was already a large crowd gathered around it. Others were wandering alone or grouping together around other graves but nothing rivalled the crowd that had formed around George's gravestone. They were tightly packed, all trying to get as close to the grave as possible. There was definitely some over lapping going in that mass of souls, Penny thought. She saw no other option than to join them if she was to ever get a chance to speak with George.

A hand gripped her shoulder, just as she was about to step into the crowd. She turned around to see Gary standing beside her. Her took her hand and placed his finger to his lips, to indicate a need for silence. Penny followed his lead unresistingly, as they left George's grave to the other souls and silently headed towards the church.

Penny hadn't been inside the church since she was a small child but it remained exactly as she remembered it, dark, damp and foreboding. The wooden beams of the arched roof curved upwards above her until it became too dark to see. It was a fading darkness, not the sharp, bold edge of shadow that she had witnessed on her kitchen ceiling. Patches of moonlight filtered through the windows, creating stepping stones of light down the aisle towards the altar. Penny could see four figures standing in a patch of light next to the altar and, as she drew closer, she recognised three of them.

May and George stood with an older woman dressed in a blue and white striped dress, that reminded Penny of an old fashioned nurses uniform. Jeremy was sat on the stone steps below them, he looked up at her as she approached.

"Hello Penny" He said as he stood up. "I'm so glad Gary managed to find you". Penny glanced back at Gary who was standing silently behind her, he smiled.

"You do know there's lots of spirits wandering around outside looking for him," Penny pointed at George.

"Oh yes, our new celebrity. We know they're out there but only a few of them are actually looking for George. Most of the still don't believe everything he says," Jeremy shrugged. "They've come here with the belief that the consecrated ground surrounding this church will protect them and keep the safe in some way".

"Will it? Are we safe here?"

"Not at all, it saddens me to say". George stepped down from the altar, leaving May alone with the woman in the striped dress. Penny noticed that May's ginger tom cat was lying outstretched on the altar cloth.

"I need to speak with you," Penny said to George.

"A statement of little surprise," George sat down on a nearby pew. His dog appeared from behind his legs and sat on the floor by his feet, slowly wagging his tail. "Join me? Please do". Penny sat sideways on the pew in front of George and turned her head to face him.

"Is my daughter safe from your Soul Stalkers George?"

"In truth, I can not admit to being all knowing. I am willing to place admission though, to owning the second greatest wisdom on the subject. The great authority on the Soul Stalkers, I am not. Only they know of their own truth. I for one know not of their true name and merely refer to them by the title I have chosen by way of description for their deeds. I stood as witness to their actions, though from afar, as they took upon a gathering of spirits. A gathering so large, I have neither seen before or since. Swooping down from the heavens and devouring souls as if sating a great hunger. With no obvious reasoning or motive, they enveloped souls as they scattered in every direction. Both fleeing across the physical landscape and attempting to transverse were failed tactics for them. From my elevated position overlooking the battle field, I saw none escape. I stood vigil until all movement had ceased. Staying longer than it was safe, I felt mesmerised by that which was taking place before me. My belief is that luck was my only saviour that night". He bent down and patted his dog on the head, he was smiling.

"So that's a no then!" Penny cried. "That's it, that's all you've got. We have no idea why they come or where they take people when they disappear. They could be out there right now stalking us. My daughter could be in danger and we are just huddling in here like rabbits in a burrow, hoping the fox can't dig!" Gary sat down next to her and took her hands in his.

"Ignorant of all possibilities we are not," George offered. "Rumoured truth you may call it. My many years have not been spent in vein. Conjecture and assumption of an education mind are our tools and, I believe, will prove our saviour. Fact is beyond our grasp but I stand firm to my likely truth".

"That's better than nothing I guess," Penny was forced to admit. She didn't like it but she liked a helpless ignorance even less. "So do you think my daughter is safe from them? What's likely to happen to us all?"

"Firstly, no evidence shows that The Soul Stalkers have ever harmed, taken or even affected a living being in any way. Some comfort should be awarded to you by this, even though much has fallen short of documentation in these regards. Secondly, I believe to feed on our energy in some fashion, is their ambition toward us. To be consumed until nothing else remains, is our fate were we to fall fowl of them. If forced to assume our resulting existence, I would impart that we become a small part of their whole. To cease to exist altogether would be the only other alterative and, either way, of an attractive fate I can not conjecture".

"Yet somehow we are drawn to them in their presence". May stepped down from the altar, the lady in the stripped nurse's uniform followed closely behind.

"Of this we have spoken May," George said "A mortal instinct in remnant which laces danger with attraction. Such a derangement is common amongst the living. I believe the phrase is: "Thrill Seeker Syndrome," though I am not familiar with such things. Even so, as I said before May: I didn't think you were the type"

"And I think you'll find she's not the type, not the type in any way you wish to spout it!" The old nurse yelled. Her voice was flooded with authority and the volume and tone reminded Penny of a large bird squawking in defence of its hatchlings.

"Undoubtedly," George apologised. "No thought was further from my mind Annie".

"I should hope it stays that way!" Annie pointed a long, bony finger directly at May.

"Come on girl! Where's your manners gone to? Aren't you going to introduce me?" Penny braced herself for a reaction that didn't come. May looked more submissive than angry; it was an expression Penny had never seen before.

"Oh yes of course Mam," May apologised. "I would like to introduce Mrs Annie Collins, my childhood mentor".

Chapter Thirty Three

She was the last person that she had ever expected to see again. May had mixed feelings. She felt surprised, confused, sorry, glad and even a little bitter. She remembered that she had felt similarly muddled emotions at the time of their parting. The only difference was that she had felt an added vulnerability as well back then. Most reunions either go well or very badly, May felt that this one was going to rock back and forth between the two.

May had arrived at George's grave to find a small crowd beginning to form around it but there had been no sign of George himself. May had just begun to plan her lecture on tardiness when Jeremy had appeared to lead her to the church.

George and Mrs Collins were already there waiting for her. George had smiled at May while gesturing towards Mrs Collins, who had looked May up and down, straight faced and critical. May had felt as if she was under some kind of inspection. How dare she make judgments about me, May had thought. She felt bitter that Mrs Collins had sent her out into the world and had never once tried to contact her or find out how she was getting on. May had spent many years trying to understand why Mrs Collins had nurtured her so intently, only to abandon her as soon as she had out grown the orphanage. May had lit a fire on her tongue and was ready to unleash half a century of frustration and bitterness but then Mrs Collins had spoke.

Her voice had instantly dulled her temper and May had suddenly felt like a small child again. She was the woman who had instilled the very foundation of who May was and how she had led her life. She was her mentor; she was the only family she had ever known. Her words hit may like a rogue wave that made her emotionally stumble.

"May Elizabeth Trump, you have done well".

There had only been time for a few words between them, before Penny had arrived at the Church and memories from the past gave way to the needs of the present.

"It's a pleasure to meet you". Penny said to Mrs Collins, after May had introduced them to each other.

"The famous Penny Saunders," Mrs Collins replied. "The only one who's ever managed to coerce my girl May, into doing anything that lacked profit for herself. So you managed to convince her into prostituting herself for your own financial gain eh! A clever ploy I grant you but hardly an honourable one". May felt mortified and Penny looked horrified.

"It wasn't like that! It wasn't like that at all!" Penny was almost teary eyed. "May offered to help; there was no coercion of any kind. I need May's help and I've been nothing but respectful and grateful for receiving it!" May felt compelled to speak on Penny's behalf but Mrs Collins spoke before she was able to muster the courage to rebuke her childhood mentor.

"Well then, if that be the case, it's a great pleasure to meet you". A moment of awkward silence followed, as both Penny and May were lost for suitable words. May had been ready with an aggressive rant about whose business concerns who and she figured Penny was loaded with similar vocal ammunition.

"Oh...um, well that's ok then I guess," Penny finally replied.

May sat on the pew next to Penny but Mrs Collins indicated that she preferred to stand.

"So then George do you think they will come for us here?" May asked, facing backwards over the pew.

"I don't think so," George replied. "If they do come they will most likely gather in the area surrounding Penny's house". Penny drew a deep breath and cupped her cheeks with her hands as George continued.

"They were drawn to that area by Wilfred's outburst, for

want of a better word; they have no reason to come over here".

"I must go back home!" Penny stood up from the pew and quickly stepped out into the aisle.

"No Penny don't go, it's not safe for you there!" Gary stepped in front of her, blocking her path.

"Quite right Mr Reed," George agreed. "The living will come to no harm, of that I'm sure. The welfare of your daughter, Miss Saunders, is not at threat. So very unlike your own I'm afraid. A single spirit alone would become easy prey should they venture there. Why risk your very soul when such a gathering of spirits resides here for your protection. If to venture here is on their agenda, we number enough to thwart them".

"Are you completely sure of that?" Penny asked.

"My belief is strong in this matter". George's reply seemed a little too vague for May's liking.

"I will go with her!" May said the words quickly and without thought. If what George said was true then the real danger lay at Penny's house and fear gripped her because of it. She felt the growing dread that she had experienced in the presence of Wilfred's Rage but this time she didn't freeze with it. This time she felt impelled to act.

"It would prove a needless action," George assured her. "There is no place safer than here".

May didn't register the first scream, it sounded far away and almost dreamlike. The second and the third scream drew her eyes to the closest window.

"What the hell was that?" She cried and then she felt the chill. It fell through the church like a stage curtain. The windows appeared to frost over in a matter of seconds and the screams became louder.

"So much for your theories George!" Jeremy yelled, as he made a mad dash for the nearest wall. Gary grabbed hold of Penny and drew her close. He looked into her eyes and then kissed her, as if it was the last chance he was ever going to get. Penny seemed startled at first but then kissed him back with equal fervour. Mere seconds passed before they parted, Gary pulled Penny towards the door.

"Come on you lot!" He cried as he looked back "We'll be trapped in here!" May, George and Mrs Collins all looked at each other, before scurrying over the pews. Gracelessly stumbling into the aisle, they chased after Gary and Penny as they disappeared through the door. May glanced back at the altar to where Mr Kibbles still sat. He returned her gaze with wide, calm eyes.

"Come on you stupid cat!" She called but Mr Kibbles made no motion to follow. He arched his back and padded around in a tight circle, as if being petted by an unseen hand. May felt George grab her arm and she was dragged through the door.

Everything outside was covered by a fine mist. Frost grew on every headstone and every tree. A dark cloud hovered above the graveyard, covering the sky for as far as May could see. Random shaped patches of shadow swooped down from the cloud, like falcons chasing their prey. They spiralled through the air and slithered across the ground before launching themselves back up and into the cloud above. Through the mist May could see ghosts rushing back and forth, they were screaming and shouting. Some seemed to be trying to reach the outer wall of the cemetery while others were zigzagging through the headstones in no discernable direction. George pulled her further into the graveyard, as she watched a shadow swoop down upon two spirits who were running towards her. The shadow grazed the ground between them. Almost immediately, it rose back into the air and the spirits were gone.

May turned to face George who was still dragging her into a run. Penny and Gary were way ahead of them, only just visible through the mist. Mrs Collins was a few yards behind them but still ahead of George and May. She had her skirt hitched up above her knees and was running like no living eighty year old woman could dream of. As if she could sense May's eyes upon her, Mrs Collins looked back.

She smiled at May, just as a shadow swooped down between them.

It a desperate attempt to stop George tumbled to the ground, bringing May with him. They rolled across the frost laden grass and managed to stop several yards short of the shadow, which drifted back up into the air leaving nothing but empty space behind it; Mrs Collins was gone.

May felt her heart twist in her chest and her eyes began to well up. She felt like she was standing outside the orphanage once again, watching Mrs Collins as she turned her back on the window. Through her tears, she could see that Gary and Penny had stopped running. They looked back at her, lying in a heap on the ground next to George and started to run back towards them.

"Keep going!" May cried, as she dragged herself to her knees. "Leave us!" They hesitated but then continued towards her. Over the shouts and screams, May could just make out Penny calling her name. May kept waving and shouting.

"Go back, save yourselves, run!" Suddenly a thick, dark shadow dropped to the ground between them.

May turned and looked backwards only to see another shadow drifting purposefully towards them. They were cut off, surrounded; there was no escape. She looked over at George, who was finally raising himself to his knees.

"At least you'll find out if all your theories are correct," May said. She smiled, the fear had vanished and so had the cold chill. Maybe it's because it's now inevitable, she thought, as she slowly lifted herself to her feet. The shadows crept closer, merging together and creating an ever decreasing circle around them. There seemed to be no urgency in its movements, as if it knew that it had them trapped.

George rose to his feet and put his arm around her shoulder. May glanced down and saw Mr Kibbles. He twisted around her feet and rubbed up against her legs, purring contently. She picked him up and held him in her arms. He didn't struggle; he just stared at her with his big round eyes. May felt George's arm leave her shoulder. She turned and saw that he had dropped back down to one knee. He was stroking Trevor, who was wagging his tail profusely.

May felt a sudden surge of energy. She watched as the wall of shadow directly in front of her dip sharply inwards, before springing back into shape like an elastic band.

George stood up and put his arm back around her shoulder. He looked into her eyes and smiled. May was about to speak but then George put his finger gently to her lips. They both turned to face forward and watched silently, as the shadow finally enveloped them.

May's world turned to darkness and she felt Georges touch slip away. Mr Kibbles vanished from her arms, yet somehow she still felt safe. Memories seemed to drift from her mind and her thoughts became simple. She felt everything that she ever knew gradually fade away. May Elizabeth Trump was gone.

Chapter Thirty Four

Alone in the séance room, Barbara begun to disassemble Madam Trump's dummy. The doorbell rang down stairs but she took no notice. I've got more than enough to do up here, someone else can answer it. She had already gathered up all her candles, wrapped them in black tissue paper and put them in a cardboard box that Chloe had kindly dug out of a cupboard for her.

"I can't believe it's over," she grumbled to herself. "My first ever, genuine contact with the other side. I was just beginning to get the hang of it as well".

She slipped the dummy's hat and veil off and gently placed them into the box. She stared at the unveiled cauliflower; it was beginning to turn brown around the edges.

"I guess you did quite well out of all of this. You would have been chopped up, boiled and served on a dinner plate before now had things turned out otherwise". She dragged the Cauliflower off its perch and placed it on the table.

"Barbara!" The voice sounded both close and distant.

"I'm busy!" She called back, as she attempted to unzip the dummy's dress. The zip was stuck; the lace trim had become jammed between its teeth. She pulled on it until she heard the material begin to tear.

"Bugger it! I'll have to get Debs up here; she's good with all the fiddly stuff".

"Barbara!"

"What now, I'm busy!" Barbara let the dress slip from her fingers and turned around to face the door; there was nobody there. I'm hearing things now, she sighed, before picking up the cauliflower. With the stale vegetable held out in front of her, like some kind of religious offering, she stepped out of the room and onto the landing.

The various sounds of a commotion were coming from

the kitchen. Barbara could hear her friend's voices, as she carried the cauliflower down the stairs. They sounded shrill and excited.

"Please do take a seat Mr Cole," Victoria's voice. "Can I get you anything? Tea, Coffee, me perhaps?"

"Do give over Vicky," Margret's voice. "leave the man be!"

Barbara entered the kitchen cauliflower first and took in the scene. Victoria was by the sink filling the kettle. Margret and Chloe were sitting around the table with a well dressed young man, who Barbara assumed was Mr Cole. Deborah was standing behind Chloe with her note book open; she was looking at Mr Cole with a great deal of suspicion in her eyes.

"A coffee would be lovely thank you". Mr Cole said with a stiff smile. He looked up at her and offered out his hand.

"Hello, I'm Richard Cole".

"I'm very sure you are," Barbara acknowledged. She lifted up the cauliflower to indicate that the shaking of hands would prove awkward at best in the current circumstances.

"This is Barbara," Margaret announced while pointing and smiling "The woman not the vegetable, obviously". Barbara gave Margret a false grin and walked over to the rubbish bin. She pressed the pedal with her foot and dropped the cauliflower into it; the lid made a loud clang as it closed.

"So just what's going on in here?" She asked, as she brushed the palms of her hands together.

"This here is Mr Cole," Chloe replied.

"Yes Chloe, we've been passed that bit now. Why is he here?"

"I think...I think I might be rich". Chloe turned her palms upwards and splayed her fingers.

"Now let's not get too far ahead of ourselves just yet," Richard Cole suggested. "I've been hunting for the heir of a rather sizable estate and it would seem that the buck stops here". He tapped on the table with his finger. "However, there's still a lot of paperwork we need to get through to be sure".

"I would like to see that paperwork, if you don't mind?" Deborah said, as she stepped forward and lent over the table.

"If Miss Saunders is in agreement?" Richard replied. He looked over at Chloe, who nodded and shrugged. He lifted his briefcase onto the table and pulled out a handful of papers. He offered them up to Deborah, who snatched them out of his hand and then turned her back on the table.

"Thank you," she said quietly. The room went silent for a few minutes; the only sounds were of pages being turned and cups being stirred. Barbara stepped over to where Victoria was making the tea. She wanted to make sure that there was a cup available for her.

"I do believe he's right," Deborah announced as she turned back to face the table. "Everything seems to be in order here and it all points towards you Chloe." She passed a sheet of paper to Margaret and pointed to the top of the page. "But this is the oddest thing of all!" Margret pulled the sheet of paper closer and began to read it out loud.

"In the matter of the estate of May Elizabeth Trump, deceased. Oh my!" She cried, as she lifted her hand to her mouth.

"Did you know her?" Richard asked.

"No one knew her better," Margaret replied through her fingers.

Victoria handed Barbara a cup of tea.

"And there was me thinking that everything was beginning to go back to normal," she said. Barbara took the cup and just shrugged. What was normal anyway? She thought.

Barbara made her excuses and went back to the séance room. She didn't feel needed downstairs anyway. Deborah was in her element, she had always been good with legislation and paperwork. She seemed to have everything under control and besides, Barbara was tired of the way Victoria kept staring at Mr Cole.

She took another look at the zip on the dummy's dress, it was still stuck fast. She gave it a couple more tugs and something definitely began to tear. She sighed, she didn't even know why she cared if she tore the dress; it belonged to a dead woman anyway.

"Barbara". The voice still sounded distant; it was as if somebody far away was talking to someone else called Barbara and a freak gust of wind had brought it just within her earshot. She ignored it because if it wasn't a distant voice caught on a swift breeze then it was closer that Barbara cared to imagine. Hearing voices in your head, she thought, is that the first or the second sign of madness?

"Barbara can you hear me?" That time it was louder and she felt a chill on the tip of her ear.

"She can hear me! I just know she can hear me". Barbara turned around and scanned the room. That had sounded very close by, she thought.

"I'm sure she has the gift, have a little faith Gary why don't you!"

"Hello," Barbara called out gingerly and felt embarrassed the moment she did. There's no one there you old fool, she scolded herself. You've sprung a leak in your marbles bag. You're finally cracking up, there's nobody...hold on one minute!

"Is that you May?" Barbara called out, the voice hadn't sounded like May's but it was worth a shot.

"No, no it's not"

"Well then there you go old girl you've finally lost the plot!" Barbara admitted out loud.

"Barbara can you hear me? It's Penny, Chloe's mother". Then Barbra felt it dawn on her, it was as if a light had just been switched on in a darkened room.

"Well I never!" Barbara smiled and clapped her hands together. "So you can do what May can do. You can speak to the living just like her".

"Not exactly no," Penny admitted. "This is through no gift

of mine".

"Oh surely not," Barbara said. "You sell yourself short. If that be the case then that would mean…" She paused, her mind became jumbled. It was as if someone was now playing around with the dimmer switch.

"Yes Barbara it means exactly what you think it means. It means that you really do have the gift; you surely are a medium".

Barbara felt the strength leave her legs and she slumped against the table. Surely not, she told herself, not after all this time. Not after all these years of pouncing on random creaks in the floorboards or freak gusts of wind blowing through the curtains and claiming them as signs of the supernatural.

"Are you alright Barbara?" Penny asked, concerned.

"Yes…yes I'm fine," Barbara replied as she pushed herself away from the table. She pulled out a chair and then dropped onto it like a sack of potatoes.

"That's good because I have a lot to tell you".

"Oh do you know that Chloe should be alright for money now?"

"Yes I heard. I was down there when Mr Cole first arrived. I think she will be ok now, if everything he says is true. I would like to stay to be sure of it but it would seem that Gary and I must leave this realm. Something terrible has happened Barbara, it's not safe here for us anymore".

"Oh my! Does it involve *Them?*" Barbara replied. May had explained to her about the Soul Stalkers and she hadn't liked the sound of *Them* one little bit.

Penny recounted the incident at the cemetery. How George's theories turned out so very wrong and how May, among others, had become lost to them.

"I can't believe she's really gone!" Barbara's stomach twisted uncomfortably and her eyes became moist with the threat of tears. She hadn't known May Trump very well at all really. Before she had died, she had always thought of her as the cantankerous old crone who she had spoken about more than had actually spoken to. An unlikely friend of Margaret's; who continued to defend her against our sour opinions even after her passing. After death she was just a disembodied voice that barked more often than spoke and now she was not even *that*. May had introduced Barbara to the real world of mediums and ghosts and for that she would always be grateful. The welling tears, however, were more for Margaret than herself. Margaret who would soon hear that she had lost one of her oldest friends for a second time and, to Barbara it seemed, it would now be a more permanent arrangement.

"I saw Mrs Collins vanish within the mist and I fear May was trapped in much the same way. When that wall of smoke fell between us; it felt like the blade of a guillotine. A solid wall of darkness; I saw no escape for her. " Penny's voice crackled as she relived the moment. "I tried to free her! George also, if he was still by her side. I drew on all the telekinetic force that I had within me and threw it towards the shadow. It was the powerful thing I have ever felt. It was as if I had thrown my very soul at that thing but it was useless; I was useless. Everything I had just bounced back at me and threw both Gary and I high into the air. The shadow caught my power, like a sail catches the wind. We finally ended up in a field about three miles away. I guess it was that which saved us but it was my intention to save May".

"You did your best by her Penny," Barbara said. She could barley understand the concept of what Penny was telling her but she understood the emotion perfectly. "I would bet that if anything, May would be glad to see that you are both safe. That is what you should concern yourself with now. May is beyond anyone's help now and let us keep an eye on Chloe for you. If These Stalkers are still out there, then you must seek haven in this other realm you speak of".

"Yes Gary says the same thing but can I really leave Chloe alone with all what's going on in her life?"

"She wont be alone Penny, we will be here. Margret, Deborah and I will be here. Even Victoria will be willing to watch over her, even though I'm not sure if her continued influence is such a great idea; your daughter will not be alone".

"I guess you're right Barbara, Gary seems to agree with you?"

"I'm sure he does and you can tell him that we've heard from his son as well. He phoned just this morning. Chloe talked with him for the best part of an hour and, by what I gather, I think he will be fine also. There was something about them meeting up for dinner next Friday but I don't know all the details. Not that it matters, neither of them will have to struggle alone through this, you have my word on it".

"Thank you Barbara. I will return as soon as it's safe, I promise. Can you explain everything to Chloe for me and give her all my love".

Chapter Thirty Five

It felt as if he had travelled a great distance but he had no grasp on measurement so he couldn't be entirely sure. It didn't really matter; distance was no obstacle for him. He had travelled to every corner of this world and he knew that he would retread the same ground many times to come. It was part of his function; he would follow her to wherever she began.

He sat on the edge of a small, white bookcase filled with children's classics and books that were guaranteed chew-proof. The room was yellow, which had surprised him, they were usually pink. He wasn't worried by this; there were other things that were different this time.

He looked down at the two cots and the two small baby twins asleep in them. He concentrated on the nearest one and felt more at ease when he saw the pale pink blanket. Familiarity in an ever changing environment. It helped him settle and made his function easier to perform.

The tiny baby girl below would sense him, see him and eventually come to love him. He already loved her as he always had. Over time she would outgrow him. She would no longer see him; she would no longer sense him. At times she would even forget about him altogether but he would always be there. He would watch over her during the good times and reappear to her and bring her comfort during the bad. This was his function. A function which he had performed on countless occasions, for an immeasurable length of time. This time however something was different; this time he was not alone.

Mr Kibbles still had fond memories of his original life. He remembered his death, though less fondly. All those years ago he had been given a choice. There were no words in the offering, more a sense of duty being thrust upon him.

He could have chosen to dessert the obligation and fallen back into the infinite rotation with everything else but reincarnation has its risks. Mr Kibbles had taken his place amongst the spirit guides because of what he was. He was a cat and the thought of returning to life as anything else was unbearable. Better a dead cat than a living door mouse, he had always thought. That was how it had started, that was when he had first set eyes on her. She was his catalyst and he was her guide. He would watch over her as she travelled through the rotation and he would stand by her at her every end. From the moment she began until the moment she ignited the culling, he would be there always.

Mr Kibbles stared down at Trevor who was lying on the floor by the foot of the second cot. He was hardly the perfect company for the spirit of a big, fluffy ginger tom cat but we all have our crosses to bear and our functions to perform.

The End

ABOUT THE AUTHOR

Peter John was born in Bromley Kent, England in 1973. He gained an interest in creative writing at the age of 14 and was published during the 1990's in several poetry anthologies. Happily Married to Jo since 1996 and currently living in Sidcup Kent, not so far from the tree.

Made in the USA
Charleston, SC
11 January 2013